THE AUTHOR

'Mark Rutherford' was the pseudonym of William Hale White. Hale White was born in Bedford in 1831 and his childhood there inspired many of his books, while his father William instilled White's love of literature, his radical socialism and his profound if defiant religious faith.

White trained as a nonconformist minister until 1852, but was expelled from New College, London for unorthodox views. He then worked for the *Westminster Review,* though in 1854 he rejected an offer of partnership and entered the Registrar-General's as a clerk: he stayed in the Civil Service almost forty years.

From 1861 until 1883 White supplemented his income by contributing columns to provincial newspapers and writing occasional pieces. He was fifty-two before he published his first major book, a translation of Spinoza's *Ethic.* This was followed by five others while he was still working, and another fourteen after he retired in 1892. The letters, criticism, translations appeared under his own name, but the journals and novels – *The Autobiography of Mark Rutherford* (1881), *Mark Rutherford's Deliverance* (1885), *Tanner's Lane, Miriam's Schooling* (1890), *Catharine Furze* (1893), *Clara Hopgood* (1896), all to be published by The Hogarth Press – were penned by 'Mark Rutherford'. To confuse matters further, White invented a fictitious editor for 'Mark Rutherford' – 'Reuben Shapcott'. Behind these two alter egos the real author hid for many years until, in 1896, the columnist Claudius Clear (W. Robertson Nicholl) revealed Hale White as the only begetter of these works.

Twenty years after the death of his first wife, Harriet, Hale White married the writer Dorothy Vernon White in 1911. He died at Groombridge two years later.

THE REVOLUTION
IN
TANNER'S LANE

Mark Rutherford

New Introduction by
Claire Tomalin

THE HOGARTH PRESS
LONDON

Published in 1984 by
The Hogarth Press
40 William IV Street, London WC2N 4DF

First published in Great Britain by Trübner & Co. 1887
Hogarth edition offset from Jonathan Cape 1927 edition
Introduction copyright © Claire Tomalin 1984

British Library Cataloguing in Publication Data

Rutherford, Mark
The revolution in Tanner's Lane.
Rn: William Hale White I. Title
823'.8 [F]   PR5795.W7

ISBN 0-7012-1901-7

Printed in Great Britain by
Redwood Burn Limited,
Trowbridge

CONTENTS

Introduction

INTRODUCTION

William Hale White is one of the oddities of English literature, and *The Revolution in Tanner's Lane* is the oddest of his books. It is the work of a man who believed in perfect truthfulness and yet felt forced to lie; a man divided between secretiveness and display, between puritanism and a passionate response to art, beauty and emancipated women; between a rejection of all organised religious observance and a deeply religious temperament; divided also between his career as a civil servant, part of the great disciplined mass of clerks who serviced the British Empire at the summit of its power, and a fervent radicalism which made him cleave to the idea of revolution and look with loathing on the permitted poverty of Victorian England.

Out of this mass of contradictions Hale White produced, late in life, six novels, of which the first two are lightly disguised spiritual autobiography and the last three studies of young women in crisis (the final volume brought down on his head the same sort of disapproval that Hardy got for his *Tess*). *The Revolution in Tanner's Lane* is a bridge between these two sets of books, containing elements of family and personal history and also sketches of a defiantly unconventional young woman. It is both romantic and realistic; a political novel containing a lament for a more glorious past, and also a rebuke to the present, although there is more despair than rebuke in the closing section.

The title itself is puzzling and indeed misleading (although one can see why Hale White and his publishers liked it). What starts off as a historical narrative moving at a fast pace, with a heroic as well as a domestic theme, is abruptly halted half-way through; years are telescoped, and the action is transported to the sleepy provincial town of Cowfold. The heroic theme disappears completely, the focus becomes almost entirely domestic and the 'revolution' appears so paltry that there has been some legitimate dispute over what Hale White meant by his use of the word.

Tanner's Lane is a back street in the town of Cowfold in which stands a Meeting house or chapel where some of the action of the second half of the book takes place, and at the end it is pulled down and replaced by a more modern building. But to call this the revolution which is supposed to have taken place in the Dissenting church will not really do. Hale White was not as feeble as this would make him out to be. He was not, in 1887, merely surveying the decay into which the church of his forefathers had fallen forty years earlier, or suggesting that the appointment of a Cambridge-educated minister with a knowledge of German biblical scholarship had reversed that decay in revolutionary fashion. The book would be ridiculous if this were its message. And it is not ridiculous.

There is no doubt that he is writing about the spirit of revolution. The book has an awkward strength, a force – lopsided maybe, but truthful and driving – which removes it altogether from the enclosed world to which Hale White is often assigned by critics more interested in the literature of the Dissenting church than in giving the book itself the sympathetic attention it deserves. It is not the work of a young revolutionary but something quieter and at the same time more desperate, that of an ageing man who reverses the revolutionary ideal but is conscious that he has neither embodied it nor in any real sense encouraged it. Hale White's contemporaries abroad – Nietzsche, Strindberg, Ibsen, Zola, Maupassant and Tolstoy among them – were exuberantly and shockingly radical in their utterances, but his own voice was simply not pitched at that level. Among his fellow writers he is closest to George Gissing and Thomas Hardy, whose tones were low and whose chronicles of urban and rural poor were never condescending but usually depressed.

At the time of its publication it was seen to be striking, powerful, unusual and, according to the fiction critic of the *Athenaeum* (April 1887), 'marvellously true'; and Hale White has found a small but persistent band of admirers ever since, among them Conrad, Gide, D. H. Lawrence and Lionel Trilling.

Trilling described *Tanner's Lane* as giving 'a shock to our usual conception of the Victorian past' and making that past 'far closer to us than we had supposed'. The book in fact begins much earlier than the Victorian era. Its span is from 1814 to the 1840s. Its hero is a printer, Zachariah Coleman, about thirty when the action starts as he sustains a blow for refusing to doff his cap to the Prince Regent's procession for the restored Bourbon Louis XVIII; and its heroine is Pauline Caillaud, a daughter of the French Revolution (in an almost literal sense), an exile, a republican, an artist (she is a dancer, though she performs in private only) and a freethinker. Like Catherine Earnshaw in *Wuthering Heights*, Pauline has a child who is her spiritual heiress, and whose dramatic action brings the plot to its climax and solution. The Paulines, mother and daughter, though given very different spheres of action, are the embodiment of the spirit of revolution: they are sceptical but passionate, full of intellectual curiosity, generous and also histrionic in their behaviour at times and, above all, capable of effective action.

There is an element of idealisation and fantasy about the Paulines, as though Hale White is creating emblems of what he admires rather than known, intimately observed women. Their inner lives and emotions are not explored and they are most vividly presented through the imaginations of the women who are jealous of them. The scene in which Zachariah's neat, pretty and virtuous nonconformist wife stands outside Pauline's lodgings in the rain, looking in with so much fascination and loathing that she scarcely notices she is being drenched to the skin, is one of the most haunting in the book. The hatred Mrs Coleman feels is partly sexual, but it is also intellectual and spiritual. Her own nature is cool and correct; she cannot forgive or even begin to understand a woman who has a mind and imagination of her own, thereby drawing to herself the men who should, Mrs Coleman thinks, be ordered and confined by the type of womanhood and wifehood she herself represents.

The contrast between revolutionary women and the petty domestic tyrants of provincial England is at the heart of the book and, as we shall see, it is drawn very closely from Hale White's private experience. It is fiercely done, but not unjustly, and never falls into caricature. Mrs Coleman is given her own anguish, unacknowledged even to herself, in her feeling for her husband's rich and gallant friend, Major Maitland; and in the second generation Priscilla Allen is treated almost as tenderly as David Copperfield's Dora. Silly and unable to think about the Corn Laws or to escape her dreadful mother's domination and be loyal to her husband in time of stress she may be, but she is also gently excused as a pretty child who lacks the very capacity for development. Her young husband comes to feel bitterly his mistake in marrying her for her shining curls and affectionate ways, but he lays the blame on no one but himself and, like Zachariah before him, is prepared to endure the consequences of his mistake, even though it shrivels his soul.

Hale White's perception of the crucial part played by women in ordering and changing society at the deepest level was very much of his age. It was also something personal experience, most of it bitter, had led him to brood on. His family history, and the situation in which he found himself at the time of writing *The Revolution in Tanner's Lane*, had a profound effect on the book, not just because he said 'I have never *created* a character in my life' but because its intensity suggests a man writing under peculiar pressure, needing to express something violently felt but always kept back. It is full of things which could be said only to strangers, to the public, never in conversation.

Hale White was a depressive to whom life gave ample reason to be depressed. The promise of any idyllically happy childhood in Bedford in the 1830s as the bright first son of a loving and beloved father – William White – had failed when young Hale was sent to a nonconformist theological college at the insistent wish of his pious and socially ambitious mother. There Hale, accused of unorthodox views on the divine inspiration and veracity of the Bible, got into trouble and was expelled. His father, a printer and bookseller and a fervent radical polemicist, took up his son's case, but to no avail. The humiliation and sense of helplessness and terror – what was he to do now? – were as crucial to his development as the break with the Calvinist orthodoxy in which he had been raised. And just as his father's love and loyalty bound him closely, his mother's part in having pushed him in an obviously unsuitable direction when he was too young to resist seems not to have been forgiven.

He had to find work for himself and, since his father was a printer, thought of publishing. Almost at once he was offered a job as assistant to John Chapman, the freethinking publisher, at No. 142 The Strand (the house still stands). Mrs Chapman kept a boarding house upstairs and Hale was given a room. Below him were the rooms of a Miss Evans who was also working for Chapman as assistant editor of the *Westminister Review*. Miss Evans was in her early thirties; she was kind to Hale and sometimes played Beethoven for him on her piano when they were alone (as Pauline was to dance in private). And he was dazzled by her, never before having met a woman who thought for herself without regard for intellectual or social convention (except for a Colchester aunt, fondly remembered from his childhood, who abandoned her husband's bakery to walk in the country, a book of poems in hand, to the scandal of her neighbours). Miss Evans urged Hale to learn French if only in order to read the *Confessions* of Jean-Jacques Rousseau; and she had obviously freed herself from the shackles of Christianity with little difficulty.

Miss Evans is better known to us now as George Eliot, but she had not yet become a novelist when Hale knew her. Upon him she acted magnetically, by her intellectual adventurousness, her courage and warmth, her music, her independence. But he was also frightened. There was a dangerous aspect to Chapman's circle. Free thought might become merely cynicism; courage in defying convention could lead to sexual anarchy: there were scandals at Chapman's and there were to be more involving Marian Evans. Hale feared to cut himself off from the values of his home and the last shreds of his Christian faith.

Marian Evans left the Chapman household in the autumn of 1853. Chapman then offered Hale a partnership which, even with the shaky finances of the *Westminster*, must have been a tempting prospect; but he retreated. Through the patronage of Samuel Whitbread, a Bedford M.P. who knew his father, Hale was offered a clerkship at Somerset House (writing out lists of names); he accepted this in place of Chapman's offer, left the Strand and took up the other work, which he found a deadly grind. He made no effort to communicate with Marian Evans again until the last years of her life. Clearly Hale had some of his mother's cautious concern for outward appearance, however much he admired his father's dash.

At this time William White's business in Bedford was failing, partly (Hale believed) because his radical political views had alienated customers. He decided to come to London also and, through the patronage of the Russell family whose cause he had supported at every election, was made Doorkeeper of the House of Commons. To pay off the debts he had left in Bedford, he turned journalist in his spare time, writing parliamentary sketches which were much admired. The son was to follow the father in this occupation, driven by equally pressing financial need.

Hale married in 1856. His wife was not a hawk like Marian Evans but a dove, the young half-sister of his much-admired landlady. Harriet appears to have been musically gifted, gentle, affectionate and pious, but very soon after the marriage she began to show signs of disseminated sclerosis and the whole of her married life was that of a tragically deteriorating invalid as the paralysis spread slowly until it killed her in 1891. The horror of this, and its effect on Hale, can be partly imagined. He fathered five children on her in the early stages of the illness; one died, but there were four to educate, constant nursing to be paid for and special accommodation to be arranged. Hale was always moving house, dissatisfied with whatever he found. Harriet endured with saintly patience, but there was no real life together, sexual or social, no holidays, no happiness or relief. Hale was transferred from Somerset House to the Admiralty (where he did well and was remembered for his toughness; on the other hand he abominated the arms race of his day, which he witnessed through the development of naval weapons). They lived mostly in Surrey; his income was supplemented for years with journalism, which drained his creative energy. Home life was gloomy. He suffered from insomnia, rose at dawn, commuted to London, and retired early in the evening to hours of jealously guarded privacy which he used for his writing. Small wonder that it sometimes emerged like scalding steam from a pressure cooker.

His first two novels were quietly successful, finding favour among critics in England and America. Yet his life became ever more painful. Harriet's illness grew worse. His elder sons, whom he had decided to send to conventional Church of England boarding school, not surprisingly grew conventional in their views. Hale loved them, but his temperament was such that he suffered bitter pangs of jealousy when they found themselves young wives. Then the late Seventies and early Eighties saw a sequence of deaths that affected him painfully: his father's patron Lord John Russell in 1878, George Eliot in 1880, his hero Carlyle and (less of a hero, but still a giant in the landscape) Disraeli in 1881; then his deeply loved father in 1882. William White left a small inheritance which, coinciding as it did with the financial independence of Hale's elder sons, released him from the necessity of taking on journalism.

His death also stimulated Hale's memory. *The Revolution in Tanner's Lane* is a tribute both to his father and to the unknown grandfather who had, like Zachariah Coleman, been a supporter of the French Revolution and opponent of the wars against France, and suffered for it. Coleman's battering at the start of *Tanner's Lane* owes something to the grandfather, just as the later part of the book owes something to William White's activities in Bedford in the 1840s, when he invited the Chartists to visit and applauded Cobden's speech against the Corn Laws, which of course enraged the Bedfordshire farmers. Another trigger to the book was the publication of John Cross's memoir of George Eliot in 1885, to which Hale objected on the grounds that it made her 'too respectable'. He was writing against the cant of respectable Victorian society, from a heart full of truth-telling memory.

The historical background is not exact. The Friends of the People who met in Red Lion Street have no true parallel, since the society of that name was active much earlier and excluded working men (its dues were too high for them). But the bribing of an informer by government officials is convincing enough; when the Corn Laws were passed in 1815 troops were needed to protect parliament from the people. And the march of the Blanketeers was a real occasion, fizzling out just as sadly, though the bloodshed happened not then but at Peterloo. It has been suggested that Maitland is founded on John Cartwright; in fact there is little resemblance beyond the military rank, and Maitland is nearly fifty years younger.

It is not a *roman à clef* in that sense; but George Allen bears some of Hale White's features, a little wistfully connecting his young self with admired paternal forebears. Indeed, the second half of the book is full of echoes and parallels. Zachariah's unhappy marriage is precisely echoed by George's. Caillaud lives alone with his adoptive daughter just as Zachariah lives alone later with his daughter. Caillaud's action in avenging Maitland is repeated when Pauline Coleman takes her revenge on Thomas Broad. The flight from London in 1815 has its parallel in the emigration from England in the 1840s. The sermon preached by the Reverend Thomas Bradshaw at the Pike Street Meeting house in 1814 on Jephthah's daughter is echoed by his sermon in the second half of the book when he tells the congregation 'You must make your own religion' and George feels he has looked right into his heart.

Bradshaw, who is held up to admiration, is a republican who has lived 'somewhere abroad' in the mid-1790s and returned 'an altered man'. He is scornful of conventional morality, drawing attention to the fact that Jephthah is the son of a whore and asks his congregation: 'To what did God elect Jephthah? To a respectable, easy, decent existence, with money at interest, regular meals, sleep after them, and un-broken rest at night? He elected him to that tremendous oath and that tremendous penalty.' And in his second sermon he feels, ' "he should not be doing his duty if he did not tell those whom he taught which way they *ought* to vote, and what he had preached to them for so many years would be poor stuff if it did not compel them into a protest against taxing the poor for the sake of the rich." '

Two more passages reveal Hale White's hatred of the system under which he lived and his delight in those who defy canting respectability. The first is his picture of the workhouse where Zachariah finds himself after his collapse, and where an old pauper tells him of his own decline into blank, apathetic nothingness produced by the prison-like place – and work-houses were of course as busy and cruel in their effects in the 1880s as in the 1820s. The other comes early in the second part of the book and simply describes a monument in the park of Cowfold Hall under which the people of the town do their courting. The monument was the work of a lord of the time of Queen Anne who had married an unsuitable and passionately loved wife, and lost her after two years. The lord became a free-thinker and put up a godless memorial to her. It is absolutely characteristic of Hale White that he should delight in the notion of an atheistical romantic as the presiding spirit over the bucolic exchanges of the dull young farmers and shopkeepers' daughters of his native town – for Cowfold is of course Bedford – lending even them a touch of glory.

Hale White's name did not appear on the title page of *The Revolution in Tanner's Lane*. Like all his novels, it was presented from the protection of a double mask, not only the pseudonym 'Mark Rutherford', but the name of a supposed editor, 'Reuben Shapcott'. No member of the Hale White family knew of its existence; nor did any of his colleagues at the Admiralty. So perfectly did he preserve his secret that when his wife died she had not read any of his books, and his daughter Molly knew nothing of them until she was grown up. His own explanation for the secrecy was that, 'I did not desire praise, blame or in fact any talk about what I had done from anybody near me. I have felt too much and am too old to care for notoriety of any kind and wanted to be quiet.' More likely Hale White, a man who prized truthfulness and sincerity above most virtues, simply could not reconcile the truth of his vision as a writer with the life he actually lived. Many years later he told his second wife that, 'if I had been given you as a wife when I was thirty I would never have let the public hear a syllable from me'. Fortunately for us, he was not.

Claire Tomalin, London 1983

'Per varios casus, per tot discrimina rerum,
Tendimus in Latium; sedes ubi fata quietas
Ostendunt. Illic fas regna resurgere Trojæ.
Durate, et vosmet rebus servate secundis.'

                                          – *Virgil.*

'By diuers casis, sere parrellis and sufferance
Unto Itaill we ettill (aim) quhare destanye
Has schap (shaped) for vs ane rest and quiet harbrye
Predestinatis thare Troye sall ryse agane.
Be stout on prosper fortoun to remane.'

                          – *Gawin Douglas's translation.*

THE
REVOLUTION IN TANNER'S LANE

CHAPTER ONE

The World Outside

*

THE 20th April, 1814, an almost cloudless, perfectly sunny day, saw all London astir. On that day Louis the Eighteenth was to come from Hartwell in triumph, summoned by France to the throne of his ancestors. London had not enjoyed too much gaiety that year. It was the year of the great frost. Nothing like it had been known in the memory of man. In the West of England, where snow is rare, roads were impassable and mails could not be delivered. Four dead men were dug out of a deep drift about ten miles west of Exeter. Even at Plymouth, close to the soft south-western ocean, the average depth of the fall was twenty inches, and there was no other way of getting eastwards than by pack-horses. The Great North Road was completely blocked, and there was a barricade over it near Godmanchester of from six to ten feet high. The Oxford coach was buried. Some passengers inside were rescued with great difficulty, and their lives were barely saved. The Solway Firth at Workington resembled the Arctic Sea, and the Thames was so completely frozen over between Blackfriars and London Bridges that people were able, not only to walk across, but to erect booths on the ice. Coals, of course, rose to famine prices in London, as it was then dependent solely upon water-carriage for its supply. The Father of his people, the Prince Regent, was much moved by the general distress of 'a large and meritorious class of industrious persons,' as he called them, and issued a circular to all Lords-Lieutenant ordering them to provide all practicable means for removing obstructions from the highways.

However, on this 20th April the London mob forgot the frost, forgot the quartern loaf and the national debt, and prepared for a holiday, inspired thereto, not so much by Louis the Eighteenth as by the warmth and brilliant sky. There are two factors in all human bliss – an object and the subject. The object may be a trifle, but the condition of the subject is most important. Turn a man out with his digestion in perfect order, with the spring in the air and in his veins, and he will cheer anything, any Louis, Lord Liverpool, dog, cat, or rat who may cross his path. Not that this is intended as a sufficient explanation of the Bourbon reception. Far from it; but it does mitigate it a trifle. At eleven o'clock in the forenoon two troops of the Oxford Blues drew up at Kilburn turnpike to await the sacred arrival. The Prince Regent himself went as far as Stanmore to meet his August Brother. When the August Brother reached the village, the excited inhabitants thereof took the horses out of the carriage and drew him through the street. The Prince, standing at the door of the principal inn, was in readiness to salute him, and this he did by embracing him! There have been some remarkable embraces in history. Joseph fell on Israel's neck, and Israel said unto Joseph, 'Now let me die, since I have seen thy face': Paul, after preaching at Ephesus, calling the elders of the church to witness that, for the space of three years, he ceased not to warn every one night and day with tears, kneeled down and prayed, so that they all wept sore and fell on his neck: Romeo took a last embrace of Juliet in the vault, and sealed the doors of breath with a righteous kiss: Penelope embraced Ulysses, who was welcome to her as land is welcome to shipwrecked swimmers escaping from the grey sea-water – there have, we say, been some remarkable embraces on this earth since time began, but none more remarkable than that on the steps of the Abercorn Arms. The Divine couple then drove in solemn procession to town. From the Park corner for three-quarters of a mile or so was a line of private carriages, filled with most fashionable people, the ladies all standing on the seats. The French royalist flag waved everywhere. All along the Kilburn Road, then thinly lined with houses, it was triumphant, and even the trees were decorated with it. Arriving by way of Cumberland Gate at Piccadilly, Louis was escorted, amidst uproarious rejoicing, to Grillon's Hotel in Albemarle Street. There, in reply to an address from the Prince, he 'ascribed, under Providence,' to His Royal Highness and the British people his present blissful condition; and soon afterwards, being extremely tired, went to bed. This was on a Wednesday. The next day, Thursday, His Sacred Majesty, or Most Christian Majesty, as he was then called, was solemnly made a Knight of the Garter, the Bishops of Salisbury and Winchester assisting. On Friday he received the Corporation of London, and on Saturday the 23rd he prepared to take his departure. There was a great crowd in the street when he came out of the hotel, and immense applause; the mob crying out, 'God bless your Majesty!' as if they owed him all they had, and even their lives. It was very touching, people thought at the time, and so it was.

Is there anything more touching than the waste of human loyalty and love? As we read the history of the Highlands or a story of Jacobite loyalty such as that of Cooper's Admiral Bluewater, dear to boys, we sadden that destiny should decree that in a world in which piety is not too plentiful it should run so pitifully to waste, and that men and women should weep hot tears and break their hearts over bran-stuffing and wax.

Amidst the hooraying multitude that Saturday April morning was one man at least, Zachariah Coleman by name, who did not hooray, and did not lift his hat even when the Sacred Majesty appeared on the hotel steps. He was a smallish, thin-faced, lean creature in workman's clothes; his complexion was white, blanched by office air, and his hands were black with printer's ink.

'Off with your tile, you b – y Corsican!' exclaimed a roaring voice behind him. Zachariah turned round, and found the request came from a drayman weighing about eighteen stone; but the tile was not removed. In an instant it was sent flying to the other side of the road, where it was trodden on, picked up, and passed forward in the air amidst laughter and jeers, till it was finally lost.

Zachariah was not pugnacious, and could not very well be so in the presence of his huge antagonist; but he was no coward, and not seeing for the moment that his hat was hopelessly gone, he turned round savagely and, laying hold of the drayman, said –

'You ruffian, give it me back; if I am a Corsican, are you an Englishman?'

'Take that for your b – y beaver,' said the other, and

dealt him a blow with the fist right in his face, which staggered and stupefied him, covering him with blood.

The bystanders, observing the disparity between the two men, instantly took Zachariah's side, and called out 'Shame, shame!' Nor did they confine themselves to ejaculations, for a young fellow of about eight-and-twenty, well dressed, with a bottle-green coat of broadcloth, buttoned close, stepped up to the drayman.

'Knock my tile off, beer-barrel.'

The drayman instantly responded by a clutch at it, but before he could touch it he had an awful cut across the lips, delivered with such scientific accuracy from the left shoulder that it was clear it came from a disciple of Jackson or Tom Cribb. The crowd now became intensely delighted and excited, and a cry of 'A ring, a ring!' was raised. The drayman, blind with rage, let out with his right arm with force enough to fell an ox, but the stroke was most artistically parried, and the response was another fearful gash over the right eye. By this time the patriot had had enough, and declined to continue the contest. His foe, too, seemed to have no desire for any further display of his powers, and retired smilingly, edging his way to the pavement, where he found poor Zachariah almost helpless.

'Holloa, my republican friend, d – n it, that's a nasty lick you've got, and from one of the people, too; that makes it harder to bear, eh? Never mind, he's worse off than you are.'

Zachariah thanked him as well as he could for defending him.

'Not a word; haven't got a scratch myself. Come along with me'; and he dragged him along Piccadilly into a public-house in Swallow Street, where apparently he was well known. Water was called for; Zachariah was sponged, the wound strapped up, some brandy given him, and the stranger, ordering a hackney coach, told the driver to take the gentleman home.

'Wait a bit,' he called, as the coach drove off. 'You may feel faint; I'll go home with you,' and in a moment he was by Zachariah's side. The coach found its way slowly through the streets to some lodgings in Clerkenwell. It was well the stranger did go, for his companion on arrival was hardly able to crawl upstairs or give a coherent account to his wife of what had happened.

Zachariah Coleman, working man, printer, was in April 1814 about thirty years old. He was employed in a jobbing office in the city, where he was compositor and pressman as well. He had been married in January 1814 to a woman a year younger than himself, who attended the meeting-house at Hackney, whither he went on the Sunday. He was a Dissenter in religion, and a fierce Radical in politics, as many of the Dissenters in that day were. He was not a ranter or revivalist, but what was called a moderate Calvinist; that is to say, he held to Calvinism as his undoubted creed, but when it came to the push in actual practice he modified it. In this respect he was inconsistent; but who is there who is not? His theology probably had no more gaps in it than that of the latest and most enlightened preacher who denies miracles and affirms the Universal Benevolence. His present biographer, from in-

timate acquaintance with the class to which Zachariah
belonged, takes this opportunity to protest against the
general assumption that the Calvinists of that day, or of
any day, arrived at their belief by putting out their eyes
and accepting blindly the authority of St. Paul or anybody
else. It may be questioned, indeed, whether any religious
body has ever stood so distinctly upon the understanding,
and has used its intellect with such rigorous activity, as
the Puritans, from whom Zachariah was a genuine descendant. Even if Calvinism had been carved on tables of
stone and handed down from heaven by the Almighty
Hand, it would not have lived if it had not been found to
agree more or less with the facts, and it was because it was
a deduction from what nobody can help seeing that it was
so vital, the Epistle to the Romans serving as the inspired
confirmation of an experience. Zachariah was a great
reader of all kinds of books – a lover especially of Bunyan
and Milton; as logical in his politics as in his religion; and
he defended the execution of Charles the First on the
ground that the people had just as much right to put a
king to death as a judge had to order the execution of any
other criminal.

The courtship between Zachariah and the lady who
became his wife had been short, for there could be no
mistake, as they had known one another so long. She was
black-haired, with a perfectly oval face, always dressed
with the most scrupulous neatness, and with a certain plain
tightness which Zachariah admired. She had exquisitely
white and perfect teeth, a pale clear complexion, and the
reputation of being a most sensible woman. She was not

a beauty, but she was good-looking; the weak points in her face being her eyes, which were mere inexpressive optic organs, and her mouth, which, when shut, seemed too much shut, just as if it were compressed by an effort of the will or by a spring. These, however, Zachariah thought minor matters, if, indeed, he ever noticed them. 'The great thing was, that she was' – sometimes this and sometimes that – and so it was settled. Unfortunately in marriage it is so difficult to be sure of what the great thing is, and what the little thing is, the little thing becoming so frightfully big afterwards! Theologically, Mrs. Zachariah was as strict as her husband, and more so, as far as outward observance went, for her strictness was not tempered by those secular interests which to him were so dear. She read little or nothing – nothing, indeed, on week-days, and even the *Morning Chronicle*, which Zachariah occasionally borrowed, was folded up when he had done with it, and put under the tea-caddy till it was returned. On Sundays she took up a book in the afternoon, but she carefully prepared herself for the operation as though it were a sacramental service. When the dinner-things were washed up, when the hearth was swept and the kettle on the fire, having put on her best Sunday dress, it was her custom to go to the window – always to the window, never to the fire – where she would open Boston's *Fourfold State* and hold it up in front of her with both hands. This, however, did not last long, for on the arrival of the milkman the volume was replaced, and it was necessary to make preparations for tea.

The hackney coach drove up to the house in Rosoman

Street where Zachariah dwelt on the first floor. He was too weak to go upstairs by himself, and he and his friend therefore walked into the front room together. It was in complete order, although it was so early in the morning. Everything was dusted; even the lower fire-bar had not a speck of ashes on it, and on the hob already was a sauce-pan in which Mrs. Coleman proposed to cook the one o'clock dinner. On the wall were portraits of Sir Francis Burdett, Major Cartwright, and the mezzotint engraving of Sadler's Bunyan. Two black silhouettes – one of Zachariah and the other of his wife – were suspended on each side of the mantelpiece.

Mrs. Coleman was busily engaged in the bedroom, but hearing the footsteps, she immediately entered. She was slightly taken aback at seeing Zachariah in such a plight, and uttered a little scream, but the bottle-green stranger, making her a profound bow, arrested her.

'Pardon me, my dear madam, there is nothing seriously the matter. Your husband has had the misfortune to be the victim of a most blackguardly assault; but I am sure that, under your care, he will be all right in a day or two; and, with your permission, I take my leave.'

Mrs. Coleman was irritated. The first emotion was not sympathy. Absolutely the first was annoyance at being seen without proper notice by such a fine-looking gentle-man. She had, however, no real cause for vexation under this head. She had tied a white handkerchief over her hair, fastening it under her chin, as her manner was when doing her morning's work, and she had on her white apron; but she was trim and faultless, and the white handkerchief did but set off her black hair and marble complexion. Her second emotion, too, was not sympathy. Zachariah was at home at the wrong time. Her ordinary household arrangements were upset. He might possibly be ill, and then there would be a mess and confusion. The thought of sickness was intolerable to her, because it put 'everything out.' Rising up at the back of these two emotions came, haltingly, a third when she looked her husband in the face. She could not help it, and she did really pity him.

'I am sure it is very kind of you,' she replied.

Zachariah had as yet spoken no word, nor had she moved towards him. The stranger was departing.

'Stop!' cried Zachariah, 'you have not told me your name. I am too faint to say how much I owe you for your protection and kindness.'

'Nonsense. My name is Maitland – Major Maitland, IA Albany. Good-bye.'

He was at the top of the stairs, when he turned round and, looking at Mrs. Coleman, observed musingly, 'I think I'll send my doctor, and, if you will permit me, will call in a day or two.'

She thanked him; he took her hand, politely pressed it to his lips, and rode off in the coach which had been waiting for him.

'What has happened, my dear? Tell me all about it,' she inquired as she went back into the parlour, with just the least colour on her cheek, and perceptibly a little happier than she was five minutes before. She did nothing more than put her hand on his shoulder, but he brightened immediately. He told her the tale, and when it was over desired to lie down and to have some tea.

Emotion number two returned to Mrs. Coleman immediately. Tea at that time, the things having been all cleared away and washed up! She did not, however, like openly to object, but she did go so far as to suggest that perhaps cold water would be better, as there might be inflammation. Zachariah, although he was accustomed to give way, begged for tea; and it was made ready, but not with water boiled there. She would not again put the copper kettle on the fire, as it was just cleaned, but she asked to be allowed to use that which belonged to the neighbour downstairs who kept the shop. The tea-things were replaced when Zachariah had finished, and his wife returned to her duties, leaving him sitting in the straight-backed Windsor-chair, looking into the grate and feeling very miserable.

In the afternoon Rosoman Street was startled to see a grand carriage stop at Zachariah's door, and out stepped the grand doctor, who, after some little hesitation and inquiry, made his way upstairs. Having examined our friend, he pronounced him free from all mortal or even serious injury— it was a case of contusion and shaken nerves, which required a little alterative medicine, and on the day after to-morrow the patient, although bruised and sore in the mouth, might go back to work.

The next morning he was better, but nevertheless he was depressed. It was now three months since his wedding-day, and the pomp and beauty of the sunrise, gold and scarlet bars with intermediate lakes of softest blue, had been obscured by leaden clouds, which showed no break and let loose a cold drizzling rain. How was it? He often asked himself that question, but could obtain no satisfactory answer. Had anything changed? Was his wife anything which he did not know her to be three months ago? Certainly not. He could not accuse her of passing herself off upon him with false pretences. What she had always represented herself to be she was now. There she stood, precisely as she stood twelve months ago, when he asked her to become his wife, and he thought when she said 'Yes' that no man was more blessed than he. It was, he feared, true he did not love her, nor she him; but why could not they have found that out before? What a cruel destiny was this which drew a veil before his eyes and led him blindfold over the precipice! He at first thought, when his joy began to ebb in February or March, that it would rise again, and that he would see matters in a different light; but the spring was here, and the tide had not turned. It never would turn now, and he became at last aware of the sad truth – the saddest a man can know – that he had missed the great delight of existence. His chance had come, and had gone. Henceforth all that was said and sung about love and home would find no echo in him. He was paralysed, dead in half of his soul, and would have to exist with the other half as well as he could. He had done no wrong: he had done his best; he had not sold himself to the flesh or the devil, and, Calvinist as he was, he was tempted at times to question the justice of such a punishment. If he put his finger in the fire and got burnt, he was able to bow to the wisdom which taught him in that plain way that he was not to put his finger in the fire. But wherein lay the beneficence of visiting a simple mistake – one which he could not avoid – with a curse worse than the Jewish curse of excommunication – 'the anathema wherewith Joshua cursed Jericho; the curse which Elisha laid upon the children; all the curses which are written in the law. Cursed be he by day, and cursed be he by night; cursed be he in sleeping, and cursed be he in waking: cursed in going out, and cursed in coming in.' Neither the wretched victim nor the world at large was any better for such a visitation, for it was neither remedial nor monitory. Ah, so it is! The murderer is hung at Newgate, and if he himself is not improved by the process, perhaps a few wicked people are frightened; but men and women are put to a worse death every day by slow strangulation which endures for a lifetime, and, as far as we can see, no lesson is learned by anybody, and no good is done.

Zachariah, however, did not give way to despair, for he was not a man to despair. His religion was a part of himself. He had immortality before him, in which he thanked God there was no marrying nor giving in marriage. This doctrine, however, did not live in him as the other dogmas of his creed, for it was not one in which his intellect had such a share. On the other hand, predestination was dear to him. God knew him as closely as He knew the angel next His throne, and had marked out his course with as much concern as that of the seraph. What God's purposes were he did not know. He took a sort of sullen pride in not knowing, and he marched along, footsore and wounded in obedience to the orders of his great Chief. Only thirty years old, and only three months a husband, he had already learned renunciation. There was to be no joy in life? Then he would be satisfied if it were tolerable, and he strove to dismiss all his dreams and do his best with what lay before him. Oh, my hero! Perhaps somewhere or other – let us hope it is true – a book is kept in which human worth is duly appraised, and in that book, if such volume there be, we shall find that the divinest heroism is not that of the man who, holding life cheap, puts his back against a wall, and is shot by Government soldiers, assured that he will live ever afterwards as a martyr and saint: a diviner heroism is that of the poor printer, who, in dingy, smoky Rosoman Street, Clerkenwell, with forty years before him, determined to live through them, as far as he could, without a murmur, although there was to be no pleasure in them. A diviner heroism is this, but divinest of all, is that of him who can in these days do what Zachariah did, and without Zachariah's faith.

The next evening, just as Zachariah and his wife were sitting down to tea, there was a tap at the door, and in walked Major Maitland. He was now in full afternoon costume, and, if not dandyish, was undeniably well dressed. Making a profound bow to Mrs. Coleman, he advanced to the fireplace and instantly shook hands with Zachariah.

'Well, my republican, you are better, although the beery loyalist has left his mark upon you.'

'Certainly, much better; but where I should have been, sir, if it had not been for you, I don't know.'

'Ah, well; it was an absolute pleasure to me to teach the blackguard that cheering a Bourbon costs something. My God, though, a man must be a fool who has to be taught that! I wonder what it *has* cost us. Why, I see you've got my friend, Major Cartwright, up there.'

Zachariah and his wife started a moment at what they considered the profane introduction of God's name; but it was not exactly swearing, and Major Maitland's relationship to them was remarkable. They were therefore silent.

'A true friend of the people,' continued Maitland, 'is Major Cartwright; but he does not go quite far enough to please me.'

'As for the people so-called,' quoth Zachariah, 'I doubt whether they are worth saving. Look at the mob we saw the day before yesterday. I think not of the people. But there is a people, even in these days of Ahab, whose feet may yet be on the necks of their enemies.'

'Why, you are an aristocrat,' said Maitland, smiling; 'only you want to abolish the present aristocracy and give us another. You must not judge us by what you saw in Piccadilly, and while you are still smarting from that smasher on your eye. London, I grant you, is not, and never was, a fair specimen. But, even in London, you must not be deceived. You don't know its real temper; and then, as to not being worth saving – why, the worse men are the more they want saving. However, we are both agreed about this – crew, Liverpool, the Prince Regent, and his friends.' A strong word was about to escape before 'crew,' but the Major saw that he was in a house where it

25

would be out of place. 'I wish you'd join our Friends of
the People. We want two or three determined fellows like
you. We are all safe.'

'What are the "Friends of the People"?'

'Oh, it's a club of – a – good fellows who meet twice a
week for a little talk about affairs. Come with me next
Friday and see.'

Zachariah hesitated a moment, and then consented.

'All right; I'll fetch you.' He was going away, and
picked up from the table a book he had brought with him.

'By the way, you will not be at work till to-morrow.
I'll leave you this to amuse you. It has not been out long.
Thirteen thousand copies were sold the first day. It is
the *Corsair* – Byron's *Corsair*. My God, it *is* poetry and
no mistake! Not exactly, perhaps, in your line; but you
are a man of sense, and if that doesn't make your heart
leap in you, I'm much mistaken. Lord Byron is a neighbour of mine in the Albany. I know him by sight. I've
waited a whole livelong morning at my window to see
him go out. So much the more fool you, you'll say. Ah,
well, wait till you have read the *Corsair*.'

The Major shook hands. Mrs. Coleman, who had been
totally silent during the interview, excepting when she
asked him if he would join in a cup of tea – an offer most
gracefully declined – followed him to the top of the stairs.
As before, he kissed her hand, made her a profound bow,
and was off. When she came back into the room the faint
flush on the cheek was repeated, and there was the same
unusual little rippling overflow of kindness to her husband.

In the evening Zachariah took up the book. Byron was

not, indeed, in his line. He took no interest in him, although, like every other Englishman, he had heard much about him. He had passed on his way to Albemarle Street the entrance to the Albany. Byron was lying there asleep, but Zachariah, although he knew he was within fifty yards of him, felt no emotion whatever. This was remarkable, for Byron's influence, even in 1814, was singular, beyond that of all predecessors and successors, in the wideness of its range. He was read by everybody. Men and women who were accessible to no other poetry were accessible to his, and old sea-captains, merchants, tradesmen, clerks, tailors, milliners, as well as the best judges in the land, repeated his verses by the page.

Mrs. Coleman, having cleared away the tea-things, sat knitting till half-past six. It was prayer-meeting night, and she never missed going. Zachariah generally accompanied her, but he was not quite presentable, and stayed at home. He went on with the *Corsair*, and as he read his heart warmed, and he unconsciously found himself declaiming several of the most glowing and eloquent lines aloud. He was by nature a poet; essentially so, for he loved everything which lifted him above what is commonplace. Isaiah, Milton, a storm, a revolution, a great passion – with these he was at home; and his education, mainly on the Old Testament, contributed greatly to the development both of the strength and weakness of his character. For such as he are weak as well as strong; weak in the absence of the innumerable little sympathies and worldlinesses which make life delightful, and but too apt to despise and tread upon those gentle flowers which are as really here as the sun and the stars, and are nearer to us. Zachariah found in the *Corsair* exactly what answered to his own inmost self, down to its very depths. The lofty style, the scorn of what is mean and base, the courage – root of all virtue – that dares and evermore dares in the very last extremity, the love of the illimitable, of freedom, and the cadences like the fall of waves on a sea-shore, were attractive to him beyond measure. More than this, there was Love. His own love was a failure, and yet it was impossible for him to indulge for a moment his imagination elsewhere. The difference between him and his wife might have risen to absolute aversion, and yet no wandering fancy would ever have been encouraged towards any woman living. But when he came to Medora's song –

> 'Deep in my soul that tender secret dwells,
>   Lonely and lost to light for evermore,
> Save when to thine my heart responsive swells,
>   Then trembles into silence as before.'

and more particularly the second verse –

> 'There, in its centre, a sepulchral lamp
>   Burns the slow flame, eternal – but unseen;
> Which not the darkness of despair can damp,
>   Though vain its ray as it had never been.'

love again asserted itself. It was not love for a person; perhaps it was hardly love so much as the capacity for love. Whatever it may be, henceforth this is what love will be in him, and it will be fully maintained, though it knows no actual object. It will manifest itself in suppressed force, seeking for exit in a thousand directions; sometimes grotesque, perhaps, but always force. It will give energy to expression, vitality to his admiration of the beautiful, devotion to his worship, enthusiasm to his zeal for freedom. More than this, it will *not* make his private life unbearable by contrast; rather the reverse. The vision of Medora will not intensify the shadow over Rosoman Street, Clerkenwell, but will soften it.

CHAPTER TWO

Outside Pike Street

★

ON the Friday evening the Major called for Zachariah. He had not yet returned, but his wife was at home. The tea-things were ready, the kettle was on the hob, and she sat knitting at the window. Her visitor knocked at the door; she rose, and he entered. This time he was a little less formal, for after making his bow he shook her hand. She, too, was not quite so stiff, and begged him to be seated.

'Upon my word, madam,' he began, 'if I were as well looked after as Mr. Coleman, I doubt if I should be so anxious as he is to change the existing order of things. You would think there is some excuse for me if you were to see the misery and privation of my lodgings. Nobody cares a straw, and as for dust and dirt, they would drive you distracted.'

Mrs. Zachariah smiled, and shifted one of her little white-stockinged feet over the other. She had on the neatest of sandals, with black ribbons, which crossed over the instep. It was one of Zachariah's weak points, she considered, that he did not seem to care sufficiently for cleanliness, and when he came in he would sometimes put his black hand, before he had washed, on the white tea-cloth, or on the back of a chair, and leave behind him a patch of printer's ink. It was bad enough to be obliged always to wipe the door-handles.

'I do my best; but as for dirt, you cannot be so badly off in the Albany as we are in Clerkenwell. Clerkenwell is very disagreeable, but we are obliged to live here.'

'If Clerkenwell is so bad, all the more honour to you for your triumph.'

'Oh, I don't know about honour; my husband says it is simply my nature.'

'Nature! All the better. I could never live with anybody who was always trying and trying and struggling. I believe in Nature. Don't you?'

This was an abstract inquiry beyond Mrs. Zachariah's scope. 'It is some people's nature to like to be tidy,' she contented herself with observing; 'and others do not care for it.'

'Oh, perhaps it is because I am a soldier, and accustomed to order, that I care for it above everything.'

Mrs. Zachariah started for a moment. She reflected. She had forgotten it – that she was talking to an officer in His Majesty's service.

'Have you seen much fighting, sir?'

'Oh, well, for the matter of that, I have had my share. I was at Talavera, and suffer a good deal now in damp weather from having slept so much in the open air.'

'Dear me, that is very hard! My husband is rheumatic, and finds Tarver's embrocation do him more good than anything. Will you try it if I give you some?'

'With profound gratitude.' Mrs. Coleman filled an empty bottle, took a piece of folded brown paper out of the fireplace cupboard, untied a coil of twine, made up a compact little parcel, and gave it to the Major.

'A thousand thanks. If faith now can really cure, I shall be well in a week.'

Mrs. Zachariah smiled again.

31

'Are you Dissenters?' he asked abruptly.

'Yes. Independents.'

'I am not surprised. Ever since Cromwell's days you have always been on the side of liberty; but are you strict – I don't know exactly what to call it – go to the prayer-meetings – and so on?'

'We are both members of the church, and Mr. Coleman is a deacon,' replied Mrs. Zachariah, with a gravity not hitherto observable.

She looked out of the window and saw him coming down the street. She placed the kettle nearer the fire, put the tea in the teapot, and sat down again. He came up-stairs, went straight into his bedroom, cleaned himself as much as possible, changed his coat, and entered. The Major, being pressed, consented to take tea, and Mrs. Zachariah was a cheerful and even talkative hostess, to the surprise of at least one member of the company. She sat next to her husband, and the Major sat opposite. Three silver spoons and silver sugar-tongs had been put on the table. Ordinarily the spoons were pewter. Zachariah, fond of sugar, was in the habit of taking it with his fingers – a practice to which Mrs. Zachariah strongly objected, and with some reason. It was dirty, and as his hands were none of the whitest, the neighbouring lumps became soiled, and acquired a flavour which did not add to their sweetness. She had told him of it a score of times; but he did not amend, and seemed to think her particularity rather a vice than a virtue. So it is that, as love gilds all defects, lack of love sees nothing but defect in what is truly estimable. Notwithstanding the sugar-tongs, Zachariah – excusable, perhaps, this time, considering the warmth of the speech he was making against the late war – pushed them aside and helped himself after the usual fashion. A cloud came over Mrs. Zachariah's face; she compressed her lips in downright anger, pushed the tongs towards him with a rattle, and trod on his foot at the same time. His oration came to an end; he looked round, became confused, and was suddenly silent; but the Major gallantly came to the rescue by jumping up to prevent Mrs. Zachariah from moving in order to put more water on the tea.

'Excuse me, pray'; but as he had risen somewhat suddenly to reach the kettle, he caught the table-cloth on his knee, and in a moment his cup and saucer and the plate were on the floor in twenty pieces, and the tea running all over the carpet. Zachariah looked at his wife and expected to see her half frantic. But no; though it was her best china, she stopped the Major's apologies, and assured him, with something almost like laughter, that it was not of the slightest consequence. 'Tea doesn't stain; I hope it has not gone on your coat'; and producing a duster from the cupboard, the evil, save the loss of the crockery, was remedied in a couple of minutes.

At half-past seven o'clock the Major and Zachariah departed. They walked across the top of Hatton Garden, and so onwards till they came to Red Lion Street. Entering a low passage at the side of a small public-house, they went up some stairs, and found themselves opposite a door, which was locked. The Major gave three taps and then paused. A moment afterwards he tapped again twice; the

33

lock was turned and he was admitted. Zachariah found himself in a spacious kind of loft. There was a table running down the middle, and round it were seated about a dozen men, most of whom were smoking and drinking beer. They welcomed the Major with rappings, and he moved towards the empty chair at the head of the board.

'You're late, chairman,' said one.

'Been to fetch a new comrade.'

'Is that the cove? He looks all right. Here's your health, guv'nor, and d – n all tyrants.' With that he took a pull at the beer.

'Swear him,' said the Major.

A disagreeable-looking man with a big round nose, small red eyes, unshaven face, and slightly unsteady voice, rose, laid down his pipe, and beckoned to Zachariah, who advanced towards him.

The Secretary – for he it was – produced a memorandum-book, and began with a stutter –

'In the sacred name of –'

'Stop!' cried Zachariah. 'I don't swear.'

'That will do,' shouted the Major across a hubbub which arose – 'religious. I'll answer for him: let him sign; that's enough.'

'You *are* answerable,' growled the Secretary; 'if he's a d – d spy we'll have his blood, that's all, and yours too, Major.' The Major took no notice, and Zachariah put his name in the book, the roll of the Red Lion Friends of the People.

'Business, Mr. Secretary – the last minutes.'

34

The minutes were read, and an adjourned debate was then renewed on a motion to organize public meetings to petition in favour of Parliamentary Reform. The reader must understand that politics in those days were somewhat different from the politics of fifty or sixty years later. Bread was thirteenpence a quartern loaf; the national debt, with a much smaller population, was what it is now; everything was taxed, and wages were very low. But what was most galling was the fact that the misery, the taxes, and the debt had been accumulated, not by the will of the people, but by a corrupt House of Commons, the property of borough-mongers, for the sake of supporting the Bourbons directly, but indirectly and chiefly the House of Hanover and the hated aristocracy. There was also a scandalous list of jobs and pensions. Years afterwards, when the Government was forced to look into abuses, the Reverend Thomas Thurlow, to take one example amongst others, was awarded, as compensation for the loss of his two offices, Patentee of Bankrupts and Keeper of Hanaper, the modest allowance annually until his death of £11,380 14s. 6d. The men and women of that time, although there were scarcely any newspapers, were not fools, and there was not a Nottingham weaver who put a morsel of bread in his hungry belly who did not know that two morsels might have gone there if there were no impost on foreign corn to maintain rents, and if there were no interest to pay on money borrowed to keep these sacred kings and lords safe in their palaces and parks. Opinion at the Red Lion Friends of the People Club was much divided. Some were for demonstrations and agitation, whilst others were for physical force. The discussion went on irregularly amidst much tumult.

'How long would they have waited over the water if they had done nothing but jaw? They met together and tore down the Bastile, and that's what we must do.'

'That may be true,' said a small white-faced man who neither smoked nor drank, 'but what followed? You don't do anything really till you've reasoned it out.'

'It's my belief, parson,' retorted the other, 'that you are in a d – d funk. This is not the place for Methodists.'

'Order, order!' shouted the chairman.

'I am not a Methodist,' quietly replied the other; 'unless you mean by Methodist a man who fears God and loves his Saviour. I am not ashamed to own that, and I am none the worse for it as far as I know. As for being a coward, we shall see.'

The Secretary meanwhile had gone on with his beer. Despite his notorious failing, he had been chosen for the post because in his sober moments he was quick with his pen. He was not a working-man; nay, it was said he had been at Oxford. His present profession was that of attorney's clerk. He got up and began a harangue about Brutus.

'There's one way of dealing with tyrants – the old way, Mr. Chairman. Death to them all, say I; the short cut; none of your palaver; what's the use of palavering?'

He was a little shaky, took hold of the rail of his chair, and as he sat down broke his pipe.

Some slight applause followed; but the majority were either against him or thought it better to be silent.

The discussion continued irregularly, and Zachariah

noticed that about half a dozen of those present took no part in it. At about ten o'clock the chairman declared the meeting at an end; and it was quite time he did so, for the smoke and the drink had done their work.

As Zachariah came out, a man stood by his side whom he had scarcely noticed during the evening. He was evidently a shoemaker. There was a smell of leather about him, and his hands and face were grimy. He had a slightly turned-up nose, smallish eyes, half-hidden under very black eyebrows, and his lips were thin and straight. His voice was exceedingly high-pitched, and had something creaking in it, like the sound of an ill-greased axle. He spoke with emphasis, but not quite like an Englishman, was fond of alliteration, and often, in the middle of a sentence, paused to search for a word which pleased him. Having found it, the remainder of the sentence was poised and cast from him like a dart. His style was a curious mixture of foreign imperfection and rhetoric – a rhetoric, however, by no means affected. It might have been so in another person, but it was not so in him.

'Going east?' said he.

'Yes.'

'If you want company, I'll walk with you. What do you think of the Friends?'

Zachariah, it will be borne in mind, although he was a Democrat, had never really seen the world. He belonged to a religious sect. He believed in the people, it is true, but it was a people of Cromwellian Independents. He purposely avoided the company of men who used profane language, and never in his life entered a tavern. He did not know what the masses really were; for although he worked with his hands, printers were rather a superior set of fellows, and his was an old-established shop which took the best of its class. When brought actually into contact with swearers and drunkards as patriots and reformers he was more than a little shocked.

'Not much,' quoth he.

'Not worse than our virtuous substitute for a sovereign?'

'No, certainly.'

'You object to giving them votes, but is not the opinion of the silliest as good as that of Lord Sidmouth?'

'That's no reason for giving them votes.'

'I should like to behold the experiment of a new form of misgovernment. If we are to be eternally enslaved to fools and swindlers, why not a change? We have had regal misrule and aristocratic swindling long enough.'

'Seriously, my friend,' he continued, 'study that immortal charter, the Declaration of the Rights of Man.'

He stopped in the street, and with an oratorical air repeated the well-known lines, 'Men are born and always continue free, and equal in respect of their rights. . . . Every citizen has a right, either by himself or by his representative, to a free voice in determining the necessity of public contributions, the appropriation of them, and their amount, mode of assessment, and duration.' He knew them by heart. 'It is the truth,' he continued; 'you must come to that, unless you believe in the Divine appointment of dynasties. There is no logical repose between Lord Liverpool and the Declaration. What is the real difference between him and you? None but a question of

38

degree. He does not believe in absolute monarchy, and stays at this point. You go a little lower. You are both alike. How dare you say, "My brother, I am more honest and more religious than you; pay me half-a-crown and I will spend it for your welfare"? You cannot tell me that. You know I should have a *right* to reject you. I refuse to be coerced. I prefer freedom to – felicity.'

Zachariah was puzzled. He was not one of those persons who can see no escape from an argument and yet are not convinced; one of those happy creatures to whom the operations of the intellect are a joke – who, if they are shown that the three angles of a triangle are equal to two right angles, decline to disprove it, but act as if they were but one. To Zachariah the appeal 'Where will you stop?' was generally successful. If his understanding told him he could not stop, he went on. And yet it so often happens that if we do go on we are dissatisfied; we cannot doubt each successive step, but we doubt the conclusion. We arrive serenely at the end, and lo! it is an absurdity which common sense, as we call it, demolishes with scoffs and laughter.

They had walked down to Holborn in order to avoid the rather dangerous quarter of Gray's Inn Lane. Presently they were overtaken by the Secretary, staggering under more liquor. He did not recognize them, and rolled on. The shoemaker instantly detached himself from Zachariah and followed the drunken official. He was about to turn into a public-house, when his friend came up to him softly, abstracted a book which was sticking out of his pocket, laid hold of him by the arm, and marched off with him across the street and through Great Turnstile.

39

Sunday came, and Zachariah and his wife attended the services at Pike Street Meeting house, conducted by that worthy servant of God, the Reverend Thomas Bradshaw. He was at that time preaching a series of sermons on the Gospel Covenant, and he enlarged upon the distinction between those with whom the covenant was made and those with whom there was none, save of judgment. The poorest and the weakest, if they were sons of God, were more blessed than the strongest who were not. These were nothing: 'they should go out like the smoke of a candle with an ill favour; whereas the weak and simple ones are upholden, and go from strength to strength, and increase with the increasings of God.' Zachariah was rather confused by what had happened during the week, and his mind, especially during the long prayer, wandered a good deal, much to his discomfort.

CHAPTER THREE
The Theatre
*

MAJOR MAITLAND was very fond of the theatre, and as he had grown fond of Zachariah, and frequently called at his house, sometimes on business and sometimes for pleasure, he often asked his friend to accompany him. But for a long time he held out. The theatre and dancing in 1814 were an abomination to the Independents. Since 1814 they have advanced, and consequently they not only go to plays and dance like other Christians, but the freer, less prejudiced, and more enlightened encourage the ballet, spend their holidays in Paris, and study French character there. Zachariah, however, had a side open to literature, and though he had never seen a play acted, he read plays. He read Shakespeare, and had often thought how wonderful one of his dramas must be on the stage. So it fell out that at last he yielded, and it was arranged that Mrs. and Mr. Coleman should go with the Major to Drury Lane to see the great Edmund Kean in 'Othello.' The day was fixed, and Mrs. Coleman was busy for a long time beforehand in furbishing up and altering her wedding-dress, so that she might make a decent figure. She was all excitement, and as happy as she could well be. For months Zachariah had not known her to be so communicative. She seemed to take an interest in politics; she discussed with him the report that Bonaparte was mad, and Zachariah, on his part, told her what had happened to him during the day, and what he had read in the newspapers. The Prince Regent had been to Oxford, and verses had been composed in his honour. Mr. Bosanquet had recited to the Prince an ode, or something of the kind, and had ventured, after dilating on the enormous services rendered by kings in general to the community during the last twenty years, to warn them –

'But ye yourselves must bow: your praise be given
   To Him, the Lord of lords, your King in heaven.'

And Mrs. Zachariah, with a smile and unwonted wit, wondered whether Mr. Bosanquet would not be prosecuted for such treasonable sentiments. Zachariah hardly knew what to make of his wife's gaiety, but he was glad. He thought that perhaps he was answerable for her silence and coldness, and he determined at all costs to try and amend, and, however weary he might be when he came home at night, that he would speak and get her to speak too.

The eventful evening arrived. Zachariah was to get away as early as he could; the Major was to call at about six. After Zachariah had washed and dressed they were to take a hackney coach together. At the appointed hour the Major appeared, and found Mrs. Zachariah already in her best clothes and tea ready. She was charming – finished from the uttermost hair on her head to the sole of her slipper – and the dove-coloured, somewhat Quaker-ish tint of her wedding-gown suited her admirably. Quarter-past six came, but there was no Zachariah, and she thought she would make the tea, as he was never long over his meals. Half-past six, and he was not there. The two now sat down, and began to listen to every sound. The coach was ordered at a quarter to seven.

'What shall we do?' said the Major. 'I cannot send you on and wait for him.'

'No. How vexing it is! It is just like –' and she stopped.

'We must stay where we are, I suppose; it is rather a pity to miss being there when Kean first comes on.'

She was in a fretful agony of impatience. She rose and looked out of the window, thought she heard somebody on the stairs, went outside on the landing, returned, walked up and down, and mentally cursed her husband, not profanely – she dared not do that – but with curses none the less intense. Poor man! he had been kept by a job he had to finish. She might have thought this possible, and, in fact, did think it possible; but it made no difference in the hatred which she permitted to rise against him. At last her animosity relaxed, and she began to regard him with more composure, and even with pleasure.

'Had you not better go, and leave me here, so that we may follow? I do not know what has happened, and I am sure he would be so sorry if you were to be disappointed.'

She turned her eyes anxiously towards the Major.

'That will never do. You know nothing about the theatre. No! no!'

She paused and stamped her little foot, and looked again out of the window.

The coachman knocked at the door, and when she went down asked her how long he had to wait.

She came back and, throwing herself on a chair, fairly gave way to her mortification, and cried out, 'It is too bad – too bad! – it is, really.'

'I'll tell you what,' replied the Major. 'Do you mind

43

coming with me? We will leave one of the tickets which I have bought, and we can add a message that he is to follow, and that we will keep his place for him. Put on your bonnet at once, and I will scribble a line to him.'

Mrs. Zachariah did not see any other course open; her wrath once more disappeared, and in another moment she was busy before the looking-glass. The note was written, and pinned to the ticket, both being stuck on the mantel-piece in a conspicuous place, so that Zachariah might see them directly he arrived. In exuberant spirits she added in her own hand, 'Make as much haste as you can, my dear,' and subscribed her initials. It was a tremendously hot afternoon, and, what with the fire and the weather and the tea, the air was very oppressive. She threw the bottom sash open a little wider therefore, and the two rolled off to Drury Lane. As the door slammed behind them, the draught caught the ticket and note, and in a moment they were in the flames and consumed.

Ten minutes afterwards in came Zachariah. He had run all the way, and was dripping with perspiration. He rushed upstairs, but there was nobody. He stared round him, looked at the plates, saw that two had been there, rushed down again, and asked the woman in the shop –

'Has Mrs. Coleman left any message?'

'No. She went off with that gentleman that comes here now and then; but she never said nothing to me,' and Zachariah thought he saw something like a grin on her face.

It may be as well to say that he never dreamed of any real injury done to him by his wife, and, in truth, the Major was incapable of doing him any. He was gay, unorthodox, a man who went about the world, romantic, republican, but he never would have condescended to seduce a woman, and least of all a woman belonging to a friend. He paid women whom he admired all kinds of attentions, but they were nothing more than the gallantry of the age. Although they were nothing, however, to him, they were a good deal more than nothing to Mrs. Zachariah. The symbolism of an act varies much, and what may be mere sport to one is sin in another. The Major's easy manners and very free courtesy were innocent so far as he was concerned; but when his rigid, religious companion in the hackney coach felt them sweet, and was better pleased with them than she had ever been with her husband's caresses, she sinned, and she knew that she sinned.

What curiously composite creatures we are! Zachariah for a moment was half-pleased, for she had now clearly wronged him. The next moment, however, he was wretched. He took up the teapot; it was empty; the tea-caddy was locked up. It was a mere trifle, but, as he said to himself, the merest trifles are important if they are significant. He brooded, therefore, over the empty teapot and locked tea-caddy for fully five minutes. She had not only gone without him, but had forgotten him. At the end of the five minutes teapot and tea-caddy had swollen to enormous dimensions and had become the basis of large generalizations. 'I would rather,' he exclaimed, 'be condemned to be led out and hung if I knew one human soul would love me for a week beforehand and honour me afterwards, than live half a century and be nothing to any living creature.' Presently, however, it occurred to him that, although in the abstract this might be true, yet at that particular moment he was a fool; and he made the best of his way to Drury Lane. He managed to find his way into the gallery just as Kean came on the stage in the second scene of the first act. Far down below him, through the misty air, he thought he could see his wife and the Major; but he was in an instant arrested by the play. It was all new to him; the huge building, the thousands of excited eager faces, the lights, and the scenery. He had not listened, moreover, to a dozen sentences from the great actor before he had forgotten himself and was in Venice, absorbed in the fortunes of the Moor. What a blessing is this for which we have to thank the playwright and his interpreters, to be able to step out of the dingy, dreary London streets, with all their wretched corrosive cares, and for at least three hours to be swayed by nobler passions. For three hours the little petty self, with all its mean surroundings, withdraws: we breathe a different atmosphere, we are jealous, glad, weep, laugh with Shakespeare's jealousy, gladness, tears, and laughter! What priggishness, too, is that which objects to Shakespeare on a stage because no acting can realize the ideal formed by solitary reading! Are we really sure of it? Are we really sure that Garrick or Kean or Siddons, with all their genius and study, fall short of a lazy dream in an arm-chair? Kean had not only a thousand things to tell Zachariah – meanings in innumerable passages which had before been overlooked – but he gave the character of Othello such vivid distinctness that it might almost be called a creation. He was exactly the kind of actor, moreover, to impress

46

him. He was great, grand, passionate, overwhelming with
a like emotion the apprentice and the critic. Everybody
after listening to a play or reading a book uses it when
he comes to himself again to fill his own pitcher, and the
Cyprus tragedy lent itself to Zachariah as an illustration
of his own Clerkenwell sorrows and as a gospel for them,
although his were so different from those of the Moor.
Why did he so easily suspect Desdemona? Is it not improbable that a man with any faith in woman, and such
a woman, should proceed to murder on such evidence?
If Othello had reflected for a moment, he would have
seen that everything might have been explained. Why did
he not question, sift, examine, before taking such tremendous revenge? – and for the moment the story seemed
unnatural. But then he considered again that men and
women, if they do not murder one another, do actually,
in everyday life, for no reason whatever, come to wrong
conclusions about each other; utterly and to the end of
their lives misconstrue and lose each other. Nay, it seems
to be a kind of luxury to them to believe that those who
could and would love them are false to them. We make
haste to doubt the divinest fidelity; we drive the dagger
into each other, and we smother the Desdemona who
would have been the light of life to us, not because of any
deadly difference or grievous injury, but because we idly
and wilfully reject.

The tale, evermore, is –

> 'Of one whose hand,
> Like the base Indian, threw a pearl away
> Richer than all his tribe.'

47

So said Zachariah to himself as he came out into Drury Lane and walked eastwards. His wife and the Major were back before him. The Major did not wait, but returned at once to Albany Street, leaving Mrs. Coleman to sit up for her husband. He was not hurrying himself, and could not free himself from the crowd so easily as those who left from below. The consequence was that he was a full half-hour behind her, and she was not particularly pleased at having been kept so long out of her bed. When she let him in all that she said was, 'Oh, here you are at last,' and immediately retired. Strange to say, she forgot all about family worship – never before omitted, however late it might be. If she had taken the trouble to ask him whether he had seen her message and the ticket so much might have been cleared up. Of course he, too, ought to have spoken to her; it was the natural thing to do, and it was extraordinary that he did not. But he let her go; she knelt down by her bed, prayed her prayer to her God, and in five minutes was asleep. Zachariah ten minutes afterwards prayed his prayer to *his* God, and lay down, but not to sleep. No sooner was his head on the pillow than the play was before his eyes, and Othello, Desdemona, and Iago moved and spoke again for hours. Then came the thoughts with which he had left the theatre and the revulsion on reaching home. Burning with excitement at what was a discovery to him, he had entered his house with even an enthusiasm for his wife, and an impatient desire to try upon her the experiment which he thought would reveal so much to him and make him wealthy for ever. But when she met him he was struck dumb. He was shut up again in his old prison, and what was so hopeful three hours before was all vanity. So he struggled through the short night, and, as soon as he could, rose and went out. This was a frequent practice, and his wife was not surprised when she woke to find he had gone. She was in the best of spirits again, and when he returned, after offering him the usual morning greeting, she inquired at once in what part of the theatre he was, and why he had not used the ticket.

'We waited for you till the last moment; we should have been too late if we had stayed an instant longer, and I made sure you would come directly.'

'Ticket – what ticket? I saw no ticket?'

'We left it on the mantelpiece, and there was a message with it.'

His face brightened, but he said nothing. A rush of blood rose to his head; he moved towards her and kissed her.

'What a wretch you must have thought me!' she said half-laughingly, as she instantly smoothed her hair again, which he had ruffled. 'But what has become of the ticket?'

'Fell in the fire most likely; the window was open when I came in, and the draught blew the picture over the mantelpiece nearly off its hook.'

The breakfast was the happiest meal they had had for months. Zachariah did his best to overcome his natural indisposition to talk. Except when he was very much excited, he always found conversation with his wife too difficult on any save the most commonplace topics, although he was eloquent enough in company which suited him.

49

She listened to him, recalling with great pleasure the events of the preceding evening. She was even affectionate – affectionate for her – and playfully patted his shoulder as he went out, warning him not to be so late again. What was the cause of her gaiety? Was she thinking improperly of the Major? No. If she had gone with Zachariah alone to the theatre would she have been so cheerful? No. Did she really think she loved her husband better? Yes. The human heart, even the heart of Mrs. Coleman, is beyond our analysis.

CHAPTER FOUR
A Friend of the People
*

THE Friends of the People continued their meetings, and
Zachariah attended regularly, although, after about three
months' experience, he began to doubt whether any advance was being made. The immediate subject of discussion now was a projected meeting in Spitalfields,
and each branch of the Society was to organize its own
contingent. All this was perfectly harmless. There was
a good deal of wild talk occasionally; but it mostly
came from Mr. Secretary, especially when he had had
his beer. One evening he had taken more than enough,
and was decidedly staggering as he walked down Lamb's
Conduit Street homewards. Zachariah was at some distance, and in front of him, in close converse, were his
shoemaking friend, the Major, and a third man whom
he could not recognize. The Secretary swayed himself
across Holborn and into Chancery Lane, the others
following. Presently they came up to him, passed him,
and turned off to the left, leaving him to continue his
troubled voyage southwards. The night air, however,
was a little too much for him, and when he got to Fleet
Street he was under the necessity of supporting himself against a wall. He became more and more seditious
as he became more and more muddled, so that at last
he attracted the attention of a constable, who laid hold
of him and locked him up for the night. In the morning he was very much surprised to find himself in a cell,
feeling very miserable, charged with being drunk and
disorderly, and, what was ten times worse, with uttering

blasphemy against the Prince Regent. It may as well be mentioned here that the greatest precautions had been taken to prevent any knowledge by the authorities of the proceedings of the Friends of the People. The Habeas Corpus Act was not yet suspended, but the times were exceedingly dangerous. The Friends, therefore, never left in a body nor by the same door. Watch was always kept with the utmost strictness, not only on the stairs, but from a window which commanded the street. No written summons was ever sent to attend any meeting, ordinary or extraordinary. Mr. Secretary, therefore, was much disconcerted when he found that his pockets were emptied of all his official documents. He languished in his cell till about twelve o'clock, very sick and very anxious, when he was put into a cab, and, to his great surprise, instead of being taken to a police court, was carried to Whitehall. There he was introduced to an elderly gentleman, who sat at the head of a long table covered with green cloth. A younger man, apparently a clerk, sat at a smaller table by the fire and wrote, seeming to take no notice whatever of what was going on. Mr. Secretary expected to hear something about transportation, and to be denounced as an enemy of the human race; but he was pleasantly disappointed.

'Sorry to see a respectable person like you in such a position.'

Mr. Secretary wondered how the gentleman knew he was respectable; but was silent. He was not now in an eloquent or seditious humour.

'You may imagine that we know you, or we should not

have taken the trouble to bring you here. We should merely have had you committed for trial.'

The Secretary thought of his empty pockets. In truth it was the Major who had emptied them before he crossed Holborn; but of course he suspected the constable.

'You must be aware that you have exposed yourself to heavy penalties. I prefer, however, to think of you as a well-meaning but misguided person. What good do you think you can do? I can assure you that the Government are fully aware of the distress which prevails, and will do all they can to alleviate it. If you have any grievances, why not seek their redress by legitimate and constitutional means?'

The Secretary was flattered. He had never been brought face to face with one of the governing classes before. He looked round; everything was so quiet, so pacific; there were no fetters nor thumbscrews; the sun was lighting up the park; children were playing in it, and the necessity for a revolution was not on that particular spot quite apparent.

A messenger now entered carrying some sandwiches and a little decanter of wine on a tray, covered with the whitest of cloths.

'It struck me,' continued the official, taking a sandwich and pouring out a glass of wine, 'when I heard of your arrest, that I should like myself to have a talk with you. We really are most loth to proceed to extremities, and you have, I understand, a wife and children. I need not tell you what we could do with you if we liked. Now, just consider, my friend. I don't want you to give up one single principle; but is it worth your while to be sent to

jail and to have your home broken up merely because you
want to achieve your object in the wrong way, and in a
foolish way? Keep your principles; we do not object; but
don't go out into the road with them. And you, as an
intelligent man, must see that you will not get what you
desire by violence as soon as you will by lawful methods.
Is the difference between us worth such a price as you
will have to pay?'

The Secretary hesitated; he could not speak; he was
very faint and nervous.

'Ah, you've had nothing to eat, I dare say.'

The bell was rung, and was answered immediately.

'Bring some bread and cheese and beer.'

The bread and cheese and beer were brought.

'Sit down there and have something; I will go on with
my work, and we will finish our talk afterwards.'

The Secretary could not eat much bread and cheese,
but he drank the beer greedily.

When he had finished the clerk left the room. The
Commissioner – for he was one of the Commissioners of
His Majesty's Treasury – followed him to the door, closed
it, not without satisfying himself that the constable was at
his post outside, returned to his seat, opened his drawer,
saw that a pistol and five guineas were there, and then
began –

'Now, look here, my dear sir, let me speak plainly with
you and come to an understanding. We have made inquiries about you; we believe you to be a good sort of
fellow, and we are not going to prosecute you. We do
hope, however, that, should you hear anything which is –

well – really treasonable, you will let us know. Treason, I am sure, is as dreadful to you as it is to me. The Government, as I said before, are most desirous of helping those who really deserve it; and to prove this, as I understand you are out of work, just accept that little trifle.'

The guineas were handed to Mr. Secretary, who looked at them doubtfully. With the beer his conscience had returned, and he broke out –

'If you want me to be a d – d spy, d – d if I do!'

The Commissioner was not in the least disconcerted.

'Spy, my man! – who mentioned the word? The money was offered you because you haven't got a sixpence. Haven't I told you you are not required to give up a single principle? Have I asked you to denounce a single companion? All I have requested you to do, as an honest citizen, is to give me a hint if you hear of anything which would be as perilous to you as to me.'

The Secretary after his brief explosion felt flaccid. He was subject to violent oscillations, and he looked at the five guineas again. He was very weak – weak naturally, and weaker through a long course of alcohol. He was, therefore, prone to obscure, crooked, silly devices, at any rate when he was sober. Half-drunk he was very bold; but when he had no liquor inside him he could *not* do what was straight. He had not strength sufficient, if two courses were open, to cast aside the one for which there were the fewer and less conclusive reasons, and to take the proper path, as if no other were before him. A sane, strong person is not the prey of reasons: a person like Mr. Secretary can never free himself from them, and after he has arrived at some kind of a determination is still uncertain and harks back. With the roar of the flames of the Cities of the Plain in his ears, he stops, and is half afraid that it was his duty after all to stay and try and put them out. The Secretary, therefore, pondered again. The money was given on no condition that was worth anything. For aught he knew, the Commissioner had his books and papers already. He could take the guineas and be just as free as he was before. He could even give a part of it to the funds of the Friends. There obtruded, moreover, visions of Newgate, and his hands slowly crept to the coins.

'I am a Radical, sir, and I don't mind who knows it.'

'Nothing penal in that. Every man has a right to his own political creed.'

The fingers crept closer and touched the gold.

'If I thought you wanted to bribe me, I'd rot before I had anything to do with you.'

The Commissioner smiled. There was no necessity to say anything more, for the guineas were disappearing, and finally, though slowly, chinked down into Mr. Secretary's pocket.

The Commissioner held out his hand.

The Secretary before he took it looked loftier than ever.

'I hope you understand me, sir, clearly.'

'I *do* understand you clearly.'

The Secretary shook the hand; the Commissioner went with him to the door.

'Show this gentleman downstairs.'

The constable, without a look of surprise, went downstairs, and Mr. Secretary found himself in the street.

A FRIEND OF THE PEOPLE

Mr. Commissioner drank another glass of wine, and then pencilled something in a little memorandum book, which he put under the pistol. The drawer had two locks, and he carefully locked both with two little keys attached to a ribbon which he wore round his neck.

CHAPTER FIVE

The Horizon Widens

*

JEAN CAILLAUD, shoemaker, whom we have met before, commonly called John Kaylow, friend of the Major and member of the Society of the Friends of the People, was by birth a Frenchman. He had originally come to this country in 1795, bringing with him a daughter, Pauline, about four or five years old. Why he came nobody knew, nor did anybody know who was the mother of the child. He soon obtained plenty of employment, for he was an admirable workman, and learned to speak English well. Pauline naturally spoke both English and French. Her education was accomplished with some difficulty, though it was not such a task as it might have been, because Jean's occupation kept him at home; his house being in one of the streets in that complication of little alleys and thoroughfares to most Londoners utterly unknown; within the sound of St. Bride's nevertheless, and lying about a hundred yards north of Fleet Street. If the explorer goes up a court nearly opposite Bouverie Street, he will emerge from a covered ditch into one that is open, about six feet wide. Presently the ditch ends in another and wider ditch running east and west. The western one turns northward, and then westward again, roofs itself over, squeezes itself till it becomes little less than a rectangular pipe, and finally discharges itself under an oil and colourman's house in Fetter Lane. The eastern arm, strange to say, suddenly expands, and one side of it, for no earthly reason, is set back with an open space in front of it, partitioned by low palings. Immediately beyond, as if in a fit of sudden con-

58

trition for such extravagance, the passage or gutter contracts itself to its very narrowest, and, diving under a printing-office, shows itself in Shoe Lane. The houses in these trenches were not by any means of the worst kind. In the aforesaid expansion they were even genteel, or at any rate aspired to be so, and each had its own brass knocker and kept its front door shut with decent sobriety and reticence. On the top floor of one of these tenements lodged Jean Caillaud and Pauline. They had three rooms between them; one was Jean's bedchamber, one Pauline's, and one was workroom and living-room, where Jean made ball-slippers and light goods – this being his branch of the trade – and Pauline helped him. The workroom faced the north, and was exactly on a level with an innumerable multitude of red chimney-pots pouring forth stinking smoke which, for the six winter months, generally darkened the air during the whole day. But occasionally Nature resumed her rights, and it was possible to feel that sky, stars, sun and moon still existed, and were not blotted out by the obscurations of what is called civilized life. There came, occasionally, wild nights in October or November, with a gale from the south-west, and then, when almost everybody had gone to bed and the fires were out, the clouds, illuminated by the moon, rushed across the heavens, and the Great Bear hung over the dismal waste of smutty tiles with the same solemnity with which it hangs over the mountain, the sea, or the desert. Early in the morning, too, in summer, between three and four o'clock in June, there were sights to be seen worth seeing. The distance was clear for miles, and the heights of Highgate were visible, proclaiming the gospel of a beyond and beyond even to Kent's Court, and that its immediate surroundings were, mercifully, not infinite. The light made even the nearest bit of soot-grimed, twisted, rotten brickwork beautiful, and occasionally, but at very rare intervals, the odour of London was vanquished, and a genuine breath from the Brixton fields was able to find its way uncontaminated across the river. Jean and Pauline were, on the whole, fond of the court. They often thought they would prefer the country, and talked about it; but it is very much to be doubted, if they had been placed in Devonshire, whether they would not have turned back uneasily after a time to their garret. They both liked the excitement of the city, and the feeling that they were so near to everything that was stirring in men's minds. The long stretch of lonely sea-shore is all very well, very beautiful, and, maybe, very instructive to many people; but to most persons half an hour's rational conversation is much more profitable. Pauline was not a particularly beautiful girl. Her hair was black, and, although there was a great deal of it, it was coarse and untidy. Her complexion was sallow – not as clear as it might be – and underneath the cheek-bones there were slight depressions. She had grown up without an attachment, so far as her father knew, and indeed so far as she knew. She had one redeeming virtue – redeeming especially to Jean, who was with her alone so much. She had an intellect, and it was one which sought for constant expression; consequently she was never dull. If she was dull, she was ill. She had none of that horrible mental constriction which makes some English women so insupportably tedious. The last thing she read, the last thing she thought, came out with vivacity and force, and she did not need the stimulus of a great excitement to reveal what was in her. Living as she did at work side by side with her father all day, she knew all his thoughts and read all his books. Neither of them ever went to church. They were not atheists, nor had they entirely pushed aside the religious questions which torment men's minds. They believed in what they called a Supreme Being, whom they thought to be just and good; but they went no further. They were revolutionary, and when Jean joined the Friends of the People, he and the Major and one other man became a kind of interior secret committee, which really directed the affairs of the branch. Companions they had none, except the Major and one or two compatriots; but they were drawn to Zachariah, and Zachariah was drawn to them, very soon after he became a member of the Society. The first time he went to Kent's Court with Jean was one night after a meeting. The two walked home together, and Zachariah turned in for an hour, as it was but ten o'clock. There had been a grand thanksgiving at St. Paul's that day. The Prince Regent had returned thanks to Almighty God for the restoration of peace. The Houses of Parliament were there, with the Foreign Ambassadors, the City Corporation, the Duke of Wellington, Field-Marshal Blucher, peeresses, and Society generally. The Royal Dukes, Sussex, Kent, York, and Gloucester, were each drawn by six horses and escorted by a separate party of the Guards. It took eight horses to drag the Prince himself to divine service, and he too was encompassed by soldiers. Arrived at the cathedral, he was marshalled to a kind of pew surmounted by a lofty crimson-and-gold canopy. There he sat alone, worshipped his Creator, and listened to a sermon by the Bishop of Chester. Neither Jean nor Pauline troubled themselves to go out, and indeed it would not have been of much use if they had tried; for it was by no means certain that Almighty God, who had been so kind as to get rid of Napoleon, would not permit a row in the streets. Consequently, every avenue which led to the line of the procession was strictly blocked. They heard the music from a distance, and although they both hated Bonaparte, it had not a pleasant sound in their ears. It was the sound of triumph over Frenchmen, and futhermore, with all their dislike to the tyrant, they were proud of his genius.

Walking towards Clerkenwell that evening, the streets being clear, save for a number of drunken men and women who were testifying to the orthodoxy of their religious and political faith by rolling about the kennel in various stages of intoxication, Jean pressed Zachariah to go upstairs with him. Pauline had prepared supper for herself and her father, and a very frugal meal it was, for neither of them could drink beer or spirits, and they could not afford wine. Pauline and Zachariah were duly introduced, and Zachariah looked round him. The room was not dirty, but it was extremely unlike his own. Shoemaking implements and unfinished jobs lay here and there without being 'put away.' An old sofa served as a seat, and on it were a pair of lasts, a bit of a French newspaper, and a plateful of small onions and lettuce, which could not find a place on the little table. Zachariah, upstairs in Rosoman Street, had often felt just as if he were in his Sunday clothes and new boots. He never could make out what was the reason for it. There are some houses in which we are always uncomfortable. Our freedom is fettered, and we can no more take our ease in them than in a glass and china shop. We breathe with a sense of oppression, and the surroundings are like repellent *chevaux de frise*. Zachariah had no such feeling here. There was disorder, it is true; but, on the other hand, there was no polished tea-caddy to stare at him and claim equal rights against him, defying him to disturb it. He was asked to sit upon the sofa, and in so doing upset the plateful of salad upon the floor. Pauline smiled, was down on her knees in an instant, before he could prevent her, picked up the vegetables and put them back again. To tell the truth, they were rather dirty; and she therefore washed them in a hand-basin. Zachariah asked her if she had been out that day.

'I? – to go with the Lord Mayor and bless the good God for giving us back Louis Bourbon? No, Mr. Coleman; if the good God did give us Louis back again, I wouldn't bless Him for it, and I don't think He had much to do with it. So there were two reasons why I didn't go.'

Zachariah was a little puzzled, a little shocked, and a little out of his element.

'I thought you night have gone to see the procession and hear the music.'

'I hate processions. Whenever I see one, and am squeezed and trampled on just because those fine people may ride by, I am humiliated and miserable. As for the music, I hate that too. It is all alike, and might as well be done by machinery. Come, you are eating nothing. What conspiracy have you and my father hatched to-night?'

'Conspiracy!' said Jean. 'Who are the conspirators? Not we. The conspirators are those thieves who have been to St. Paul's.'

'To give thanks,' said Pauline. 'If I were up there in the sky, shouldn't I laugh at them. How comical it is! Did they give thanks for Austerlitz or Jena?'

'That's about the worst of it,' replied Jean. 'It is one vast plot to make the people believe lies. I shouldn't so much mind their robbing the country of its money to keep themselves comfortable, but what is the meaning of their *Te Deums*? I tell you again' – and he repeated the words with much emphasis – 'it is a vast plot to make men believe a lie. I abhor them for that ten times more than for taking my money to replace Louis.'

'Oh,' resumed Pauline, '*if* I were only up in the sky for an hour, I would have thundered and lightened on them just as they got to the top of Ludgate Hill, and scattered a score or so of them. I wonder if they would have thanked Providence for their escape? O father, such a joke! The Major told me the other day of an old gentleman he knew who was riding along in his carriage. A fire-ball fell and killed the coachman. The old gentleman, talking about it afterwards, said that "*providentially* it struck the box-seat."'

Zachariah, although a firm believer in his faith, and not

a coward, was tempted to be silent. He was heavy and slow in action, and this kind of company was strange to him. Furthermore, Pauline was not an open enemy, and notwithstanding her little blasphemies, she was attractive. But then he remembered with shame that he was ordered to testify to the truth wherever he might be, and unable to find anything of his own by which he could express himself, a text of the Bible came into his mind, and, half to himself, he repeated it aloud –

'I form the light and create darkness: I make peace and create evil; I the Lord do all these things.'

'What is that?' said Jean. 'Repeat it.'

Zachariah slowly repeated it. He had intended to add to it something which might satisfy his conscience and rebuke Pauline, but he could not.

'Whence is that?' said Jean.

'From the Bible; give me one and I will show it to you.'

There was no English Bible in the house. It was a book not much used; but Pauline presently produced a French version, and Jean read the passage – '*Qui forme la lumière, et qui crée les ténèbres; qui fait la paix, et qui crée l'adversité; c'est moi, l'Éternel, qui fais toutes les choses là.*'

Pauline bent over her father and read it again.

' "*Qui crée l'adversité*," ' she said. 'Do you believe that?'

'If it is there, I do,' said Zachariah.

'Well, I don't.'

'What's adversity to hell-fire? If He made hell-fire, why not adversity? Besides, if He did not, who did?'

'Don't know a bit, and don't mean to bother myself about it.'

'Right!' broke in Jean – 'right, my child; bother – that is a good word. Don't bother yourself about anything when – bothering will not benefit. There is so much in the world which will – bear a botheration out of which some profit will arise. Now, then, clear the room, and let Zachariah see your art.'

The plates and dishes were all put in a heap and the table pushed aside. Pauline retired for a few moments, and presently came back in a short dress of black velvet, which reached about half-way down from the knee to the ankle. It was trimmed with red: she had stuck a red artificial flower in her hair, and had on a pair of red stockings with dancing slippers probably of her own make. Over her shoulders was a light gauzy shawl. Her father took his station in a corner, and motioned to Zachariah to compress himself into another. By dint of some little management and piling up the chairs, an unoccupied space of about twelve feet square was obtained. Pauline began dancing, her father accompanying her with an oboe. It was a very curious performance. It was nothing like ordinary opera-dancing, and equally unlike any movement ever seen at a ball. It was a series of graceful evolutions with the shawl, which was flung now on one shoulder and now on the other, each movement exquisitely resolving itself, with the most perfect ease, into the one following, and designed apparently to show the capacity of a beautiful figure for poetic expression. Wave fell into wave along every line of her body, and occasionally a posture was arrested, to pass away in an instant into some new combination. There was no definite character in the dance

66

beyond mere beauty. It was melody for melody's sake.
A remarkable change, too, came over the face of the per-
former. She looked serious; but it was not a seriousness
produced by any strain. It was rather the calm which is
found on the face of the statue of a goddess. In none of
her attitudes was there a trace of coquettishness, although
some were most attractive. One in particular was so. She
held a corner of the shawl high above her with her right
hand, and her right foot was advanced so as to show her
whole frame extended, excepting the neck; the head being
bent downwards and sideways.

Suddenly Jean ceased; Pauline threw the shawl over
both her shoulders, made a profound curtsy, and retired;
but in five minutes she was back again in her ordinary
clothes. Zachariah was in sore confusion. He had never
seen anything of the kind before. He had been brought
up in a school which would have considered such an exhi-
bition as the work of the devil. He was distressed, too, to
find that the old Adam was still so strong within him that
he detected a secret pleasure in what he had seen. He
would have liked to have got up and denounced Jean and
Pauline, but somehow he could not. His great-great-
grandfather would have done it, beyond a doubt, but
Zachariah sat still.

'Did you ever perform in public?' he asked.

'No. I was taught when I was very young; but I have
never danced except to please father and his friends.'

This was a relief, and some kind of an excuse. He felt
not quite such a reprobate; but again he reflected that
when he was looking at her he did not know that she was

not in a theatre every night in the week. He expected that
Jean would offer some further explanation of the unusual
accomplishment which his daughter had acquired; but he
was silent, and Zachariah rose to depart, for it was eleven
o'clock. Jean apparently was a little restless at the absence
of approval on Zachariah's part, and at last he said
abruptly: –

'What do you think of her?'

Zachariah hesitated, and Pauline came to the rescue.

'Father, what a shame! Don't put him in such an awkward position.'

'It was very wonderful,' stammered Zachariah, 'but we
are not used to that kind of thing.'

'Who are the "we"?' said Pauline. 'Ah, of course you
are Puritans. I am a – what do you call it? – a daughter –
no, that isn't it – a child of the devil. I won't have that,
though. My father isn't the devil. Even *you* wouldn't say
that, Mr. Coleman. Ah, I have no business to joke, you
look so solemn; you think my tricks are satanic; but what
was it in your book, '*C'est moi, l'Éternel, qui fais toutes les
choses là*"?' and as Zachariah advanced to the door she
made him a bow with a grace which no lady of quality
could have surpassed.

He walked home with many unusual thoughts. It was
the first time he had ever been in the company of a woman
of any liveliness of temperament, and with an intellect
which was on equal terms with that of a man. In his own
Calvinistic Dissenting society, the pious women who were
members of the church took little or no interest in the
mental life of their husbands. They read no books, knew

nothing of politics, were astonishingly ignorant, and lived in their household duties. To be with a woman who could stand up against him was a new experience. Here was a girl to whom every thought her father possessed was familiar!

But there was another experience. From his youth upwards he had been trained with every weapon in the chapel armoury, and yet he now found himself as powerless as the merest novice to prevent the very sinful occupation of dwelling upon every attitude of Pauline, and outlining every one of her limbs. Do what he might, her image was for ever before his eyes, and reconstructed itself after every attempt to abolish it, just as a reflected image in a pool slowly but inevitably gathers itself together again after each disturbance of the water. When he got home, he found, to his surprise, that his wife was still sitting up. She had been to the weekly prayer-meeting, and was not in a very pleasant temper. She was not spiteful, but unusually frigid. She felt herself to be better than her husband, and she asked him if he could not arrange in future that his political meetings might not interfere with his religious duties.

'Your absence, too, was noticed, and Mrs. Carver asked me how it was that Mr. Coleman could let me go home alone. She offered to tell Mr. Carver to come home with me, but I refused.'

Delightfully generous of Mrs. Carver! That was the sort of kindness for which she and many of her Pike Street friends were so distinguished; and Mrs. Coleman not only felt it deeply, but was glad of the opportunity of letting Mr. Coleman know how good the Carvers were.

It was late, but Mrs. Coleman produced the Bible. Zachariah opened it rather mechanically. They were going regularly through it at family worship, and had got into Numbers. The portion for that evening was part of the 26th chapter: 'And these are they that were numbered of the Levites after their families: of Gershon, the family of the Gershonites: of Kohath, the family of the Kohathites: of Merari, the family of the Merarites,' etc., etc. Zachariah, having read about a dozen verses, knelt down and prayed; but, alas! even in his prayer he saw Pauline's red stockings.

The next morning his wife was more pleasant, and even talkative – talkative, that is to say, for her. Something had struck her.

'My dear,' quoth she, as they sat at breakfast, 'what a pity it is that the Major is not a converted character!'

Zachariah could not but think so, too.

'I have been wondering if we could get him to attend our chapel. Who knows? – some word might go to his heart which might be as the seed sown on good ground.'

'Have you tried to convert him yourself?'

'Oh no, Zachariah! I don't think that would be quite proper.'

She screwed up her lips a little, and then, looking down at her knees very demurely, smoothed her apron.

'Why not, my dear? Surely it is our duty to testify to the belief that is in us. Poor Christiana, left alone, says, as you will remember, "O neighbour, knew you but as much as I do, I doubt not but that you would go with me."'

'Ah, yes, that was all very well then.' She again smoothed her apron. 'Besides, you know,' she added suddenly, 'there were no public means of grace in the City of Destruction. Have *you* said anything to the Major?'

'No.'

She did not push her advantage, and the unpleasant fact again stood before Zachariah's eyes, as it had stood a hundred times before them lately, that when he had been with sinners he had been just what they were, barring the use of profane language. What had he done for his Master with the Major, with Jean, and with Pauline? – and the awful figure of the Crucified seemed to rise before him and rebuke him. He was wretched: he had resolved over and over again to break out against those who belonged to the world, to abjure them and all their works. Somehow or other, though, he had not done it.

'Suppose,' said Mrs. Zachariah, 'we were to ask the Major here on Sunday afternoon to tea, and to chapel afterwards.'

'Certainly.' He was rather pleased with the proposition. He would be able to bear witness in this way, at any rate, to the truth.

'Perhaps we might at the same time ask Jean Caillaud, his friend. Would to God' – his wife started – 'would to God,' he exclaimed fervently, 'that these men could be brought into the Church of Christ!'

'To be sure. Ask Mr. Caillaud, then, too.'

'If we do, we must ask his daughter also; he would not go out without her.'

71

'I was not aware he had a daughter. You never told me anything about her.'

'I never saw her till the other evening.'

'I don't know anything of her. She is a foreigner too. I hope she is a respectable young person.'

'I know very little; but she is more English than foreign. Jean has been here a good many years, and she came over when she was quite young. I think she must come.'

'Very well.' And so it was settled.

Zachariah that night vowed to his Redeemer that, come what might, he would never again give Him occasion to look at him with averted face and ask if he was ashamed of Him. The text ran in his ears: '*Whosoever therefore shall be ashamed of Me and of My words in this adulterous and sinful generation, of him also shall the Son of man be ashamed, when He cometh in the glory of His Father with the holy angels.*'

CHAPTER SIX

Tea à la Mode

*

SUNDAY afternoon came. It was the strangest party. Pauline, on being introduced to Mrs. Coleman, made a profound curtsy, which Mrs. Coleman returned by an inclination of her head, as if she consented to recognize Pauline, but to go no further. Tea was served early, as chapel began at half-past six. Mrs. Coleman, although it was Sunday, was very busy. She had made hot buttered toast, and she had bought some muffins, but had appeased her conscience by telling the boy that she would not pay for them till Monday. The milk was always obtained on the same terms. She also purchased some water-cresses; but the water-cress man demanded prompt cash settlement, and she was in a strait. At last the desire for water-cresses prevailed, and she said:

'How much?'

'Three-halfpence.'

'Now, mind I give you twopence for yourself – mind I give it you. I do not approve of buying and selling on Sunday. We will settle about the other ha'porth another time.'

'All right, ma'am; if you like it that way, it's no odds to me'; and Mrs. Coleman went her way upstairs really believing that she had prevented the commission of a crime.

Let those of us cast the stone who can take oath that in their own morality there is no casuistry. Probably ours is worse than hers, because hers was traditional and ours is self-manufactured.

73

Everything being at last in order, Mrs. Coleman, looking rather warm, but still very neat and very charming, sat at the head of the table, with her back to the fireplace; the Major was on her right, Jean on her left, Pauline next to him, and opposite to her Zachariah. Zachariah and his wife believed in asking a blessing on their food; but, curiously enough, in 1814, even amongst the strictest sort, it had come to be the custom not to ask it at breakfast or tea, but only at dinner; although breakfast and tea in those days certainly needed a blessing as much as dinner, for they were substantial meals. An exception was made in favour of public tea-meetings. At a public tea-meeting a blessing was always asked and a hymn was always sung.

For some time nothing remarkable was said. The weather was very hot, and Mrs. Coleman complained. It had been necessary to keep up a fire for the sake of the kettle. The Major promptly responded to her confession of faintness by opening the window wider, by getting a shawl to put over the back of her chair; and these little attentions she rewarded by smiles and particular watchfulness over his plate and cup. At last he and Jean fell to talking about the jubilee which was to take place on the first of the next month to celebrate the centenary of the 'accession of the illustrious family of Brunswick to the throne' – so ran the public notice. There was to be a grand display in the parks, a sham naval action on the Serpentine, and a balloon ascent.

'Are you going, Caillaud?' said the Major. 'It will be a holiday.'

'We,' cried Pauline – 'we! I should think not. *We* go

74

to rejoice over your House of Brunswick; and it is to be the anniversary of your battle of the Nile, too! *We* go! No, no.'

'What's your objection to the House of Brunswick? And as for the battle of the Nile, you are no friend to Napoleon.' So replied the Major, who always took a pleasure in exciting Pauline.

'The House of Brunswick! Why should we thank God for them; thank God for the stupidest race that ever sat upon a throne; thank God for stupidity – and in a king, Major? God, the Maker of the sun and stars – to call upon the nation to bless Him for your Prince Regent. As for the Nile, I am, as you say, no friend to Napoleon, but I am French. It is horrible to me to think – I saw him the other day – that your Brunswick Prince is in London and Napoleon is in Elba.'

'God, after all,' said the Major, laughing, 'is not so hostile to stupidity, then, as you suppose.'

'Ah! don't plague me, Major; that's what you are always trying to do. I'm not going to thank the Supreme for the Brunswicks. I don't believe He wanted them here.'

Pauline's religion was full of the most lamentable inconsistencies, which the Major was very fond of exposing, but without much effect, and her faith was restored after every assault with wonderful celerity. By way of excuse for her, we may be permitted to say that a perfectly consistent, unassailable creed, in which conclusion follows from premiss in unimpeachable order, is impossible. We cannot construct such a creed about any man or woman we know, and least of all about the universe. We acknowledge opposites which we have no power to bring together; and Pauline, although she knew nothing of philosophy, may not have been completely wrong with her Supreme who hated the Brunswicks and nevertheless sanctioned Carlton House.

Pauline surprised Mrs. Zachariah considerably. A woman, and more particularly a young woman, even supposing her to be quite orthodox, who behaved in that style amongst the members of Pike Street, would have been like a wild seagull in a farm-yard of peaceful, clucking, brown-speckled fowls. All the chapel maidens and matrons, of course, were serious; but their seriousness was decent and in order. Mrs. Coleman was therefore scandalized, nervous, and dumb. Jean, as his manner was when his daughter expressed herself strongly, was also silent. His love for her was a consuming, hungry fire. It utterly extinguished all trace, not merely of selfishness, but of self, in him, and he was perfectly content, when Pauline spoke well, to remain quiet, and not allow a word of his to disturb the effect which he thought she ought to produce.

The Major, as a man of the world, thought the conversation was becoming a little too metaphysical, and asked Mrs. Coleman gaily if she would like to see the *fête*.

'Really, I hardly know what to say. I suppose' – and this was said with a peculiar acidity – 'there is nothing wrong in it? Zachariah, my dear, would you like to go?'

Zachariah did not reply. His thoughts were elsewhere. But at last the spirit moved in him –

'Miss Pauline, your Supreme Being won't help you very

far. There is no light save in God's Holy Word. God
hath concluded them all in unbelief that He might have
mercy upon all. As by one man's disobedience many were
made sinners, so by the obedience of One shall many be
made righteous. That is the explanation; that is the gospel.
God allows all this wickedness that His own glory may
be manifested thereby, and His own love in sending Jesus
Christ to save us: that, as sin hath reigned unto death,
even so might grace reign through righteousness unto
eternal life by Jesus Christ our Lord. Do you ask me why
does God wink at the crimes of kings and murderers? What
if God, willing to show His wrath, and to make His power
known, endured with much long-suffering the vessels of
wrath fitted to destruction, and that He might make known
the riches of His glory on the vessels of mercy which He
had afore prepared unto glory, even us whom He had
called? Miss Pauline, the mere light of human reason will
never save you or give you peace. Unless you believe
God's Word you are lost; lost here and hereafter; lost *here*
even, for until you believe it you wander in a fog of ever-
deepening confusion. All is dark and inexplicable.'

Being very much excited, he used largely the words
of St. Paul, and not his own. How clear it all seemed to
him, how indisputable! Childish association and years of
unquestioning repetition gave an absolute certainty to
what was almost unmeaning to other people.

Mrs. Zachariah, although she had expressed a strong
desire for the Major's conversion, and was the only other
representative of the chapel present, was very fidgety and
uncomfortable during this speech. She had an exquisite

art, which she sometimes practised, of dropping her husband, or rather bringing him down. So, when there was a pause, everybody being moved at least by his earnestness, she said:

'My dear, will you take any more tea?'

He was looking on the table-cloth, with his head on his hands, and did not answer.

'Major Maitland, may I give you some more tea?'

'No, thank you.' The Major, too, was impressed – more impressed than the lady who sat next to him, and she felt rebuffed and annoyed. To Pauline, Zachariah had spoken Hebrew; but his passion was human, and her heart leapt out to meet him, although she knew not what answer to make. Her father was in the same position; but the Major's case was a little different. He had certainly at some time or other read the Epistle to the Romans, and some expressions were not entirely unfamiliar to him.

' "Vessels of wrath fitted to destruction!" – a strong and noble phrase. Who are your vessels of wrath, Coleman?'

Caillaud and Pauline saw a little light, but it was speedily eclipsed again.

'The unregenerate.'

'Who are they?'

'Those whom God has not called.'

'Castlereagh, Liverpool, Sidmouth, and the rest of the gang, for example?'

Zachariah felt that the moment had come.

'Yes, yes; but not only they. More than they. God help me if I deny the Cross of Christ – all of us into whose hearts God's grace has not been poured – we, you, all of

78

us, if we have not been born of the Spirit and redeemed by the sacrifice of His Son.'

Zachariah put in the 'us' and the 'we', it will be observed. It was a concession to blunt the sharpness of that dreadful dividing-line.

'We? Not yourself, Caillaud, and Pauline?'

He could not face the question. Something within him said that he ought to have gone further; that he ought to have singled out the Major, Caillaud, and Pauline; held them fast, looked straight into their eyes, and told them each one there and then that they were in the bonds of iniquity, sold unto Satan, and in danger of hell-fire. But, alas! he was at least a century and a half too late. He struggled, wrestled, self against self, and failed, not through want of courage, but because he wanted a deeper conviction. The system was still the same, even to its smallest details, but the application had become difficult. The application, indeed, was a good deal left to the sinner himself. That was the difference. Phrases had been invented or discovered which served to express modern hesitation to bring the accepted doctrine into actual, direct, week-day practice. It was in that way that it was gradually bled into impotence. One of these phrases came into his mind. It was from his favourite author –

' "Who art thou that judgest?" It is not for me, Major Maitland.'

Ah, but, Zachariah, do you remember that Paul is not speaking of those who deny the Lord, but of the weak in faith; of differences in eating and drinking, and the observation of days? Whether he remembered it or not, he could say no more. Caillaud, the Major, Pauline, condemned to the everlasting consequences of the wrath of the Almighty! He could not pronounce such a sentence, and yet his conscience whispered that just for the want of the last nail in a sure place what he had built would come tumbling to the ground. During the conversation the time had stolen away, and, to their horror, Zachariah and his wife discovered that it was a quarter-past six. He hastily informed his guests that he had hoped they would attend him to his chapel. Would they go? The Major consented; he had nothing particular on hand; but Caillaud and Pauline refused. Zachariah was particularly urgent that these two should accompany him, but they were steadfast, for all set religious performances were hateful to them.

'No, Coleman, no more; I know what it all means.'

'And I,' added Pauline, 'cannot sit still with so many respectable people; I never could. I have been to church, and always felt impelled to do something peculiar in it which would have made them turn me out. I cannot, too, endure preaching. I cannot tolerate that man up in the pulpit looking down over all the people – so wise and so self-satisfied. I want to pull him out and say, "Here, you, sir, come here and let me see if you can tell me two or three things I want to know." Then, Mr. Coleman, I am never well in a great building, especially in a church; I have such a weight upon my head, as if the roof were resting on it.'

He looked mournfully at her, but there was no time to remonstrate. Mrs. Zachariah was ready, in her Sunday best of sober bluish cloud-colour. Although it was her

Sunday best, there was not a single thread of finery on it, and there was not a single crease nor spot. She bade Caillaud and Pauline good-bye with much cheerfulness, and tripped downstairs. The Major had preceded her, but Zachariah lingered for a moment with the other two.

'Come, my dear, make haste, we shall be so late.'

'Go on with the Major; I shall catch you in a moment; I walk faster than you. I must close the window a trifle, and take two or three of the coals off the fire.'

Caillaud and Pauline lingered too. The three were infinitely nearer to one another than they knew. Zachariah thought he was so far, and yet he was so close. The man rose up behind the Calvinist and reached out arms to touch and embrace his friends.

'Good-bye, Caillaud; good-bye, Pauline! May God in His mercy bless and save you. God bless you!'

Caillaud looked steadfastly at him for a moment, and then, in his half-forgotten French fashion, threw his arms round his neck, and the two remained for a moment locked together, Pauline standing by herself apart. She came forward, took Zachariah's hand, when it was free, in both her own, held her head back a little, as if for clearness of survey, and said slowly, 'God bless you, Mr. Coleman.' She then went downstairs. Her father followed her, and Zachariah went after his wife and the Major, whom, however, he did not overtake till he reached the chapel door, where they were both waiting for him.

CHAPTER SEVEN

Jephthah

★

THE Reverend Thomas Bradshaw, of Pike Street Meeting-house, was not a descendant from Bradshaw the regicide, but claimed that he belonged to the same family. He was in 1814 about fifty years old, and minister of one of the most important churches in the eastern part of London. He was tall and spare, and showed his height in the pulpit, for he always spoke without a note, and used a small Bible, which he held close to his eyes. He was a good classical scholar, and he understood Hebrew, too, as well as few men in that day understood it. He had a commanding figure, ruled his church like a despot; had a crowded congregation, of which the larger portion was masculine; and believed in predestination and the final perseverance of the saints. He was rather unequal in his discourses, for he had a tendency to moodiness and, at times, even to hypochondria. When this temper was upon him he was combative or melancholy; and sometimes, to the disgust of many who came from all parts of London to listen to him, he did not preach in the proper sense of the word, but read a chapter, made a comment or two upon it, caused a hymn to be sung, and then dismissed his congregation with the briefest of prayers. Although he took no active part in politics, he was republican through and through, and never hesitated for a moment in those degenerate days to say what he thought about any scandal. In this respect he differed from his fellow-ministers, who, under the pretence of increasing zeal for religion, had daily fewer and fewer points of contact with

82

the world outside. Mr. Bradshaw had been married when he was about thirty; but his wife died in giving birth to a daughter, who also died; and for twenty years he had been a widower, with no thought of changing his condition. He was understood to have peculiar opinions about second marriages, although he kept them very much to himself. One thing, however, was known, that for a twelvemonth after the death of his wife he was away from England, and that he came back an altered man to his people in Bedford-shire, where at that time he was settled. His discourses were remarkably strong, and of a kind seldom, or indeed never, heard now. They taxed the whole mental powers of his audience, and were utterly unlike the simple stuff which became fashionable with the Evangelistic move-ment. Many of them, taken down by some of his hearers, survive in manuscript to the present day. They will not, as a rule, bear printing, because the assumption on which they rest is not now assumed; but if it be granted, they are unanswerable; and it is curious that every now and then, although they are never for a moment any-thing else than a strict deduction from what we in the latter half of the century consider unproven or even false, they express themselves in the same terms as the newest philosophy. Occasionally, too, more particularly when he sets himself the task of getting into the interior of a Bible character, he is intensely dramatic, and what are shadows to the careless reader become living human beings, with the reddest of blood visible under their skin.

On this particular evening Mr. Bradshaw took the story of Jephthah's daughter: – 'The Spirit of the Lord came upon Jephthah.' Here is an abstract of his discourse. 'It *was* the Spirit of the Lord, notwithstanding what happened. I beg you also to note that there is a mistranslation in our version. The Hebrew has it, "Then it shall be, that *whosoever*" – not *whatsoever* – "cometh forth of the doors of my house to meet me, when I return in peace from the children of Ammon, shall surely be the Lord's, and I will offer *him*" – not *it* – "up for a burnt-offering." Nevertheless I believe my text – it *was* the Spirit of the Lord. This Hebrew soldier was the son of a harlot. He was driven by his brethren out of his father's house. Ammon made war upon Israel, and in their distress the elders of Israel went to fetch Jephthah. Mark, my friends, God's election. The children of the lawful wife are passed by, and the child of the harlot is chosen. Jephthah forgets his grievances and becomes captain of the host. Ammon is over against him. Jephthah's rash vow – this is sometimes called. I say it is not a rash vow. It may be rash to those who have never been brought to extremity by the children of Ammon – to those who have not cared whether Ammon or Christ wins. Men and women sitting here in comfortable pews' – this was said with a kind of snarl – 'may talk of Jephthah's rash vow. God be with them, what do they know of the struggles of such a soul? It does not say so directly in the Bible, but we are led to infer it, that Jephthah was successful because of his vow. "The Lord delivered them into his hands." He would not have done it if He had been displeased with the "rash vow" ' (another snarl). 'He smote them from Aroer even till thou come to Minnith. Ah, but what follows? The

84

Omnipotent and Omniscient might have ordered it, surely, that a slave might have met Jephthah. Why, in His mercy, did He not do it? Who are we that we should question what He did? But if we may not inquire too closely into His designs, it is permitted us, my friends, when His reason accords with ours, to try and show it. Jephthah had played for a great stake. Ought the Almighty – let us speak it with reverence – to have let him off with an ox, or even with a serf? I say that if we are to conquer Ammon we must pay for it, and we ought to pay for it. Yes, and perhaps God wanted the girl – who can tell? Jephthah comes back in triumph. Let me read the passage to you: "Behold his daughter came out to meet him with timbrels and with dances: *and she was his only child: beside her he had neither son nor daughter.* And it came to pass, when he saw her, that he rent his clothes, and said, Alas, my daughter! thou hast brought me very low, and thou art one of them that trouble me: for I have opened my mouth unto the Lord, and I cannot go back." Now, you read poetry, I dare say – what you call poetry. I say in all of it – all, at least, I have seen – nothing comes up to that. "*She was his only child: beside her he had neither son nor daughter.*" ' – (Mr. Bradshaw's voice broke a little as he went over the words again with great deliberation and infinite pathos.) – 'The inspired writer leaves the fact just as it stands, and is content. Inspiration itself can do nothing to make it more touching than it is in its own bare nakedness. There is no thought in Jephthah of recantation, nor in the maiden of revolt, but nevertheless he has his own sorrow. *He is brought very low.* God does not rebuke him for his grief. He knows well enough, my dear friends, the nature which He took upon Himself – nay, are we not the breath of His nostrils, created in His image? He does not anywhere, therefore, I say, forbid that we should even break our hearts over those we love and lose. She asks for two months by herself upon the mountains before her death. What a time for him! At the end of the two months God held him still to his vow; he did not shrink; she submitted, and was slain. But you will want me to tell you in conclusion where the gospel is in all this. Gospel! I say that the blessed gospel is in the Old Testament as well as in the New. I say that the Word of God is one, and that His message is here this night for you and me, as distinctly as it is at the end of the sacred volume. Observe, as I have told you before, that Jephthah is the son of the harlot. He hath mercy on whom He will have mercy. He calls them His people who are not His people; and He calls her beloved which was not beloved. God at any rate is no stickler for hereditary rights. Moreover, it does not follow because you, my hearers, have God-fearing parents that God has elected you. He may have chosen, instead of you, instead of me, the wretchedest creature outside, whose rags we will not touch. But to what did God elect Jephthah? To a respectable, easy, decent existence, with money at interest, regular meals, sleep after them, and unbroken rest at night? He elected him to that tremendous oath and that tremendous penalty. He elected him to the agony he endured while she was away upon the hills! That is God's election; an election to the cross and to the cry, "Eli, Eli, lama Sabachthani." "Yes," you will

say, "but He elected him to the victory over Ammon."
Doubtless He did; but what cared Jephthah for his victory
over Ammon when she came to meet him, or, indeed, for
the rest of his life? What is a victory, what are triumphal
arches and the praise of all creation to a lonely man? Be
sure, if God elects you, He elects you to suffering. Whom
He loveth He chasteneth, and His stripes are not play-
work. Ammon will not be conquered unless your heart
be wellnigh broken. I tell you, too, as Christ's minister,
that you are not to direct your course according to your
own desires. You are not to say, "I will give up this and
that so that I may be saved." Did not St. Paul wish himself accursed from Christ for his brethren? If God should
command you to go down to the bottomless pit in fulfilment of His blessed designs, it is your place to go. Out
with self – I was about to say this damned self; and if
Israel calls, if Christ calls, take not a sheep or ox – that is
easy enough – but take your choicest possession, take your
own heart, your own blood, your very self, to the altar.'

During the sermon the Major was much excited. Apart
altogether from the effect of the actual words spoken, Mr.
Bradshaw had a singular and contagious power over men.
The three, Mrs. Coleman, the Major, and Zachariah, came
out together. Mrs. Zachariah stayed behind in the lobby
for some female friends to whom she wished to speak
about a Sunday-school tea-meeting which was to take
place that week. The other two stood aside, ill at ease,
amongst the crowd pressing out into the street. Presently
Mrs. Coleman found her friend, whom she at once informed that Major Maitland and her husband were wait-

ing for her, and that therefore she had not a moment to spare. That little triumph accomplished, she had nothing of importance to say about the tea-meeting, and rejoined her party with great good-humour. She walked between the Major and Zachariah, and at once asked the Major how he 'enjoyed the service.' The phrase was very unpleasant to Zachariah, but he was silent.

'Well, ma'am,' said the Major, 'Mr. Bradshaw is a very remarkable man. It is a long time since any speaker stirred me as he did. He is a born orator, if ever there was one.'

'I could have wished,' said Zachariah, 'as you are not often in chapel, that his sermon had been founded on some passage in the New Testament which would have given him the opportunity of more simply expounding the gospel of Christ.'

'He could not have been better, I should think. He went to my heart, though it is rather a difficult passage in the case of a man about town like me; and I tell you what, Coleman, he made me determine I would read the Bible again. What a story that is!'

'Major, I thank God if you will read it; and not for the stories in it, save as all are part of one story – the story of God's redeeming mercy.'

The Major made no reply, for the word was unwinged.

Mrs. Zachariah was silent, but when they came to their door both she and her husband pressed him to come in. He refused, however; he would stroll homeward, he said, and have a smoke as he went.

'He touched me, Coleman, he did. I thought, between you and me' – and he spoke softly – 'I had not now got

88

such a tender place; I thought it was all healed over long ago. I cannot come in. You'll excuse me. Yes, I'll just wander back to Piccadilly. I could not talk.'

They parted, and Zachariah and his wife went upstairs. Their supper was soon ready.

'Jane,' he said slowly, 'I did not receive much assistance from you in my endeavours to bring our friends to a knowledge of the truth. I thought that, as you desired the attempt, you would have helped me a little.'

'There is a reason for everything; and what is more, I do not consider it right to take upon myself what belongs to a minister. It may do more harm than good.'

'Take upon yourself what belongs to a minister! My dear Jane, is nobody but a minister to bear witness for the Master?'

'Of course I did not mean to say that; you know I did not. Why do you catch at my words? Perhaps, if you had not been quite so forward, Mr. Caillaud and his daughter might have gone to chapel.'

After supper, and when he was alone, Zachariah sat for some time without moving. He presently rose and opened the Bible again, which lay on the table – the Bible which belonged to his father – and turned to the fly-leaf on which was written the family history. There was the record of his father's marriage, dated on the day of the event. There was the record of his own birth. There was the record of his mother's death, still in his father's writing, but in an altered hand, the letters not so distinct, and the strokes crooked and formed with difficulty. There was the record of Zachariah's own marriage. A cloud of shapeless, inarticulate sentiment obscured the man's eyes and brain. He could not define what he felt, but he did feel. He could not bear it, and he shut the book, opening it again at the Twenty-second Psalm – the one which the disciples of Jesus called to mind on the night of the crucifixion. It was one which Mr. Bradshaw often read, and Zachariah had noted in it a few corrections made in the translation: –

'My God, my God, why hast Thou forsaken me?. . . Our fathers trusted in Thee; they trusted, and Thou didst deliver them. . . . Be not far from me; for trouble is near; for there is none to help. . . . Be Thou not far from me, O Lord: O my strength, haste Thee to help me. . . . Save me from the lion's mouth: and from the horns of the wild oxen Thou hast answered me.'

'From the horns of the wild oxen' – that correction had often been precious to Zachariah. When at the point of being pinned to the ground – so he understood it – help had arisen; risen up from the earth, and might again arise. It was upon the first part of the text he dwelt now. It came upon him with fearful distinctness that he was alone – that he could never hope for sympathy from his wife as long as he lived. Mr. Bradshaw's words that evening recurred to him. God's purpose in choosing to smite Jephthah in that way was partly intelligible; and, after all, Jephthah was elected to redeem his country too. But what could be God's purpose in electing one of His servants to indifference and absence of affection where he had a right to expect it? Could anybody be better for not being loved? Even Zachariah could not think it possible. But Mr. Bradshaw's words again recurred. Who was he that he should question God's designs? It might be part of the Divine design that he, Zachariah Coleman, should not be made better by anything. It might be part of that design, part of the fulfilment of a plan devised by the Infinite One, that he should be broken, nay, perhaps not saved. Mr. Bradshaw's doctrine that night was nothing new. Zachariah had believed from his childhood, or had thought he believed, that the potter had power over the clay – of the same lump to make one vessel unto honour, and another unto dishonour; and that the thing formed unto dishonour could not reply and say to him that formed it, 'Why hast thou made me thus?' Nevertheless, to believe it generally was one thing; to believe it as a truth for him was another. Darkness, the darkness as of the crucifixion night, seemed over and around him. Poor wretch! he thought he was struggling with his weakness; but he was in reality struggling against his own strength. *Why* had God so decreed? Do what he could, that fatal *why*, the protest of his reason, asserted itself; and yet he cursed himself for permitting it, believing it to be a sin. He walked about his room for some relief. He looked out of the window. It was getting late; the sky was clearing, as it does in London at that hour, and he saw the stars. There was nothing to help him there. They mocked him rather with their imperturbable, obstinate stillness. At last he turned round, fell upon his knees, and poured out himself before his Maker, entreating Him for light. He rose from the ground, looked again out of the window, and the first flush of the morning was just visible. Light was coming to the world in obedience to the Divine command, but not to him. He was exhausted, and crept into his bedroom, undressing without candle, and without a sound. For a few minutes he thought he should never sleep again, save in his grave; but an unseen Hand presently touched him, and he knew nothing till he was awakened by the broad day streaming over him.

CHAPTER EIGHT
Unconventional Justice
★

In December 1814 a steamboat was set in motion on the Limehouse Canal, the Lord Mayor and other distinguished persons being on board. In the same month Joanna Southcott died. She had announced that on the 19th October she was to be delivered of the Prince of Peace, although she was then sixty years old. Thousands of persons believed her, and a cradle was made. The Prince of Peace did not arrive, and in a little more than two months poor Joanna had departed, the cause of her departure having been certified as dropsy. Death did not diminish the number of her disciples, for they took refuge in the hope of her resurrection. 'The arm of the Lord is not shortened,' they truly affirmed; and even to this day there are people who are waiting for the fulfilment of Joanna's prophecies and the appearance of the 'second Shiloh.' Zachariah had been frequently twitted in joke by his profane companions in the printing-office upon his supposed belief in the delusion. It was their delight to assume that all the 'pious ones,' as they called them, were alike; and on the morning of the 30th of December, the day after Joanna expired, they were more than usually tormenting. Zachariah did not remonstrate. In his conscientious eagerness to bear witness for his Master, he had often tried his hand upon his mates; but he had never had the smallest success, and had now desisted. Moreover, his thoughts were that morning with his comrades, the Friends of the People. He hummed to himself the lines from *Laura* –

'Within that land was many a malcontent,
Who cursed the tyranny to which he bent;
That soil full many a wringing despot saw,
Who worked his wantonness in form of law;
Long war without and frequent broil within
Had made a path for blood and giant sin.'

The last meeting had been unusually exciting. Differences of opinion had arisen as to future procedure, many of the members, the Secretary included, advocating action; but what they understood by it is very difficult to say. A special call had been made for that night, and Zachariah was in a difficulty. His native sternness and detestation of kings and their ministers would have led him almost to any length; but he had a sober head on his shoulders. So had the Major, and so had Caillaud. Consequently they held back, and insisted, before stirring a step towards actual revolution, that there should be some fair chance of support and success. The Major in particular warned them of the necessity of drill; and plainly told them also that not only were the middle classes all against them, but their own class was hostile. This was perfectly true, although it was a truth so unpleasant that he had to endure some very strong language, and even hints of treason. No wonder: for it is undoubtedly very bitter to be obliged to believe that the men whom we want to help do not themselves wish to be helped. To work hard for those who will thank us, to head a majority against oppressors, is a brave thing; but far more honour is due to the Maitlands, Caillauds, Colemans, and others of that stamp who strove for thirty years from the outbreak of the French Revolution onwards not merely to rend the chains of the prisoners, but had to achieve the more difficult task of convincing them that they would be happier if they were free. These heroes are forgotten, or nearly so. Who remembers the poor creatures who met in the early mornings on the Lancashire moors or were shot by the yeomanry? They sleep in graves over which stands no tombstone, or probably their bodies have been carted away to make room for a railway which has been driven through their resting-place. They saw the truth before those whom the world delights to honour as its political redeemers; but they have perished utterly from our recollection, and will never be mentioned in history. Will there ever be a great Day of Assize when a just judgment shall be pronounced; when all the impostors who have been crowned for what they did not deserve will be stripped, and the Divine word will be heard calling upon the faithful to inherit the Kingdom, – who, when 'I was an hungered gave me meat, when I was thirsty gave me drink; when I was a stranger took me in; when I was naked visited me; when I was in prison came unto me'? Never! It was a dream of an enthusiastic Galilean youth, and let us not desire that it may ever come true. Let us rather gladly consent to be crushed into indistinguishable dust, with no hope of record; rejoicing only if some infinitesimal portion of the good work may be achieved by our obliteration, and content to be remembered only in that anthem which in the future it will be ordained shall be sung in our religious services in honour of all holy apostles and martyrs who have left no name.

The night before the special meeting a gentleman in a cloak, and with a cigar in his mouth, sauntered past the entrance to Carter's Rents, where Mr. Secretary lived. It was getting late, but he was evidently not in a hurry, and seemed to enjoy the coolness of the air, for presently he turned and walked past the entrance again. He took out his watch – it was a quarter to eleven o'clock – and he cursed Mr. Secretary and the beer-shops which had probably detained him. A constable came by, but never showed himself in the least degree inquisitive, although it was odd that anybody should select Carter's Rents for a stroll. Presently Mr. Secretary came in sight, a trifle, but not much, the worse for liquor. It was odd, also, that he took no notice of the blue cloak and cigar, but went straight to his own lodging. The other, after a few moments, followed; and it was a third time odd that he should find the door unbolted and go upstairs. All this, we say, would have been strange to a spectator, but it was not so to these three persons. Presently the one first named found himself in Mr. Secretary's somewhat squalid room. He then stood disclosed as the assistant whom the Secretary had first seen at Whitehall sitting in the Commissioner's office. This was not the second nor third interview which had taken place since then.

'Well, Mr. Hardy, what do you want here to-night?'

'Well, my friend, you know, I suppose. How goes the game?'

'D – n me if I *do* know. If you think I am going to split, you are very much mistaken.'

'Split! Who wants you to split? Why, there's nothing

to split about. I can tell you just as much as you can tell me.'

'Why do you come here, then?'

'For the pleasure of seeing you, and to' – Mr. Hardy. put his hand carelessly in his pocket, a movement which was followed by a metallic jingle – 'and just to – to – explain one or two little matters.'

The Secretary observed that he was very tired.

'Are you? I believe I am tired, too.'

Mr. Hardy took out a little case-bottle with brandy in it, and the Secretary, without saying a word, produced two mugs and a jug of water. The brandy was mixed by Mr. Hardy; but his share of the spirit differed from that assigned to his friend.

'Split!' he continued; 'no, I should think not. But we want you to help us. The Major and one or two more had better be kept out of harm's way for a little while; and we propose not to hurt them, but to take care of them a bit, you understand? And if, the next time, he and the others will be there – we have been looking for the Major for three or four days, but he is not to be found in his old quarters – we will just give them a call. When will you have your next meeting? They will all be handy then.'

'You can find that out without my help. It's to-morrow.'

'Ah! I suppose you've had a stormy discussion. I hope your moderate counsels prevailed.'

Mr. Secretary winked and gave his head a twist on one side, as if he meant thereby to say, 'You don't catch me.'

'It's a pity,' continued Mr. Hardy, taking no notice,

'that some men are always for rushing into extremities. Why don't they try and redress their grievances, if they have any, in the legitimate way which you yourself propose – by petition?'

It so happened that a couple of hours before, Mr. Secretary having been somewhat noisy and insubordinate, the Major had been obliged to rule him out of order and request his silence. The insult – for so he considered it – was rankling in him.

'Because,' he replied, 'we have amongst us two or three d – d conceited, stuck-up fools, who think they are going to ride over us. By God, they are mistaken though! They are the chaps who do all the mischief. Not that I'd say anything against them – no, notwithstanding I stand up against them.'

'Do all the mischief – yes, you've just hit it. I do believe that if it were not for these fellows the others would be quiet enough.'

The Secretary took a little more brandy and water. The sense of wrong within him was like an open wound, and the brandy inflamed it. He also began to think that it would not be a bad thing for him if he could seclude the Major, Caillaud, and Zachariah for a season. Zachariah in particular he mortally hated.

'What some of these fine folks would like to do, you see, Mr. Hardy, is to persuade us poor devils to get up the row, while they *direct* it. *Direct* it, that's their word; but we're not going to be humbugged.'

'Too wide awake, I should say.'

'I should say so too. We are to be told off for the Bank

of England, and they are to show it to us at the other end of Cheapside.'

'Bank of England,' said Mr. Hardy, laughing; 'that's a joke. You might run your heads a long while against that before you get in. You don't drink your brandy and water.'

The Secretary took another gulp. 'And he's a military man – a military man – a military man.' He was getting rather stupid now, and repeated the phrase each of the three times with increasing unsteadiness, but also with increasing contempt.

Mr. Hardy took out his watch. It was getting on towards midnight. 'Good-bye; glad to see you all right,' and he turned to leave. There was a jingling of coin again, and when he had left Mr. Secretary took up the five sovereigns which had found their way to the table and put them in his pocket. His visitor picked his way downstairs. The constable was still pacing up and down Carter's Rents, but again did not seem to observe him, and he walked meditatively to Jermyn Street. He was at his office by half-past nine, and his chief was only half an hour later.

The Major had thought it prudent to change his address; and, furthermore, it was the object of the Government to make his arrest, with that of his colleagues, at the place of meeting, not only to save trouble, but because it would look better. Mr. Hardy had found out, therefore, all he wanted to know, and was enabled to confirm his opinion that the Major was the head of the conspiracy.

But underneath Mr. Secretary's mine was a deeper

mine; for as the Major sat at breakfast the next morning a note came for him, the messenger leaving directly he delivered it to the servant. It was very brief: – 'No meeting to-night. Warn all except the Secretary, who has already been acquainted.' There was no signature, and he did not know the handwriting. He reflected for a little while, and then determined to consult Caillaud and Coleman, who were his informal Cabinet. He had no difficulty in finding Coleman, but the Caillauds were not at home, and it was agreed that postponement could do no harm. A message was therefore left at Caillaud's house, and one was sent to every one of the members, but two or three could not be discovered.

Meanwhile Mr. Secretary, who, strange to say, had *not* been acquainted, had been a little overcome by Mr. Hardy's brandy on the top of the beer he had taken beforehand, and woke in the morning very miserable. Finding the five sovereigns in his pocket, he was tempted to a public-house hard by, in order that he might cool his stomach and raise his spirits with a draught or two of ale. He remained there a little too long, and on reaching home was obliged to go to bed again. He awoke about six, and then it came into his still somewhat confused brain that he had to attend the meeting. At half-past seven he accordingly took his departure. Meanwhile the Major and Zachariah had determined to post themselves in Red Lion Street, to intercept those of their comrades with whom they had not been able to communicate, and also to see what was going to happen. At a quarter to eight the Secretary turned out of Holborn, and when he came a little nearer, Zachariah saw that at a distance of fifty yards there was a constable following him. He came on slowly until he was abreast of a narrow court, when suddenly there was a pistol-shot, and he was dead on the pavement. Zachariah's first impulse was to rush forward, but he saw the constable running, followed by others, and he discerned in an instant that to attempt to assist would lead to his own arrest and do no good. He managed, however, to reach the Major, and for two or three moments they stood stock-still on the edge of the pavement struck with amazement. Presently a woman passed them with a thick veil over her face.

'Home,' she said; 'don't stay here like fools. Pack up your things and be off. You'll be in prison to-morrow morning.'

'Be off!' gasped Zachariah; 'be off! – where?'

'Anywhere,' and she had gone.

The constables, after putting the corpse in a hackney coach, proceeded to the room; but it was dark and empty. They had no directions to do anything more that night, and returned to Bow Street. The next morning, however, as soon as it was light, a Secretary of State's warrant, backed by sufficient force, was presented at the lodgings of Caillaud and Zachariah. The birds had flown, and not a soul could tell what had become of them. In Zachariah's street, which was rather a Radical quarter, the official inquiries were not answered politely, and one of the constables received on the top of his head an old pail with slops in it. The minutest investigation failed to discover to whom the pail belonged.

CHAPTER NINE

A Strain on the Cable

★

Bow Street was completely at fault, and never discovered the secret of that assassination. It was clear that neither the Major nor Coleman were the murderers, as they had been noticed at some distance from the spot where the Secretary fell by several persons who described them accurately. Nor was Caillaud suspected, as the constable testified that he passed him on the opposite side of the street as he followed the Secretary. The only conclusion, according to Bow Street, which was free from all doubt was, that whoever did the deed was a committee consisting of a single member. A reward of £500 did not bring forward anybody who knew anything about the business. As for Caillaud, his daughter, and the Major, the next morning saw them far on the way to Dover, and eventually they arrived at Paris in safety. Zachariah, when he reached home, found his wife gone. A note lay for him there, probably from the same hand which warned the Major, telling him not to lose an instant, but to join in Islington one of the mails to Manchester. His wife would start that night from St. Martin's-le-Grand by a coach which went by another road. He was always prompt, and in five minutes he was out of the house. The fare was carefully folded by his unknown friend in the letter. He just managed, as directed, to secure a place, not by the regular Manchester mail, but by one which went through Barnet and stopped to take up passengers at the 'Angel'. He climbed upon the roof, and presently was travelling rapidly through Holloway and Highgate. He found, to his relief, that nobody had heard of the murder, and he was left pretty much to his own reflections. His first thoughts were an attempt to unravel the mystery. Why was it so sudden? Why had no word nor hint of what was intended reached him? He could not guess. In those days the clubs were so beset with spies that frequently the most important resolutions were taken by one man, who confided in nobody. It was winter, but fortunately Zachariah was well wrapped up. He journeyed on, hour after hour, in a state of mazed bewilderment, one thought tumbling over another, and when morning broke over the flats he had not advanced a single step in the determination of his future path. Nothing is more painful to a man of any energy than the inability to put things in order in himself – to place before himself what he has to do, and arrange the means for doing it. To be the passive victim of a rushing stream of disconnected impressions is torture, especially if the emergency be urgent. So when the sun came up Zachariah began to be ashamed of himself that the night had passed in these idiotic moonings, which had left him just where he was, and he tried to settle what he was to do when he reached Manchester. He did not know a soul; but he could conjecture why he was advised to go thither. It was a disaffected town, and Friends of the People were very strong there. His first duty was to get a lodging, his second to get work, and his third to find out a minister of God under whom he could worship. He put this last, not because it was the least important, but because he had the most time to decide upon it. At about ten o'clock at night he came to his journey's end, and to his joy saw his wife waiting for him. They went at once to a small inn hard by, and Mrs. Coleman began to overwhelm him with interrogation; but he quietly suggested that not a syllable should be spoken till they had had some rest, and that they should swallow their supper and go to bed. In the morning Zachariah rose and looked out of the window. He saw nothing but a small backyard in which some miserable, scraggy fowls were crouching under a cart to protect themselves from the rain, which was falling heavily through the dim, smoky air. His spirits sank. He had no fear of apprehension or prosecution, but the prospect before him was depressing. Although he was a poor man, he had not been accustomed to oscillations of fortune, and he was in an utterly strange place, with five pounds in his pocket and nothing to do.

He was, however, resolved not to yield, and thought it best to begin with his wife before she could begin with him.

'Now, my dear, tell me what has happened, who sent you here, and what kind of a journey you have had.'

'Mr. Bradshaw came about seven o'clock, and told me the Government was about to suppress the Friends of the People; that you did not know it; that I must go to Manchester; that you would come after me; and that a message would be left for you. He took me to the coach, and paid for me.'

'Mr. Bradshaw! Did he tell you anything more?'

'No; except that he did not think we should be pursued, and that he would send our things after us when he knew where we were.'

'You have not heard anything more, then?'

'No.'

'You haven't heard that the Secretary was shot?'

'Shot! Oh dear! Zachariah, what will become of us?'

Her husband then told her what he knew, she listening with great eagerness and in silence.

'Oh, Zachariah, what will become of us?' she broke out again.

'There is no reason to worry yourself, Jane; it is perfectly easy for me to prove my innocence. It is better for us, however, to stay here for a time. The Government won't go any further with us; they will search for the murderer – that's all.'

'Why, then, are we sent here and the others are let alone? I suppose the Major is not here?'

'I cannot say.'

'To think I should ever come to this; I haven't got a rag with me beyond what I have on. I haven't got any clean things; a nice sort of creature I am to go out of doors. And it all had nothing to do with us.'

'Nothing to do with us! My dear Jane, do you mean that we are not to help other people, but sit at home and enjoy ourselves? Besides, if you thought it wrong, why did you not say so before?'

'How was I to know what you were doing. You never told me anything; you never do. One thing I do know is, that we shall starve, and I suppose I shall have to go about and beg. I haven't even another pair of shoes or stockings to my feet.'

Zachariah pondered for a moment. His first impulse

was something very different; but at last he rose, went up
to his wife, kissed her softly on the forehead, and said :

'Never mind, my dear; courage, you will have your
clothes next week. Come with me and look out for a
lodging.'

Mrs. Zachariah, however, shook herself free – not violently, but still decidedly – from his caresses.

'Most likely seized by the Government. Look for a
lodging! That's just like you! How can I go out in this
pouring rain?'

Zachariah, lately at any rate, had ceased to expect much
affection in his wife for him; but he thought she was
sensible, and equal to any complexity of circumstances,
or even to disaster. He thought this, not on any positive
evidence; but he concluded, somewhat absurdly, that her
coldness meant common sense and capacity for facing
trouble courageously and with deliberation. He had now
to find out his mistake, and to learn that the absence of
emotion neither proves, nor is even a ground for suspecting, any good whatever of a person; that, on the contrary, it is a ground for suspecting weakness, and possibly
imbecility.

Mrs. Coleman refused to go out, and after breakfast
Zachariah went by himself, having first inquired what was
a likely quarter. As he wandered along, much that had
been before him again and again once more recurred to
him. He had been overtaken by calamity, and he had not
heard from his wife one single expression of sympathy,
nor had he received one single idea which could help him.
She had thought of nothing but herself, and even of her-

self not reasonably. She was not the helpmeet which he felt he had a right to expect. He could have endured any defect, so it seemed, if only he could have had love; he could have endured the want of love if only he could have had a counsellor. But he had neither, and he rebelled, questioning the justice of his lot. Then he fell into the old familiar controversy with himself, and it was curiously characteristic of him that, as he paced those dismal Manchester pavements, all their gloom disappeared as he re-argued the universal problem of which his case was an example. He admitted the unquestionable right of the Almighty to damn three parts of creation to eternal hell if so He willed; why not, then, one sinner like Zachariah Coleman to a weary pilgrimage for thirty or forty years? He rebuked himself when he found that he had all his life assented so easily to the doctrine of God's absolute authority in the election and disposal of the creatures He had made, and yet that he revolted when God touched him and awarded him a punishment which, in comparison with the eternal loss of His presence, was as nothing. At last – and here, through his religion, he came down to the only consolation possible for him – he said to himself, 'Thus hath He decreed; it is foolish to struggle against His ordinances; we can but submit.' 'A poor gospel,' says his critic. Poor! – yes, it may be; but it is the gospel according to Job, and any other is a mere mirage. 'Doth the hawk fly by thy wisdom and stretch her wings towards the south?' Confess ignorance and the folly of insurrection, and there is a chance that even the irremediable will be somewhat mitigated. Poor! – yes; but it is genuine; and this at least must be said for Puritanism, that of all the theologies and philosophies it is the most honest in its recognition of the facts; the most real, if we penetrate to the heart of it, in the remedy which it offers.

He found two small furnished rooms which would answer his purpose till his own furniture should arrive, and he and his wife took possession that same morning. He then wrote to his landlord in London – a man whom he knew he could trust – and directed him to send his goods. For the present, although he had no fear whatever of any prosecution, he thought fit to adopt a feigned name, with which we need not trouble ourselves. In the afternoon, he sallied out to seek employment. The weather had cleared, but Mrs. Coleman still refused to accompany him, and she occupied herself moodily with setting the place to rights, as she called it, although, as it happened, it was particularly neat and clean. There was not so much printing done in Manchester then as now, and Zachariah had no success. He came home about seven o'clock, weary and disheartened. His wife was one of those women who under misfortune show all that is worst in them, as many women in misfortune show all that is best.

'You might have been sure you would get nothing to do here. If, as you say, there is no danger, why did you not stay in London?'

'You know all about it, my dear; we were warned to come.'

'Yes, but why in such a hurry? Why didn't you stop to think?'

'It is all very well to say so now, but there were only a

few minutes in which to decide. Besides, when I got home I found you gone.'

Mrs. Zachariah conveniently took no notice of the last part of this remark, which, of course, settled the whole question, but continued:

'Ah, well, I suppose it's all right; but I'm sure we shall starve; I am convinced we shall. Oh! I wish my poor dear mother were alive! I have no home to go to. What *will* become of us?'

He lost his patience a little.

'Jane,' he said, 'what is our religion worth if it does not support us in times like these? Does it not teach us to bow to God's will? Surely we, who have had such advantages, ought to behave under our trials better than those who have been brought up like heathens. God will not leave us. Don't you remember Mr. Bradshaw's sermon upon the passage through the Red Sea? When the Israelites were brought down to the very shore with nothing but destruction before them, a way was opened. What did Mr. Bradshaw bid us observe? The Egyptians were close behind – so close that the Israelites saw them; the sea was in front. The road was not made till the enemy was upon them, and then the waters were divided and became a wall unto them on their right hand and on their left; the very waters, Mr. Bradshaw remarked, which before were their terror. God, too, might have sent them a different way; no doubt He might, but He chose *that* way.'

'Zachariah, I heard Mr. Bradshaw as well as yourself; I am a member of the church just as much as you are, and I don't think it becoming of you to preach to me as if you were a minister.' Her voice rose and became shriller as she went on. 'I will not stand it. Who are you that you should talk to me so? – bad enough to bring me down here to die, without treating me as if I were an unconverted character. Oh! if I had but a home to go to!' and she covered her face with her apron and became hysterical.

What a revelation! By this time he had looked often into the soul of the woman whom he had chosen, the woman with whom he was to be for ever in this world, and had discovered that there was nothing, nothing, absolutely nothing which answered anything in himself with a smile of recognition; but he now looked again, and found something worse than emptiness. He found lurking in the obscure darkness a reptile with cruel fangs which at any moment might turn upon him when he was at his weakest and least able to defend himself. He had that in him by nature which would have prompted him to desperate deeds. He could have flung himself from her with a curse, or even have killed himself in order to escape from his difficulty. But whatever there was in him originally had been changed. Upon the wild stem had been grafted a nobler slip, which drew all its sap from the old root, but had civilized and sweetened its acrid juices. He leaned over his wife, caressed her, gave her water, and restored her.

'God knows,' he said, 'I did not mean to preach to you. God in heaven knows I need that somebody should preach to me.' He knelt down before her as she remained leaning back in the chair, and he repeated the Lord's Prayer. '*Give us this day our daily bread. Forgive us our trespasses as we forgive them that trespass against us.*' But will it be believed that as he rose from his knees, before he had actually straightened his limbs, two lines from the *Corsair* flashed into his mind, not particularly apposite, but there they were –

'She rose – she sprung – she clung to his embrace
Till his heart heaved beneath her hidden face?'

Whence had they descended? He was troubled at their sudden intrusion, and he went silently to the window, moodily gazing into the street. His wife, left to herself, recovered, and prepared supper. There was no reconciliation, at least on her side. She was not capable of reconciliation. Her temper exhausted itself gradually. With her the storm never broke up nobly and with magnificent forgetfulness into clear spaces of azure, with the singing of birds and with hot sunshine turning into diamonds every remaining drop of the deluge which had threatened ruin; the change was always rather to a uniformly obscured sky and a cold drizzle which lasted all day.

The next morning he renewed his quest. He was away all day long, but he had no success. He was now getting very anxious. He was expecting his furniture, which he had directed to be sent to the inn where they had first stayed, and he would have to pay for the carriage. His landlord had insisted on a week's rent beforehand, so that, putting aside the sum for the carrier, he had now two pounds left. He thought of appealing to his friends; but he had a great horror of asking for charity, and could not bring himself to do it. The third, fourth, and fifth day passed, with no result. On the seventh day he found that his goods had come; but he decided not to move, as it meant expense. He took away a chest of clothes, and remained where he was. By way of recoil from the older doctrine that suffering does men good, it has been said that it does no good. Both statements are true, and both untrue. Many it merely brutalizes. Half the crime of this world is caused by suffering, and half its virtues are due to happiness. Nevertheless, suffering, actual personal suffering, is the mother of innumerable beneficial experiences, and unless we are so weak that we yield and break, it extracts from us genuine answers to many questions which, without it, we either do not put to ourselves, or, if they are asked, are turned aside with traditional replies. A man who is strong and survives can hardly pace the pavements of a city for days searching for employment, his pocket every day becoming lighter, without feeling in after life that he is richer by something which all the universities in the world could not have given him. The most dramatic of poets cannot imagine, even afar off, what such a man feels and thinks, especially if his temperament be nervous and foreboding. How foreign, hard, repellent, are the streets in which he is a stranger, alone amidst a crowd of people all intent upon their own occupation whilst he has none! At noon, when business is at its height, he, with nothing to do, sits down on a seat in an open place, or, maybe, on the doorstep of an empty house, unties the little parcel he has brought with him and eats his dry bread. He casts up in his mind the shops he has visited; he reflects that he has taken all the more promising first, and that not more than two or three are left. He thinks of the vast waste of the city all round him; its miles of houses; and he has a more vivid sense of abandonment than if he were on a plank in the middle of the Atlantic. Towards the end of the afternoon the pressure in the offices and banks increases; the clerks hurry hither and thither; he has no share whatever in the excitement; he is an intrusion. He lingers about aimlessly, and presently the great tide turns outwards and flows towards the suburbs. Every vehicle which passes him is crowded with happy folk who have earned their living and are going home. He has earned nothing. Let anybody who wants to test the strength of the stalk of carle hemp in him try it by the wringing strain of a day thus spent! How humiliating are the repulses he encounters! Most employers to whom a request is made for something to do prefer to treat it as a petition for alms, and answer accordingly. They understand what is wanted before a word is spoken, and bawl out, 'No! Shut the door after you.' One man to whom Zachariah applied was opening his letters. For a moment he did not pay the slightest attention, but as Zachariah continued waiting, he shouted with an oath, 'What do you stand staring there for? Be off!' There was once a time when Zachariah would have stood up against the wretch; but he could not do it now, and he retreated in silence. Nevertheless, when he got out into the street he felt as if he could have rushed back and gripped the brute's throat till he had squeezed the soul out of his carcass. Those of us who have craved unsuccessfully for permission to do what the Maker of us all has fitted us to do alone understand how revolutions are generated. Talk about the atrocities of the Revolution! All the atrocities of the democracy heaped together ever since the world began would not equal, if we had any gauge by which to measure them, the atrocities perpetrated in a week upon the poor, simply because they are poor; and the marvel rather is, not that there is every now and then a September massacre at which all the world shrieks, but that such horrors are so infrequent. Again, I say, let no man judge communist or anarchist *till he has asked for leave to work*, and a 'Damn your eyes!' has rung in his ears.

Zachariah had some self-respect; he was cared for by God, and in God's Book was a registered decree concerning him. These men treated him as if he were not a person, an individual soul, but as an atom of a mass to be swept out anywhere, into the gutter – into the river. He was staggered for a time. Hundreds and thousands of human beings swarmed past him, and he could not help saying to himself as he looked up to the grey sky, 'Is it true, then? Does God really know anything about me? Are we not born by the million every week, like spawn, and crushed out of existence like spawn? Is not humanity the commonest and cheapest thing in the world?' But as yet his faith was unshaken, and he repelled the doubt as a temptation of Satan. Blessed is the man who can assign promptly everything which is not in harmony with himself to a devil, and so get rid of it. The pitiful case is that of the distracted mortal who knows not what is the degree of authority which his thoughts and impulses possess; who is constantly bewildered by contrary messages, and has no evidence as to their authenticity. Zachariah had his rule still; the suggestion in the street was tried by it; found to be false; was labelled accordingly, and he was relieved.

The dread of the real, obvious danger was not so horrible as a vague, shapeless fear which haunted him. It was a coward enemy, for it seized him when he was most tired and most depressed. What is that nameless terror? Is it a momentary revelation of the infinite abyss which surrounds us, from the sight of which we are mercifully protected by a painted vapour, by an illusion; that unspeakable darkness which we all of us know to exist, but which we hypocritically deny, and determine never to confess to one another? Here again, however, Zachariah had his advantage over others. He had his precedent. He remembered that quagmire in the immortal *Progress*, into which, if even a good man falls, he can find no bottom; he remembered that gloom so profound 'that ofttimes, when he lifted up his foot to set forward, he knew not where or upon what he should set it next'; he remembered the flame and smoke, the sparks and hideous noises, the things that cared not for Christian's sword, so that he was forced to betake himself to another weapon called All-prayer; he remembered how that Christian *'was so confounded that he did not know his own voice'*; he remembered the voice of a man as going before, saying, *'Though I walk through the valley of the shadow of death I will fear none ill, for Thou art with me.'* Lastly, he remembered that by and by the day broke, and Christian cried, *'He hath turned the shadow of death into the morning.'* He remembered all this; he could connect his trouble with the trouble of others; he could give it a place in the dispensation of things, and could therefore lift himself above it.

He had now been in Manchester a fortnight, and his little store had dwindled down to five shillings. It was Saturday night. On the Sunday, as his last chance, he meant to write to Mr. Bradshaw. He went out on the Sunday morning, and had persuaded his wife to accompany him. They entered the first place of worship they saw. It was a Methodist chapel, and the preacher was Arminian in the extreme. It was the first time Zachariah had ever been present at a Methodist service. The congregation sang with much fervour, and during the prayer, which was very long, they broke in upon it with ejaculations of their own, such as, 'Hear him, O Lord!' – 'Lord, have mercy on us!'

The preacher spoke a broad Lancashire dialect and was very dramatic. He pictured God's efforts to save a soul. Under the pulpit ledge was the imaginary bottomless pit of this world – not of the next. He leaned over and pretended to be drawing the soul up with a cord. 'He comes, he comes!' he cried; 'God be praised he is safe!' and he landed him on the Bible. The congregation gave a great groan of relief. 'There he is on the Rock of Ages! No, no, he slips; the Devil has him!' The preacher tried to rescue him. 'He is gone – gone!' and he bent over the pulpit in agony. The people almost shrieked. 'Gone – gone!' he said again with most moving pathos, and was still for a moment. Then gathering himself up, he solemnly repeated the terrible verses: '*For it is impossible for those who were once enlightened, and have tasted of the heavenly gift, and were made partakers of the Holy Ghost, and have tasted the good word of God, and the powers of the world to come, if they shall fall away, to renew them again unto repentance; seeing they crucify to themselves the Son of God afresh, and put Him to an open shame.*' Zachariah knew that text well. Round it had raged the polemics of ages. Mr. Bradshaw had never referred to it but once, and all the elder members of his congregation were eager in the extreme to hear what he had to say about it. He boldly declared that it had nothing to do with the elect. He was compelled to do so. Following his master, Calvin, he made it apply to outsiders. The elect, says Calvin, are beyond the risk of fatal fall. But 'I deny,' he goes on to say, that 'there is any reason why God may not bestow even on the reprobate a taste of His favour; may irradiate their minds with some scintillations of His light; may touch them with some sense of His goodness; may somehow engrave His word on their minds.' Horrible, most horrible, we scream, that the Almighty should thus play with those whom He means to destroy; but let us once more remember that these men did not idly believe in such cruelty. They were forced into their belief by the demands of their understanding, and their assent was more meritorious than the weak protests of so-called enlightenment. Zachariah, pondering absently on what he had heard, was passing out of the chapel when a hand was gently laid on his shoulder.

'Ah, friend, what are you doing here?'

He turned round and recognized William Ogden, who had been sent by the Hampden Club in Manchester some six months before as a delegate to the Friends of the People in London. The two walked some distance together, and Zachariah gave him the history of the last three weeks. With the murder he was, of course, acquainted. Ogden was a letterpress printer, and when he heard that Zachariah was in such straits, he said that he thought he might perhaps find him a job for the present, and told him to come to his office on the following morning. Zachariah's heart rejoiced that his bread would not fail, but he characteristically rejoiced even more at this signal proof that his trust in his God was justified. When he reached home he proposed to his wife that they should at once kneel down and thank God for His mercy.

'Of course, Zachariah; but you are not yet sure you will get anything. I will take off my things directly.'

'Need you wait to take off your things, my dear?'

'Really, Zachariah, you do make such strange remarks sometimes. I need not wait; but I am sure it will be more becoming, and it will give you an opportunity to think over what you are going to say.'

Accordingly Mrs. Coleman retired for about five minutes. On her return she observed that it was the time for regular family prayer, and she produced the Bible. Zachariah had indeed had the opportunity to think, and he had thought very rapidly. The mere opening of the sacred Book, however, always acted as a spell, and when its heavy lids fell down on either side the room cleared itself of all haunting, intrusive evil spirits. He read the seventeenth chapter of Exodus, the story of the water brought out of the rock; and he thanked the Almighty with great earnestness for the favour shown him, never once expressing a doubt that he would not be successful. He was not mistaken, for Ogden had a place for him, just as good and just as permanent as the one he had left in London.

CHAPTER TEN

Disintegration by Degrees

*

WE must now advance a little more rapidly. It was in the beginning of 1815 that Zachariah found himself settled in Manchester. That eventful year passed without any external change, so far as he was concerned. He became a member of the Hampden Club, to which Ogden and Bamford belonged; but he heard nothing of Maitland nor of Caillaud. He had a letter now and then from Mr. Bradshaw, and it was a sore trial to him that nobody could be found in Manchester to take the place of that worthy man of God. He could not attach himself definitively to any church in the town, and the habit grew upon him of wandering into this or the other chapel as his fancy led him. His comrades often met on Sunday evenings. At first he would not go; but he was afterwards persuaded to do so. The reasons which induced him to alter his mind were, in the first place, the piety, Methodistic most of it, which was then mixed up with politics; and secondly, a growing fierceness of temper, which made the cause of the people a religion. From 1816 downwards it may be questioned whether he would not have felt himself more akin with any of his democratic friends, who were really in earnest over the great struggle, than with a sleek half-Tory professor of the gospel, however orthodox he might have been. In 1816 the situation of the working classes had become almost intolerable. Towards the end of the year wheat rose to 103*s.* a quarter, and incendiarism was common all over England. A sense of insecurity and terror took possession of everybody. Secret outrages, especially fires by night, chill the courage of the bravest, as those know well enough who have lived in an agricultural county, when, just before going to bed, great lights are seen on the horizon; when men and women collect on bridges or on hill-tops, asking 'Where is it?' and when fire-engines tearing through the streets arrive useless at their journey's end because the hose has been cut. One evening in November, 1816, Zachariah was walking home to his lodgings. A special meeting of the club had been called for the following Sunday to consider a proposal made for a march of the unemployed upon London. Three persons passed him – two men and a woman – who turned round and looked at him and then went on. He did not recognize them, but he noticed that they stopped opposite a window, and as he came up they looked at him again. He could not be mistaken; they were the Major, Caillaud, and his daughter. The most joyous recognition followed, and Zachariah insisted on their going home with him. It often happens that we become increasingly intimate with one another even when we are shut out from all inter-course. Zachariah had not seen the Major nor Caillaud nor Pauline for two years, and not a single thought had been interchanged. Nevertheless he was much nearer and dearer to them than he was before. He had uncon-sciously moved on a line rapidly sweeping round into parallelism with theirs. The relationship between him-self and his wife during those two years had become, not openly hostile, it is true, but it was neutral. Long ago he had given up the habit of talking to her about politics, the thing which lay nearest to his heart just then. The pumping effort of bringing out a single sentence in her presence on any abstract topic was incredible, and so he learned at last to come home, though his heart and mind were full to bursting, and say nothing more to her than that he had seen her friend Mrs. Sykes, or bought his tea at a different shop. On the other hand, the revolutionary literature of the time, and more particularly Byron, increasingly interested him. The very wildness and remoteness of Byron's romance was just what suited him. It is all very well for the happy and well-to-do to talk scornfully of poetic sentimentality. Those to whom a natural outlet for their affection is denied know better. They instinctively turn to books which are the farthest removed from commonplace and are in a sense unreal. Not to the prosperous man, a dweller in beautiful scenery, well married to an intelligent wife, is Byron precious, but to the poor wretch, say some City clerk, with an aspiration beyond his desk, who has two rooms in Camberwell; and who, before he knew what he was doing made a marriage – well – which was a mistake, but who is able to turn to that island in the summer sea where dwells Kaled, his mistress – Kaled, the Dark Page disguised as a man, who watches her beloved dying:

'Who nothing fears, nor feels, nor heeds, nor sees,
Save that damp brow which rests upon his knees;
Save that pale aspect, where the eye, though dim,
Held all the light that shone on earth for him.'

When they came indoors, and Mrs. Zachariah heard on the stairs the tramp of other feet besides those of her husband, she prepared herself to be put out of temper. Not that she could ever be really surprised. She was not one of those persons who keep a house orderly for the sake of appearances. She would have been just the same if she had been living alone, shipwrecked on a solitary island in the Pacific. She was the born natural enemy of dirt, dust, untidiness, and of every kind of irregularity, as the cat is the born natural enemy of the mouse. The sight of dirt, in fact, gave her a quiet kind of delight, because she foresaw the pleasure of annihilating it. Irregularity was just as hateful to her. She could not sit still if one ornament on the mantelpiece looked one way and the other another way, and she would have risen from her death-bed, if she could have done so, to put a chair straight. She was not, therefore, aggrieved in expectancy because she was not fit to be seen. It was rather because she resented any interruption of domestic order of which she had not been previously forewarned. As it happened, however, the Major came first, and striding into the room, he shook her hand with considerable fervour and kissed it gallantly. Her gathering ill-temper disappeared with the promptitude of a flash. It was a muddy night; the Major had not carefully wiped his boots and the footmarks were all over the floor. She saw them, but they were nothing.

'My dear Mrs. Coleman, how are you? What a blessing to be here again in your comfortable quarters.'

'Really, Major Maitland, it is very good of you to say

so. I am very glad to see you again. Where *have* you been? I thought we had lost you for ever.'

Caillaud and his daughter had followed. They bowed to her formally, and she begged them to be seated.

'Then, my dear madam,' continued the Major, laughing, 'you must have thought me dead. You might have known that if I had not been dead I must have come back.'

She coloured just a trifle, but made no reply further than to invite all the company to have supper.

Zachariah was somewhat surprised. He did not know what sort of a supper it could be; but he was silent. She asked Pauline to take off her bonnet, and then proceeded to lay the cloth. For five minutes, or perhaps ten minutes, she disappeared, and then there came, not only bread and cheese, but cold ham, a plentiful supply of beer, and, more wonderful still, a small cold beefsteak pie. Everything was produced as easily as if it had been the ordinary fare, and Zachariah was astonished at his wife's equality to the emergency. Whence she obtained the ham and beefsteak pie he could not conjecture. She apologized for having nothing hot, would have had something better if she had known, etc. etc., and then sat down at the head of the table. The Major sat on her right, Pauline next to him, and opposite to Pauline, Caillaud and Zachariah. Their hostess immediately began to ask questions about the events of that fatal night when they all left London. The Major, however, interposed, and said that it would perhaps be better if nothing was said upon that subject.

'A dismal topic,' he observed; 'talking about it can do no good, and I for one don't want to be upset by thinking about it just before I go to bed.'

'At least,' said Zachariah, 'you can tell us why you are in Manchester?'

'Certainly,' replied the Major. 'In the first place, Paris is not quite so pleasant as it used to be; London, too, is not attractive; and we thought that, on the whole, Manchester was to be preferred. Moreover, a good deal will have to be done during the next twelvemonth, and Manchester will do it. You will hear all about it when your club meets next time.'

'You've been in Paris?' said Mrs. Zachariah. 'Isn't it very wicked?'

'Well, that depends on what you call wicked.'

'Surely there cannot be two opinions on that point.'

'It does seem so; and yet when you live abroad you find that things which are made a great deal of here are not thought so much of there; and, what is very curious, they think other things very wrong there of which we take no account here.'

'Is that because they are not Christians?'

'Oh dear, no; I am speaking of good Christian people; at least, so I take them to be. And really, when you come to consider it, we all of us make a great fuss about our own little bit of virtue, and undervalue the rest – I cannot tell upon whose authority.'

'But are they not, Major, dreadfully immoral in France?'

Pauline leaned over her plate and looked Mrs. Coleman straight in the face.

'Mrs. Coleman, you are English; you –'

Her father put up his hand; he foresaw what was coming, and that upon this subject Pauline would have defied all the rules of hospitality. So he replied calmly, but with the calm of suppressed force:

'Mrs. Coleman, as my daughter says, you are English; you are excusable. I will not dispute with you, but I will tell you a little story.'

'Will you not take some more beer, Mr. Caillaud, before you begin?'

'No, thank you, madam, I have finished.'

Caillaud pushed away his plate, on which three parts of what was given him, including all the ham, remained untouched, and began – his Gallicisms and broken English have been corrected in the version now before the reader:

'In 1790 a young man named Dupin was living in Paris, in the house of his father, who was a banker there. The Dupins were rich, and the son kept a mistress, a girl named Victorine. Dupin the younger had developed into one of the worst of men. He was strictly correct in all his dealings, sober, guilty of none of the riotous excesses which often distinguish youth at that age, and most attentive to business but he was utterly self-regarding, hard, and emotionless. What could have induced Victorine to love him, I do not know; but love him she did, and her love, instead of being a folly, was her glory. If love were always to be in proportion to desert, measured out in strictest and justest huckstering conformity therewith, what a poor thing it would be! The love at least of a woman is as the love of the Supreme Himself, and just as magnificent. Victorine was faithful to Dupin, and, poor and handsome as she was, never wronged him by a loose look. Well, Dupin's father said his son must marry, and the son saw how reasonable and how necessary the proposal was. He did marry, and he cut himself adrift from Victorine without the least compunction, allowing her a small sum weekly, insufficient to keep her. There was no scene when they parted, for his determination was communicated to her by letter. Three months afterwards she had a child, of whom he was the father. Did she quietly take the money and say nothing? Did she tear up the letter in a frenzy and return him the fragments? She did neither. She wrote to him and told him that she would not touch his gold. She would never forget him, but she could not be beholden to him now for a crust of bread. She had done no wrong hitherto – so she said, Mrs. Coleman ; I only repeat her words – they are not mine. But to live on him after he had left her would be a mortal crime. So they separated, a victim she – both victims, I may say – to this cursed thing we call Society. One of the conditions on which the money was to have been given was, that she should never again recognize him in any way whatever. This half of the bargain she faithfully observed. For some months she was alone, trying to keep herself and her child, but at last she was taken up by a working stonemason named Legouvé. In 1793 came the Terror, and the Dupins were denounced and thrown into the Luxembourg. Legouvé was one of the Committee of Public Safety. It came to the recollection of the younger Dupin as he lay expecting death that he had heard that the girl Victorine had gone to live with Legouvé, and a ray of light dawned on him in his dungeon. He commissioned his wife to call on Victorine and implore her to help them. She did so. Ah, that was a wonderful sight – so like the Revolution! Madame Dupin, in her silks and satins, had often passed the ragged Victorine in the streets, and, of course, had never taken the slightest notice of her. Now Madame was kneeling to her! Respectability was in the dust before that which was not by any means respectable; the legitimate before the illegitimate! Oh, it was, I say, a wonderful sight in Victorine's wretched garret! She was touched with pity, and, furthermore, the memory of her old days with Dupin and her love for him revived. Legouvé was frightfully jealous, and she knew that if she pleaded Dupin's cause before him she would make matters worse. A sudden thought struck her. She went to Couthon and demanded an audience.

' "Couthon," she said, "are the Dupins to die?"

' "Yes, to-morrow."

' "Dupin the younger is the father of my child.'

' "And he deserted you, and you hate him. He shall die."

' "Pardon me, I do not hate him."

' "Ah, you love him still; but that is no reason why he should be spared, my pretty one. We must do our duty. They are plotters against the Republic, and must go."

' "Couthon, they must live. Consider; shall that man ascend the scaffold with the thought in his heart that I could have rescued him, and that I did not; that I have had my revenge? Besides, what will be said? – that the Republic uses justice to satisfy private vengeance. All the women in my quarter know who I am."

' "That is a fancy."

' "Fancy! Is it a fancy to murder Dupin's wife – murder all that is good in her – murder the belief in her for ever that there is such a thing as generosity? You do not wish to kill the soul? That is the way with tyrants, but not with the Republic."

'Thus Victorine strove with Couthon, and he at last yielded. Dupin and his father were released that night, and before daybreak they were all out of Paris and safe. In the morning Legouvé found that they were liberated, and on asking Couthon the reason was answered with a smile that they had an eloquent advocate. Victorine had warned Couthon not to mention her name, and he kept his promise; but Legouvé conjectured but too truly. He went home, and in a furious rage taxed Victorine with infidelity to him, in favour of the man who had abandoned her. He would not listen to her, and thrust her from him with curses. I say nothing more about her history. I will only say this, that Pauline is that child who was born to her after Dupin left her. I say it because I am so proud that Pauline has had such a mother!'

'Pauline her daughter!' said Zachariah. 'I thought she was your daughter.'

'She is my daughter: I became her father.'

Everybody was silent.

'Ah, you say nothing,' said Caillaud; 'I am not surprised. You are astonished. Well may you be so that such a creature should ever have lived. What would Jesus Christ have said to her?'

The company soon afterwards rose to go.

'Good-bye, Mrs. Coleman,' said the Major in his careless way; 'I am glad to find Manchester does not disagree with you. At least, I should think it does not.'

'Oh no, Major Maitland, I like it quite as well as London. Mind, you promise to come again soon—*very* soon.'

The Major had gone downstairs first. She had followed him to the first landing, and then returned to bid Pauline and Caillaud good-bye. She stood like a statue while Pauline put on her hat.

'Good night, madam,' said Caillaud, slightly bowing.

'Good night, madam,' said Pauline, not bowing in the least.

'Good night,' she replied, without relaxing her rigidity.

As soon as they were in the street, Pauline said: 'Father, I abhor that woman. If she lives she will kill her husband.'

Mrs. Coleman, on the other hand, at the same moment said, 'Zachariah, Pauline and Caillaud cannot come to this house again.'

'Why not?'

'Why not, Zachariah? I am astonished at you! The child of a woman who lived in open sin!'

He made no reply. Years ago not a doubt would have

crossed his mind. That a member of Mr. Bradshaw's church could receive such people as Caillaud and Pauline would have seemed impossible. Nevertheless, neither Caillaud nor Pauline were now repugnant to him; nor did he feel that any soundless gulf separated them from him, although, so far as he knew, his opinions had undergone no change.

Mrs. Coleman forbore to pursue the subject, for her thoughts went off upon another theme, and she was inwardly wondering whether the Major would ever invite her to the theatre again. Just as she was going to sleep, the figure of the Major hovering before her eyes, she suddenly bethought herself that Pauline, if not handsome, was attractive. She started, and lay awake for an hour. When she rose in the morning the same thought again presented itself, to dwell with her henceforward, and to gnaw her continually like vitriol.

CHAPTER ELEVEN
Politics and Pauline
*

SOON after this visit debates arose in Zachariah's club, which afterwards ended in the famous march of the Blanketeers, as they were called. Matters were becoming very serious, and the Government was thoroughly alarmed, as well it might be, at the discontent which was manifest all over the country. The Prince Regent was insulted as he went to open Parliament, and the windows of his carriage were broken. It was thought, and with some reason, that the army could not be trusted. One thing is certain, that the reformers found their way into the barracks at Knightsbridge and had lunch there at the expense of the soldiers, who discussed Hone's pamphlets and roared with laughter over the *Political Litany*. The Prince Regent communicated to both Houses certain papers, and recommended that they should at once be taken into consideration. They contained evidence, so the royal message asserted, of treasonable combinations 'to alienate the affections of His Majesty's subjects from His Majesty's person and Government,' etc. Secret committees were appointed to consider them, both by Lords and Commons, and in about a fortnight they made their reports. The text was the Spitalfields meeting of the preceding 2nd of December. A mob had made it an excuse to march through the city and plunder some shops. Some of the charges brought against the clubs by the Lords Committee do not now seem so very appalling. One was, that they were agitating for universal suffrage and annual Parliaments – 'projects,' say the Committee, 'which evidently involve, not any qualified or partial change, but a total subversion of the British constitution.' Another charge was the advocacy of 'parochial partnership in land, on the principle that the landholders are not proprietors in chief; that they are but stewards of the public; that the land is the people's farm; that landed monopoly is contrary to the spirit of Christianity and destructive of the independence and morality of mankind.' The Reform party in Parliament endeavoured to prove that the country was in no real danger, and that the singularly harsh measures proposed were altogether unnecessary. That was true. There was nothing to be feared, because there was no organization; but nevertheless, especially in the manufacturing towns, the suffering was fearful and the hatred of the Government most bitter. What is so lamentable in the history of those times is the undisciplined wildness and feebleness of the attempts made by the people to better themselves. Nothing is more saddening than the spectacle of a huge mass of humanity goaded, writhing, starving, and yet so ignorant that it cannot choose capable leaders, cannot obey them if perchance it gets them, and does not even know how to name its wrongs. The governing classes are apt to mistake the absurdity of the manner in which a popular demand expresses itself for absurdity of the demand itself; but in truth the absurdity of the expression makes the demand more noteworthy and terrible. Bamford, when he came to London in the beginning of 1817, records the impression which the clubs made upon him. He went to several, and found them all alike; 'each man with his porter-pot before him and a pipe in his mouth; many speaking at once; more talkers than thinkers; more speakers than listeners. Presently "Order" would be called, and comparative silence would ensue; a speaker, stranger or citizen, would be announced with much courtesy and compliment. "Hear, hear, hear," would follow, with clapping of hands and knocking of knuckles on the tables, till the half-pints danced; then a speech, with compliments to some brother orator or popular statesman; next a resolution in favour of Parliamentary Reform, and a speech to second it; an amendment on some minor point would follow; a seconding of that; a breach of order by some individual of warm temperament; half a dozen would rise to set him right; a dozen to put them down; and the vociferation and gesticulation would become loud and confounding.'

The Manchester clubs had set their hearts upon an expedition to London – thousands strong; each man with a blanket to protect him and a petition in his hand. The discussion on this project was long and eager. The Major, Caillaud and Zachariah steadfastly opposed it; not because of its hardihood, but because of its folly. They were out-voted, but they conceived themselves loyally bound to make it a success. Zachariah and Caillaud were not of much use in organization, and the whole burden fell upon the Major. Externally gay, and to most persons justifying the charge of frivolity, he was really nothing of the kind when he had once settled down to the work he was born to do. His levity was the mere idle sport of a mind unattached and seeking its own proper object. He was like a cat, which will play with a ball or its own tail in the sunshine, but if a mouse or a bird crosses its path will fasten on it with sudden ferocity. He wrought like a slave during the two months before the eventful 10th March, 1817, and wellnigh broke his heart over the business. Everything had to be done subterraneously; for though the Habeas Corpus Act was not yet suspended, preparations for what looked like war were perilous. But this was not the greatest difficulty. He pleaded for dictatorial powers, and at once found he had made himself suspected thereby. He was told bluntly that working-men did not mean to exchange one despot for another, and that they were just as good as he was. Any other man would have thrown up his commission in disgust, but not so Major Maitland. He persevered unflaggingly, although a sub-committee had been appointed to act with him and check his proceedings. The secretary of this very sub-committee, who was also treasurer, was one of the causes of the failure of the enterprise; for when the march began neither he nor the funds with which he had been entrusted could be found. After the club meetings in the evening there was often an adjournment to Caillaud's lodgings, where the Major, Zachariah, Caillaud and Pauline sat up till close upon midnight. One evening there was an informal conference of this kind prior to the club meeting on the following night. The Major was not present, for he was engaged in making some arrangements for the commissariat on the march. He had always insisted on it that they were indispensable, and he had been bitterly opposed the week before by some of his brethren, who were in favour of extempore foraging which looked very much like plunder. He carried his point, notwithstanding some sarcastic abuse and insinuations of half-heartedness, which had touched also Caillaud and Zachariah, who supported him. Zachariah was much depressed.

'Mr. Coleman, you are dull,' said Pauline. 'What is the matter?'

'Dull! – that's not exactly the word. I was thinking of to-morrow.'

'Ah! I thought so. Well?'

Zachariah hesitated a little. 'Is it worth all the trouble?' at last he said, an old familiar doubt recurring to him – 'is it worth all the trouble to save them? What are they – and, after all, what can we do for them? Suppose we succeed, and a hundred thousand creatures like those who blackguarded us last week get votes, and get their taxes reduced, and get all they want, what then?'

Pauline broke in with all the eagerness of a woman who is struck with an idea: 'Stop, stop, Mr. Coleman. Here is the mistake you make. Grant it all – grant your achievement is ridiculously small – is it not worth the sacrifice of two or three like you and me to accomplish it? That is our error. We think ourselves of such mighty importance. The question is, whether we *are* of such importance, and whether the progress of the world one inch will not be cheaply purchased by the annihilation of a score of us. You believe in what you call salvation! You would struggle and die to save a soul; but in reality you can never save a man; you must be content to struggle and die to save a little bit of him – to prevent one habit from descending to his children. You won't save him wholly, but you may arrest the propagation of an evil trick, and so improve a trifle – just a trifle – whole generations to come. Besides, I don't believe what you will do is nothing. "Give a hundred thousand blackguard creatures votes" – well, that is something. You are disappointed they do not at once become converted and all go to chapel. That is not the way of the Supreme. Your hundred thousand get votes, and perhaps are none the better, and die as they were before they had votes. But the Supreme has a million, or millions, of years before Him.'

Zachariah was silent. Fond of dialectic, he generally strove to present the other side; but he felt no disposition to do so now, and he tried rather to connect what she had said with something which he already believed.

'True,' he said at last; 'true, or true in part. What are we? – what are we?' and so Pauline's philosophy seemed to reconcile itself with one of his favourite dogmas, but it had not quite the same meaning which it had for him ten years ago.

'Besides,' said Caillaud, 'we hate Liverpool and all his crew. When I think of that speech at the opening of Parliament, I become violent. There it is; I have stuck it up over the mantelpiece:

' "*Deeply as I lament the pressure of these evils upon the country, I am sensible that they are of a nature not to admit of an immediate remedy. But whilst I observe with*

137

peculiar satisfaction the fortitude with which so many priva-
tions have been borne, and the active benevolence which has
been employed to mitigate them, I am persuaded that the
great sources of our national prosperity are essentially unim-
paired; and I entertain a confident expectation that the
native energy of the country will at no distant period sur-
mount all the difficulties in which we are involved." '

'My God,' continued Caillaud, 'I could drive a knife
into the heart of the man who thus talks!'

'No murder, Caillaud,' said Zachariah.

'Well, no. What is it but a word? Let us say sacrifice.
Do you call the death of your Charles a murder? No;
and the reason why you do not is what? Not that it was
decreed by a Court. There have been many murders
decreed by Courts according to law. Was not the death
of your Jesus Christ a murder? Murder means death for
base, selfish ends. What said Jesus – that He came to
send a sword? Of course He did. Every idea is a sword.
What a God He was! He was the first who ever cared
for the people – for the real people, the poor, the ignorant,
the fools, the weak-minded, the slaves. The Greeks and
Romans thought nothing of these. I salute thee, O Thou
Son of the People!' and Caillaud took down a little cruci-
fix which, strange to say, always hung in his room and
reverently inclined himself to it. 'A child of the people,'
he continued, 'in everything, simple, foolish, wise,
ragged, Divine, martyred Hero.'

Zachariah was not astonished at this melodramatic display, for he knew Caillaud well; and although this was

a little more theatrical than anything he had ever seen
before, it was not out of keeping with his friend's character. Nor was it insincere, for Caillaud was not an
Englishman. Moreover, there is often more insincerity
in purposely lowering the expression beneath the thought,
and denying the thought thereby, than in a little exaggera-
tion. Zachariah, although he was a Briton, had no liking
for that hypocrisy which takes a pride in reducing the
extraordinary to the commonplace, and in forcing an
ignoble form upon that which is highest. The conversation went no further. At last Caillaud said:

'Come, Pauline, a tune; we have not had one for a
long time.'

Pauline smiled, and went into her little room. Meanwhile her father removed chairs and table, piling them
one on another so as to leave a clear space. He and
Zachariah crouched into the recess by the fireplace. Pauline entered in the selfsame short black dress trimmed
with red, with the red artificial flower, wearing the same
red stockings and dancing-slippers, but without the
shawl. The performance this time was not quite what
it was when Zachariah had seen it in London. Between
herself and the corner where Zachariah and her father
were seated she now had an imaginary partner, before
whom she advanced, receded, bowed, displayed herself
in the most exquisitely graceful attitudes, never once
overstepping the mark, and yet showing every limb and
line to the utmost advantage. Zachariah, as before, followed every movement with eager – shall we say with
hungry – eyes? He was so unused to exhibitions of this

kind that their grace was not, as it should have been, their only charm; for, as we before observed, in his chapel circle even ordinary dancing was a thing prohibited. The severity of manners to which he had been accustomed tended to produce an effect the very opposite to that which was designed; for it can hardly be doubted that if it were the custom in England for women to conceal the face, a glimpse of an eye or a nose would excite unpleasant thoughts.

The dance came to an end, and as it was getting late Zachariah rose.

'Stop,' said Caillaud. 'It is agreed that if they persist on this march one or the other of us goes too. The Major will be sure to go. Which shall it be, you or me?'

'We will draw lots.'

'Good.' And Zachariah departed, Pauline laughingly making him one of her costume curtsies. He was very awkward. He never knew how to conduct himself becomingly, or even with good manner, on commonplace occasions. When he was excited in argument he was completely equal to the best company, and he would have held his own on level terms at a Duke's dinner-party, provided only the conversation were interesting. But when he was not intellectually excited he was lubberly. He did not know what response to make to Pauline's graceful adieu, and retreated sheepishly. When he got home he found his wife waiting for him. The supper was cleared away and, as usual, she was reading, or pretending to be reading, the Bible.

'You have had supper, of course?' There was a peculiar

tone in the 'of course,' as if she meant to imply not merely that it was late, but that he had preferred to have it with somebody else.

'I do not want any.'

'Then we had better have prayers.'

CHAPTER TWELVE
One Body and One Spirit
★

NEXT week Zachariah found it necessary to consult with Caillaud again. The Major was to be there. The intended meeting was announced to Mrs. Coleman by her husband at breakfast on the day before, and he informed her that he should probably be late, and that no supper need be kept for him.

'Why do you never meet here, Zachariah? Why must it always be at Caillaud's?'

'Did you not say that they should not come to this house again?'

'Yes; but I meant I did not want to see them as friends. On business there is no reason why Caillaud should not come.'

'I cannot draw the line.'

'Zachariah, do you mean to call unconverted infidels your friends?'

They were his friends – he felt they were – and they were dear to him; but he was hardly able as yet to confess it, even to himself.

'It will not do,' he said. 'Besides, Caillaud will be sure to bring his daughter.'

'She will not be so bold as to come if she is not asked. Do *I* go with you anywhere except when I am asked?'

'She has always been used to go out with her father wherever he goes. She knows all his affairs, and is very useful to him.'

'So it seems. She must be *very* useful. Well, if it must be so, and it is on business, invite her, too.'

'I think still it will be better at Caillaud's; there is more room. There would be five of us.'

'How do you make five?'

'There is the Major. And why, by the way, do you object to Caillaud and Pauline more than the Major? He is not converted.'

'There is plenty of room here. I didn't say I didn't object to the Major. Besides, there is a difference between French infidels and English people, even if they are not church members. But I see how it is. You want to go there, and you will go. I am of no use to you. You care nothing for me. You can talk to such dreadful creatures as Caillaud and that woman who lives with him, and you never talk to me. Oh, I wish Mr. Bradshaw were here, or I were back again at home! What would Mr. Bradshaw say?'

Mrs. Coleman covered her face in her hands.

Zachariah felt no pity. His anger was roused. He was able to say hard things at times, and there was even a touch of brutality in him.

'Whose fault is it that I do not talk to you? When did I ever get any help from you? What do you understand about what concerns me, and when have you ever tried to understand anything? Your home is no home to me. My life is blasted, and it might have been different. The meeting shall not be here, and I will do as I please.'

He went out of the room in a rage, and downstairs into the street, going straight to his work. It is a terrible moment when the first bitter quarrel takes place, and when hatred, even if it be hatred for the moment

143

only, first finds expression. That moment can never be recalled! Is it ever really forgotten, or really forgiven? Some of us can call to mind a word, just one word, spoken twenty, thirty, forty, fifty years ago, which rings in our ears even to-day as distinctly as when it was uttered, and forces the blood into the head as it did then. When Zachariah returned that night he and his wife spoke to each other as if nothing had happened, but they spoke only about indifferent things. The next day Mrs. Coleman wondered whether, after all, he would repent; but the evening came, and she waited and waited in vain. The poor woman for hours and hours had thought one thought, and one thought only, until at last she could bear it no longer. At about eight o'clock she rose, put on her cloak, and went out of doors. She made straight for Caillaud's house. It was cold, and the sky was clear at intervals, with masses of clouds sweeping over the nearly full moon. What she was to do when she got to Caillaud's had not entered her head. She came to the door and stopped. It had just begun to rain heavily. The sitting-room was on the ground floor, abutting on the pavement. The blind was drawn down, but not closely, and she could see inside. Caillaud, Pauline, and Zachariah were there, but not the Major. Caillaud was sitting by the fireside; her husband and Pauline were talking earnestly across the table. Apparently both of them were much interested, and his face was lighted up as she never saw it when he was with her. She was fascinated and could not move. It was a full, lonely street and nobody was to be seen that wet night. She had no protection from the weather but her cloak, and in ten minutes, as the rain came down more and more heavily, she was wet through and shivering from head to foot – she who was usually so careful, so precise, so singularly averse from anything like disorder. Still she watched – watched every movement of those two – every smile, every gesture; and when Caillaud went out of the room, perhaps to fetch something, she watched with increasing and self-forgetting intensity. She had not heard footsteps approaching. The wind had risen, the storm was ever fiercer and fiercer, and the feverish energy which poured itself into her eyes had drained and deadened every other sense.

'Well, my good woman, what do you want?'

She turned with a start, and it was the Major!

'Mrs. Coleman! Good God! what are you doing here? You are soaked. Why don't you come in?'

'Oh no, Major Maitland; indeed, I cannot. I – I had been out, and I had just stopped a moment. I didn't know it was going to rain.'

'But I say you are dripping. Come in and see your husband; he will go with you.'

'Oh no, Major, please don't; please don't mention it to him. Oh no, please don't; he would be very vexed. I shall be all right; I will go on at once and dry myself.'

'You cannot go alone. I will see you as far as your house. Here, take my coat and put it over your shoulders.'

The Major took off a heavy cloak with capes, wrapped

it round her, drew her arm through his, and they went to her lodgings. She forgot Zachariah, Caillaud, and Pauline. When they arrived she returned the cloak and thanked him. She dared not ask him upstairs, and he made no offer to stay.

'Please say nothing to my husband; promise you will not. He would be in such a way if he thought I had been out; but I could not help it.'

'Oh, certainly not, Mrs. Coleman, if you wish it; though I am sure he wouldn't, he couldn't be angry with you.'

She lingered as he took the coat.

'Come inside and put it on, Major Maitland; why, it is you who are dripping now. You will not wear that over your sopped clothes. Cannot I lend you something? Won't you have something hot to drink?'

'No, thank you; I think not; it is not so bad as all that.'

He shook hands with her, and had gone.

She went upstairs into her dark room. The fire was out. She lighted no candle, but sat down just as she was, put her head on the table, and sobbed as if her heart would break. She was very seldom overcome by emotion of this kind, and used to be proud that she had never once in her life fainted, and was not given to hysterics. Checked at last by a deadly shivering which came over her, she took off her wet garments, threw them over a chair, and crept into bed, revolving in her mind the explanation which she could give to her husband. When she saw him, and he inquired about her clothes, she offered some trifling excuse, which seemed very readily to satisfy him, for he made scarcely any reply, and was soon asleep. This time it was her turn to lie awake, and the morning found her restless, and with every symptom of a serious illness approaching.

CHAPTER THIRTEEN

To the Greeks Foolishness

★

Neither Mrs. Coleman nor her husband thought it anything worse than a feverish cold, and he went to his work. It was a club night, the night on which the final arrangements for the march were to be made, and he did not like to be away. His wife was to lie in bed; but a woman in the house offered to wait upon her and bring what little food she wanted. It was settled at the club that the Major should accompany the expedition, and Zachariah and Caillaud having drawn lots, the lot fell upon Caillaud. A last attempt was made to dissuade the majority from the undertaking; but it had been made before, not only by our three friends, but by other Lancashire societies, and had failed. The only effect its renewal had now was a disagreeable and groundless insinuation which was unendurable. On his return from the meeting Zachariah was alarmed. His wife was in great pain, and had taken next to nothing all day. Late as it was, he went for a doctor, who would give no opinion as to the nature of the disease then, but merely ordered her some kind of sedative mixture, which happily gave her a little sleep. Zachariah was a working-man and a poor man. Occasionally it does happen that a working-man and a poor man has nerves, and never does his poverty appear so hateful to him as when he has sickness in his house.

The mere discomforts of poverty are bad enough – the hunger and cold of it – but worse than all is the impossibility of being decently ill, or decently dying, or of paying any attention to those who take it into their heads to be ill or to die. A man tolerably well off can at least get his wife some help when she is laid up, and when she is near her end can remain with her to take her last kiss and blessing. Not so the bricklayer's labourer. If his wife is in bed, he must depend upon charity for medicine and attendance. And although he knows he will never see her again, he is forced away to the job on which he is employed; for if he does not go he will lose it, and must apply to the parish for a funeral. Happily the poor are not slow to help one another. The present writer has known women who have to toil hard all day long sit up night after night with their neighbours, and watch them with the most tender care. Zachariah found it so in his case. A fellow-lodger, the mother of half a dozen children, a woman against whom the Colemans had conceived a prejudice and whom they had avoided, came forward and modestly asked Zachariah if she might 'look after' Mrs. Coleman while he was away. He thought for a moment of sundry harsh things which he had said about her, and then a well-known parable came into his mind about a certain Samaritan, and he could have hugged her with joy for her offer.

Mrs. Carter was one of those healthy, somewhat red-faced, gay creatures whom nothing represses. She was never melancholy with those who were suffering; not because she had no sympathy – for she was profoundly sympathetic – but because she was unsubduable. Her pulse was quick, and her heart so sound that her blood, rich and strong – blood with never a taint in it – renewed every moment every fibre of her brain. Her very presence to those who were desponding was a magnetic charm, and she could put to flight legions of hypochondriacal fancies with a cheery word. Critics said she ruled her husband; but what husband would not rejoice in being so ruled? He came home weary, and he did not want to rule. He wanted to be directed, and he gladly saw the reins in the hands of his 'missus,' of whom he was justly proud. She conducted all the conversation; she spent his money, and even bought him his own clothes; and although she said a sharp thing or two now and then, she never really quarrelled with him. The eldest of her six children was only twelve years old, and she was not over-methodical, so that her apartments were rather confused and disorderly. She was not, however, dirty, and would not tolerate dirt even in her boys, to whom, by the way, she administered very short and sharp corrections sometimes. If they came to the table with grimy paws, the first intimation they had that their mother noticed it was a rap on the knuckles with the handle of a knife, which sent the bread and butter flying out of their fingers. She read no books, and, what was odd in those days, did not go to chapel or church; but she had her 'opinions,' as she called them, upon everything which was stirring in the world, and never was behindhand in the news. She was really happier when she found that she had to look after Mrs. Coleman. She bustled about, taking directions from the doctor – not without some scepticism, for she had notions of her own on the subject of disease – and going up and down stairs continually to see how her patient was getting on. It was curious that although she was a heavy woman she was so active. She was always on her legs from morning to night, and never seemed fatigued. Indeed, when she sat still she was rather uncomfortable; and this was her weak point, for her restlessness interfered with sewing and mending, which she abominated.

The time for the march was close at hand. The Habeas Corpus Act had meanwhile been suspended, and every reformer had to walk very warily. Ogden, in whose office it will be remembered that Zachariah was engaged, had issued a handbill informing all the inhabitants of Manchester and its neighbourhood that on the 10th March a meeting would be held near St. Peter's Church of those persons who had determined to carry their petitions to London. Zachariah, going to his shop as usual on the morning of the 10th – a Monday – was astonished to find that Ogden was arrested and in prison.

We must, however, for a time, follow the fortunes of Caillaud and the Major on that day. They were both astir at five o'clock, and joined one another at the club. All the members were to assemble there at seven. Never was the Major more despondent. As for organization, there was none, and every proposal he had made had been thwarted. He saw well enough, as a soldier, that ten times the enthusiasm at his command would never carry a hundred men to London in that cold weather, and that if twenty thousand started, the number would be the difficulty. The Yeomanry cavalry were under orders to oppose them, and what could an undisciplined mob do against a semi-military force? The end of it would be the prompt dispersion of the pilgrims and the discredit of the cause. Nevertheless, both he and Caillaud had determined not to desert it. The absence of all preparations on the part of these poor Blanketeers was, in truth, very touching, as it showed the innocent confidence which they had in the justice of their contention. Their avowed object was to present a petition personally to the Prince Regent, that they might 'undeceive' him; as if such a thing were possible, or, being possible, would be of the slightest service. The whole country would rise and help them, their journey would be a triumphal procession; they were not a hostile army; the women would come to the doors and offer them bread and milk; they would reach London, Lord Liverpool would resign, and they would come back to Manchester with banners flying, having saved their country. At nine o'clock the club was in St. Peter's Fields, and a kind of platform had been erected, from which an address was to be given. Caillaud and the Major were down below. Both of them were aghast at what they saw. Thousands of men were present with whom they were unacquainted, who had been attracted by Ogden's proclamation; some with coats, others without coats; some with sticks; some with petitions; but most of them with blankets, which they had rolled up like knapsacks. The Major's heart sank within him. What on earth could he do? Nothing, except accompany them and try to prevent collision with the troops. The magistrates were distracted by no doubts whatever. They read the Riot Act, although there was no riot, nor the semblance of one, and forthwith surrounded the platform and carried off every one on it to prison. The crowd was then chased by the soldiers and special constables till all power of combination was at an end. About three hundred, however, were collected, and found their way to Ardwick Green. They had been joined by others on their route, and the Major informally reviewed his men. Never, surely, was there such a regiment! Never, surely, did any regiment go on such an errand! Ragged many of them, ignorant all; fanatical, penniless, they determined, in spite of all arguments, to proceed. He pointed out that if they could be so easily scattered when they were thousands strong, every one of them would be cut down or captured before they were twenty miles on the road. He was answered as before with contempt and suspicions of cowardice. A Methodist, half-starved, grey-haired, with black rings round his eyes and a yellow face, harangued them.

'My friends,' he said, 'we have been told to go back; that we are too few to accomplish the task to which we have set ourselves. What said the Lord unto Gideon Judges vii.: "The people that are with thee are too many for me to give the Midianites into their hands, lest Israel vaunt themselves against me, saying, Mine own hand hath saved me. Now therefore go to, proclaim in the ears of the people, saying, Whosoever is fearful and afraid, let him return and depart early from Mount Gilead." Well, twenty-two thousand went back, and at last Gideon had only the three hundred who lapped the water. By those three hundred Israel was saved from the Midianites.

Our thousands have left us, but we shall triumph. It may be the Lord's will that more should depart. It may be that there are yet too many. I say, then, in the words of Gideon, "Whosoever is fearful and afraid, let him return." Is there anybody?' (Loud shouts answered 'None.') 'The Lord is with us,' continued the speaker – 'the sword of the Lord and of Gideon!' Every one shouted again.

Respectable Manchester was frightened when the Blanketeers met, and laughed them to scorn when they were dispersed. No wonder at the laughter! What could be more absurd? And yet, when we call to mind the THING then on the throne; the THING that gave £180 for an evening coat, and incurred enormous debts while his people were perishing; the THING that drank and lied and whored; the THING that never did nor said nor thought anything that was not utterly brutish and contemptible – when we think that the THING was a monarch, Heaven-ordained, so it was said, on which side does the absurdity really lie? Of a truth, not only is the wisdom of this world foolishness, as it ever was, but that which to this world is foolishness is adjudged wisdom by the Eternal Arbiter. The Blanketeers shivering on Ardwick Green, the weavers who afterwards drilled on the Lancashire moors, and were hung according to law, or killed at Peterloo, are less ridiculous than those who hung or sabred them, less ridiculous than the Crimean war and numberless dignified events in human history, the united achievements of the sovereigns and ministries of Europe.

The route of the three hundred was towards Stockport; but when they reached the bridge they found it occupied by the Yeomanry and a troop of the Life Guards. To attempt to force a passage was impossible; but numbers threw themselves into the river and so crossed. The soldiers then withdrew into Stockport town, and the bridge was left open to the main body. When they got into the street on the other side the soldiers and police dashed at them, and arrested everybody whom they could catch. The Major was foremost in the crowd, endeavouring to preserve some sort of discipline, and one of the Yeomanry, suspecting him to be a leader, rode up to him and, leaning from his horse, collared him. He was unarmed; but he was a powerful man, and wrenched himself free. The soldier drew his sword, and although Caillaud was close by and attempted to parry the blow with a stick, the Major lay a dead man on the ground. The next moment, however, the soldier himself was dead – dead from a pistol-shot fired by Caillaud, who was instantly seized, handed over to a guard, and marched off with a score of others to Manchester jail. A remnant only of the Blanketeers escaped from Stockport, and a smaller remnant got to Macclesfield. There there was no shelter for them, and many of them lay in the streets all night. When the morning dawned only twenty went on into Staffordshire, and these shortly afterwards separated and wandered back to Manchester. The sword of Gideon was, alas! not the sword of the Lord, and aching hearts in that bitter March weather felt that there was something worse than the cold to be borne as they struggled homewards. Others, amongst whom was our Methodist orator, were not discouraged. It is a poor religion which makes no provision for disaster, and even for apparently final failure. The test of faith is its power under defeat, and these silly God-fearing souls argued to themselves that their Master's time was not their time; that perhaps they were being punished for their sins, and that when it pleased Him they would triumph. Essentially right they were, right in every particular, excepting, perhaps, that it was not for their own sins that this sore visitation came upon them. Visitation for sin it was certainly, but a visitation for the sins of others – such is the way of Providence, and has been ever since the world began, much to the amazement of many reflective persons. Thou hast laid on Him the iniquity of us all, and Jesus is crucified rather than the Scribes and Pharisees! Yet could we really wish it otherwise? Would it have been better in the end that Caiaphas and the elders should have been nailed upon Calvary, and Jesus die at a good old age, crowned with honour? It was not yet God's time in 1817, but God's time was helped forward, as it generally is, by this anticipation of it. It is a commonplace that a premature outbreak puts back the hands of the clock and is a blunder. Nine times out of ten this is untrue, and a revolt instantaneously quenched in blood is not merely the precursor but the direct progenitor of success.

We will spend no time over the death of Major Maitland. The tragic interest, as one of our greatest masters has said, lies not with the corpse but with the mourners; and we turn back to Zachariah. Ogden's office was shut. On the night after the breakdown at Stockport a note in pencil was left at Zachariah's house, in Pauline's hand-writing. It was very short: 'Fly for your life – they will have you to-night. – P.'

Fly for his life! But how could he fly, with his wife in bed and with no work before him? Would it not be base to leave her? Then it occurred to him that, if he were taken and imprisoned, he would be altogether incapable of helping her. He determined to speak to Mrs. Carter. He showed her the note, and she was troubled with no hesitation of any kind.

'My good man,' she said, 'you be off this minute. That's what you've got to do. Never mind your wife; I'll see after her. Expense? Lord, Mr. Coleman, what's that? She don't eat much. Besides, we'll settle all about that afterwards.'

Zachariah hesitated.

'Now, don't stand shilly-shallying and a-thinking and a-thinking – that never did anybody any good. I can't a-bear a man as thinks and thinks when there's anything to be done as plain as the nose in his face. Where's your bag?'

Mrs. Carter was out of the room in an instant, and in ten minutes came back with a change of clothes.

'Now, let us know where you are; but don't send your letters here. You write to my sister; there's her address. You needn't go up there; your wife's asleep. I'll bid her good-bye for you. Take my advice – get out of this county somewhere, and get out of Manchester to-night.'

'I must go upstairs to get some money,' and Zachariah

157

stole into his bedroom to take half a little hoard which was in a desk there. His wife, as Mrs. Carter had said, was asleep. He went to her bedside and looked at her. She was pale and worn. Lying there unconscious, all the defects which had separated him from her vanished. In sleep and death the divine element of which we are compounded reappears, and we cease to hate or criticize; we can only weep or pray. He looked and looked again. The hours of first love and courtship passed before him; he remembered what she was to him then, and he thought that perhaps the fault, after all, might have been on his side, and that he had perhaps not tried to understand her. He thought of her loneliness – taken away by him into a land of strangers – and now he was about to desert her; he thought, too, that she also was one of God's children just as much as he was; perhaps more so. The tears filled his eyes, although he was a hard, strong man not used to tears, and something rose in his throat and almost choked him. He was about to embrace her, but he dared not disturb her. He knelt down at the foot of the bed, and in an agony besought his God to have mercy on him. 'God have mercy on me! God have mercy on her!' That was all he could say – nothing else, although he had been used to praying habitually. His face was upon her feet as she lay stretched out there, and he softly uncovered one of them, so gently that she could not perceive it. Spotlessly white it was, and once upon a time she was so attractive to him because she was so exquisitely scrupulous! He bent his lips over it, kissed it – she stirred, but did not wake; a great cry almost broke from him, but he stifled it and rose. There was a knock at the door, and he started. It was Mrs. Carter.

'Come,' she said as he went out, 'you have been here long enough. Poor dear man! – there, there – of course it's hard to bear – poor dear man!' – and the good creature put her hand affectionately on his shoulder.

'I don't know how it is,' she continued, wiping her eyes with her apron, 'I can't a-bear to see a man cry. It always upsets me. My husband ain't done it above once or twice in his life, and, Lord, I'd sooner a-cried myself all night long. Good-bye, my dear, good-bye, good-bye; God bless you! It will all come right.'

In another minute Zachariah was out of doors. It was dark, and getting late. The cold air revived him, but he could not for some time come to any determination as to what he ought to do next. He was not well acquainted with the country round Manchester, and he could not decide to what point of the compass it would be safest to bend his steps. At last he remembered that at any rate he must escape from the town boundaries and get a night's lodging somewhere outside them. With the morning some light would possibly dawn upon him.

Pauline's warning was well-timed, for the constables made a descent upon Caillaud's lodgings as soon as they got him into jail, and thence proceeded to Coleman's. They insisted on a search, and Mrs. Carter gave them a bit of her mind, for they went into every room of the house, and even into Mrs. Coleman's bedroom.

'I'll tell you what it is, Mr. Nadin,' she said, turning towards the notorious chief constable, 'if God A'mighty had to settle who was to be hung in Manchester, it wouldn't be any of them poor Blanketeers. Wouldn't you like to strip the clothes off the bed? That would be just in your line.'

'Hold your damned tongue!' quoth Mr. Nadin; but, nevertheless, seeing his men grinning and a little ashamed of themselves, he ordered them back.

Meanwhile, Zachariah pursued his way north-westward unchallenged, and at last came to a roadside inn, which he thought looked safe. He walked in, and found half a dozen decent-looking men sitting round a fire and smoking. One of them was a parson, and another was one of the parish overseers. It was about half-past ten, and they were not merry, but a trifle boozy and stupid. Zachariah called for a pint of beer and some bread and cheese, and asked if he could have a bed. The man who served him didn't know, but would go and see. Presently the overseer was beckoned out of the room, and the man came back again and informed Zachariah that there was no bed for him, and that he had better make haste with his supper, as the house would close at eleven. In a minute or two the door opened again, and a poor, emaciated weaver entered and asked the overseer for some help. His wife, he said, was down with the fever; he had no work; he had had no victuals all day, and he and his family were starving. He was evidently known to the company.

'Ah,' said the overseer, 'no work, and the fever, and starving; that's what they always say. I'll bet a sovereign you've been after them Blanketeers.'

'It's a judgment on you,' observed the parson. 'You and your like go setting class against class; you never come near the church, and then you wonder God Almighty punishes you.'

'You can come on your knees to us when it suits you, and you'd burn my rick to-morrow,' said a third.

'There's a lot of fever amongst 'em down my way,' said another, whose voice was rather thick, 'and a damned lot of expense they are, too, for physic and funerals. It's my belief that they catch it out of spite.'

'Aren't you going to give me nothing?' said the man. 'There isn't a mouthful of food in the place, and the wife may be dead before the morning.'

'Well, what do you say, parson?' said the overseer.

'I say we've got quite enough to do to help those who deserve help,' he replied, 'and that it's flying in the face of Providence to interfere with its judgment.' With that he knocked the ashes out of his pipe and took a great gulp of his brandy-and-water.

There was an echo of assent.

'God have mercy on me!' said the man, as he sat down on the form by the table. Zachariah touched him gently, and pushed the plate and jug to him. He looked at Zachariah, and, without saying a word, devoured it greedily. He just had time to finish, for the landlord, entering the room, roughly ordered them to turn out. Out they went accordingly.

'The Lord in heaven curse them!' exclaimed Zachariah's companion when they were in the road. 'I could have ripped 'em up, every one of 'em. My wife is in bed with her wits a-wandering, and there a'nt a lump of coal, nor a crumb of bread, nor a farthing in the house.'

'Hush, my friend, cursing is of no use.'

'Ah! it's all very well to talk; you've got money, maybe.'

'Not much. I, too, have no work, no lodging, and I'm driven away from home. Here's half of what's left.'

'What a sinner I am!' said the other. 'You wouldn't think it, to hear me go on as I did, but I am a Methodist. The last two or three days, though, I've been like a raving madman. That's the worst of it. Starvation has brought the devil into me. I'm not a-going to take all that though, master; I'll take some of it; and if ever I prayed to the Throne of Grace in my life, I'll pray for you. Who are you? Where are you going?'

Zachariah felt that he could safely trust him, and told him what had happened.

'I haven't got a bit of straw myself on which to put you, but you come along with me.'

They walked together for about half a mile till they came to a barn. There was a haystack close by, and they dragged some of the dry hay into it.

'You'd better be away from these parts afore it's light, and, if you take my advice, Liverpool is the best place for you.'

He was right. Liverpool was a large town, and, what was of more consequence, it was not so revolutionary as Manchester, and the search there for the suspected was not so strict. The road was explained, so far as Zachariah's friend knew it, and they parted.

Zachariah slept but little, and at four o'clock, with a

bright moon, he started. He met with no particular adventure, and in the evening found himself once more in a wilderness of strange streets, with no outlook, face to face with the Red Sea. Happy is the man who, if he is to have an experience of this kind, is trained to it when young, and is not suddenly brought to it after a life of security. Zachariah, although he was desponding, could now say he had been in the same straits before, and had survived. That is the consolation of all consolations to us. We have actually touched and handled the skeleton, and after all we have not been struck dead.

[1] 'O socii, neque enim ignari sumus ante malorum,
O passi graviora, dabit Deus his quoque finem.

---

[1] 'O ze (ye) my feris (companions) and deir freyndis, quod he,
Of bywent perillis not ignorant ben we,
Ze have sustenit gretir dangeris unkend,
Like as hereof God sall make sone ane end:
The rage of Silla, that huge sweste (whirlpool) in the se
Ze have eschapit and passit eik (each) have ze:
The euer (pot) routand (roaring) Caribdis rokkis fell
The craggis quhare monstruous Cyclopes dwell:
Ze are expert: pluk up zour harts, I zou pray,
This dolorous drede expell and do away.
Sum tyme hereon to think may help perchance.'
– *Gawin Douglas.*

'Endure and conquer! Jove will soon dispose
To future good, our past and present woes.
With me, the rocks of Scylla you have tried;
Th' inhuman Cyclops, and his den defied.
What greater ills hereafter can you bear?
Resume your courage, and dismiss your care.
An hour will come, with pleasure to relate.
Your sorrows past, as benefits of fate.'–*Dryden.*

Vos et Scyllæam rabiem penitusque sonantes
Accestis scopulos; vos et Cyclopia saxa
Experti. Revocate animos, moestumque timorem
Mittite; forsan et hæc olim meminisse juvabit.'

He wandered down to the water and saw a ship cleared
for some port across the Atlantic. A longing seized him
to go with her. Over the sea – he thought there he would
be at rest. So we all think, and as we watch the vessels
dropping below the horizon in the sunset cloud, we
imagine them bound with a happy crew to islands of the
blest, the truth being that the cloud is a storm, and the
destined port is as commonplace and full of misery as
the one they have left. Zachariah, however, did not
suffer himself to dream. He went diligently and system-
atically to work; but this time all his efforts were fruitless.
He called on every printing-office he could find, and
there was not one which wanted a hand, or saw any
prospect of wanting one. He thought of trying the river-
side; but he stood no chance there, as he had never
been accustomed to carry heavy weights. His money was
running short, and at last, when evening came on the
third day, and he was faint with fatigue, his heart sank.
He was ill, too, and sickness began to cloud his brain.
As the power of internal resistance diminishes, the cir-
cumstance of the external world presses on us like the
air upon an exhausted glass ball, and finally crushes us.
It saddened him, too, to think, as it has saddened thousands before him, that the fight which he fought, and the
death which, perhaps, was in front of him, were so mean.

Ophelia dies; Juliet dies; and we fancy that their fate, although terrible, is more enviable than that of a pauper who drops undramatically on London stones. He came to his lodging at the close of the third day, wet, tired, hungry, and with a headache. There was nobody to suggest anything to him or offer him anything. He went to bed, and a thousand images, uncontrolled, rushed backwards and forwards before him. He became excited, so that he could not rest, and after walking about his room till nearly daylight turned into bed again. When morning had fairly arrived he tried to rise, but he was beaten. He lay still till about eleven, and then the woman who kept the lodging-house appeared and asked him if he was going to stay all day where he was. He told her he was very bad; but she went away without a word, and he saw nothing more of her. Towards night he became worse, and finally delirious.

CHAPTER FOURTEEN
The School of Adversity: the Sixth Form thereof

★

WHEN Zachariah came to himself he was in a large, long, whitewashed room, with twenty beds or more in it. A woman in a greyish check dress was standing near him.

'Where am I?' he said.

'Where are yer?' she said; 'why, in the workus infirmary, to be sure, with me a-looking after yer. Where would yer be?'

Zachariah relapsed and was still. The next time he opened his eyes the woman had left him. It was true he was in the workhouse, and a workhouse then was not what it is now. Who can possibly describe what it was? Who can possibly convey to anybody who has not known what it was by actual imprisonment in it any adequate sense of its gloom; of the utter, callous, brutal indifference of the so-called nurses; of the neglect of the poor patients by those who were paid to attend to them; of the absence of even common decency; of the desperate persistent attempts made by everybody concerned to impress upon the wretched mortals who were brought there that they were chargeable to the parish and put there for form's sake, prior to being shovelled into a hole in the adjoining churchyard? The infirmary nurses were taken from the other side of the building – sometimes for very strange reasons. The master appointed them, and was not bound to account to anybody for his preferences. One woman had given him much trouble. She was a stout, lazy brute, who had no business in the

House, and who went in and out just as she liked. One day something displeased her, and she attacked him with such fury and suddenness that he would have been a dead man in a few minutes if she had not been pulled off. But he dared not report her. She knew too much about him, and she was moved a few days afterwards to look after the sick. She it was who spoke to Zachariah. She, however, was not by any means the worst. Worse than her were the old, degraded, sodden, gin-drinking hags, who had all their lives breathed pauper air and pauper contamination; women with not one single vestige of their Maker's hand left upon them, and incapable, even under the greatest provocation, of any human emotion; who would see a dying mother call upon Christ, or cry for her husband and children, and would swear at her and try to smother her into silence. As for the doctor, he was hired at the lowest possible rate, and was allowed a certain sum for drugs. It was utterly insufficient to provide anything except the very commonest physic; and what could he do in the midst of such a system, even if he had been inclined to do anything? He accordingly did next to nothing: walked through the wards, and left his patients pretty much to Providence. They were robbed even of their food. They were not much to be pitied for being robbed of the stimulants, for every drop, including the 'port wine,' was obtained by the directors from those of their number or from their friends who were in the trade, and it was mostly poisonous. Death is always terrible – terrible on the battlefield; terrible in a sinking ship; terrible to the exile – but the present writer, who has seen Death in the 'House' of years gone by, cannot imagine that he can ever be so distinctively the King of Terrors as he was there. The thought that thousands and thousands of human beings, some of them tender-hearted, have had to face him there is more horrifying than the thought of French soldiers freezing in their blood on the Borodino, or of Inquisitional tortures. It is one of those thoughts which ought not to be thought – a thought to be suppressed, for it leads to atheism, or even something worse than mere denial of a God. Thank Heaven that the present generation of the poor has been relieved at least of one argument in favour of the creed that the world is governed by the Devil! Thank Heaven that the modern hospital, with its sisters gently nurtured, devoted to their duty with that pious earnestness which is a true religion, has supplied some evidence of a Theocracy.

Zachariah looked round again. There was an old male attendant near him. He had on a brown rough coat with brass buttons, and shoes which were much too big for him. They were supplied in sizes, and never fitted. The old men always took those that were too large. They had as their place of exercise a paved courtyard surrounded by high brick walls, and they all collected on the sunny side and walked up and down there, making a clapping noise with their feet as the shoes slipped off their heels. This sound was characteristic of the whole building. It was to be heard everywhere.

'You've been very bad,' said the old man, 'but you'll get better now; it a'nt many as get better here.'

He was a poor-looking, half-fed creature, with a cadaverous face. He had the special, workhouse, bloodless aspect – just as if he had lived on nothing stronger than gruel and had never smelt fresh air. The air, by the way, of those wards was something peculiar. It had no distinctive odour – that is to say, no odour which was specially this or that; but it had one that bore the same relation to ordinary odours which well-ground London mud bears to ordinary colours. The old man's face, too, had nothing distinctive in it. The only thing certainly predicable of him was that nothing could be predicated of him. He was neither selfish nor generous; neither a liar nor truthful; neither believed anything, nor disbelieved anything; was neither good nor bad; had no hope hereafter, nor any doubt.

'Who are you?' said Zachariah.

'Well, that a'nt easy to say. I does odd jobs here as the nurses don't do, and I gets a little extra ration.'

'How long have I been here?'

'About a fortnight.'

Zachariah was too weak to say anything more, and fell asleep again. Next day he was better, and he then thought of his wife; he thought of Caillaud, the Major, and Pauline; but he had no power to reflect connectedly. He was in that miserable condition in which objects present themselves in a tumbling crowd, one following the other with inconceivable rapidity, the brain possessing no power to disentangle the chaos. He could not detach the condition of his wife, for example, and determine what ought to be done; he could not even bring himself to decide if it would be best to let her know where he was.

No sooner did he try to turn his attention to her, even for a moment, than the Major came before him, and then his other friends, and then the workhouse and the dread of death there. Mercifully, he went to sleep again, and after another long night's rest he was much stronger. He was able now – first sign of restored power – to settle that he ought before everything to communicate with Mrs. Carter, and he inquired of the old man if he could write.

'Oh yes, I can write,' said he, and something like a gleam of light passed over his countenance at being asked to practise an art almost forgotten in those walls.

A letter was accordingly written to Mrs. Carter, at her sister's address, telling her briefly what had happened, but that she was not to be alarmed, as the writer was rapidly recovering. He was able to sign his name; but when the letter was finished, he reflected that he had not got a coin in his pocket with which to pay the postage. One of the institutions of the workhouse was, however, a kind of pawnshop kept by one of the under-masters, as they were called, and Zachariah got a shilling advanced on a pocket-knife. The letter, therefore, was duly dispatched, and he gave his secretary a penny for his trouble. This led to a little further intimacy, and Zachariah asked him how he came there.

'I don't know,' he replied. 'I was born in the country, and when I was fourteen my father apprenticed me to the watchmaking. He was well off – my father was – and when I was out of my time he set me up in business in Liverpool. It was a business as had been established some time – a fairish business it was. But when I came to Liverpool I felt dull.'

'What do you mean by dull? Stupid?'

'No, not exactly that. You know what dull means, don't you? – low-spirited like – got nothing to talk about. Well, I can't tell how it come about, but I was always dull, and have been so ever since. I got married soon after I was settled. My wife was a good sort of woman, but she wasn't cheerful, and she wasn't very strong. Somehow the business fell off. Customers as used to come didn't come, and I got no new ones. I did my work pretty well; but still, for all that, things went down and down by degrees. I never could make out why, except that people like to be talked to, and I had nothing particular to say to any of them when they came in. The shop, too, ought to have been painted more often, and I ought to have had something in the window; but, as I say, I was always dull, and my wife wasn't strong. At last I was obliged to give up and go to journey-work; but when I got old I couldn't see, and was put in here.'

'But,' said Zachariah, 'is that all? Why, you are nearly seventy years old. You must have something more to tell me.'

'No; I don't know as I have; That seems about all.'

'But what became of your father? He was well off. What became of his money when he died?'

'I'd had my share.'

'Had you no brothers nor sisters to help you?'

'Yes, I had some.'

'Did they let you come here?'

'Why, you see, as I've told you before, I was dull, and my wife wasn't strong. They never came much to see me. It was my fault; I never had nothing to say to them.'

'Had you no children?'

'Yes; I had a son and daughter.'

'Are they alive now?'

'Yes – both of them; at least, I haven't heard as they are dead.'

'And able to keep themselves?'

'They used to be.'

'And do you mean that your son and daughter let you go to the workhouse?'

The old man was a little disturbed, and for a moment some slight sign of nervous excitement revealed itself in his lustreless eyes.

'I haven't seen anything of 'em for years.'

'Did you quarrel?'

'No, we didn't quarrel; but they left off visiting us. They both of them married, and went out a good bit, and were gayer than we were. We used to ask them, and then they'd look in sometimes; but never except when they were asked, and always seemed to wish to get away. We never had nothing to show anybody, nor nothing to give anybody; for we didn't drink, and I never smoked. They went away, too, both of them, from Liverpool, somewhere towards London.'

'But when you broke down didn't you inform them?'

'No. I hadn't heard anything of them for so long. I thought I might as well get into the House. It will do very well.'

'Didn't you know anybody belonging to your church or chapel?'

'Well, we went to church; but when the business dropped we left off going, for nothing much seemed to come of it, and nobody ever spoke to us.'

'Wouldn't you like to get out of this place?'

'No – I don't know as I should now; I shouldn't know what to do, and it won't last long.'

'How old are you?'

'Sixty-five.'

It puzzled Zachariah that the man's story of his life was so short – all told in five minutes.

'But did you never have any adventures? Did you never hear about anything or see anybody worth remembering? Tell me all about yourself. We've got nothing to do.'

'I don't recollect anything particular after I came to Liverpool. Things seemed to go on pretty much in the same way.'

'But you got married, and your wife died?'

'Yes – I got married, and she died.'

'What was your wife's name?'

'Her name was Jenkins; she was the daughter of the saddler that lived next door.'

'Couldn't her friends have helped you?'

'After she died they had nothing more to do with me.'

'And you really cannot tell me any more?'

'No – how can I? What more is there to tell? It's all alike.'

173

The old pauper was called away, and went shuffling along to the door, leaving Zachariah to his meditations.

Another day passed, and he was lying half-asleep when a visitor was announced, and close upon the announcement stood before him – who should it be? – no other than Mrs. Carter, out of breath, radiant, healthy, impetuous.

'God bless the poor dear man!' she burst out; 'to think of finding you here, and not to have told us before. But I suppose you couldn't. Directly as I got your letter, off I came, and here I am, you see.'

Her presence was like the south-west wind and sunlight after long north-easterly gloom and frost. Astonishing is that happy power which some people possess which enables them at once to dispel depression and even disease. A woman like Mrs. Carter comes into a house where there is misery and darkness; where the sufferer is possessed by demons; unnameable apprehensions, which thicken his blood and make him cry for death, and they retreat precipitately, as their brethren were fabled to retreat at the sign of the cross. No man who is so blessed as to have a friend with that magnetic force in him need disbelieve in much of what is recorded as miraculous. Zachariah felt as if a draught of good wine had been poured down his throat. But he instantly asked:

'How is my wife?'

'She is all right; but you mustn't bother about her. You must come out at once. You mustn't go back to Manchester just yet – not as they'd care much about you now; Nadin's got plenty of work to do and wouldn't concern himself about you – but you aren't well enough, and are better away. Now, look here – I'll tell you what I've been and done. I've got a cousin living here in Liverpool, as good a soul as ever lived. I goes to her and tells her you must stay there.'

'But how can I? Just think of the trouble and expense. I don't know her.'

'Lord a mercy, there you are again – trouble and expense! What trouble will you be? And as for expense, one would think you'd been living like a Lord Mayor to hear you talk. What are we made for, if not to help one another?'

'I can't walk; and shouldn't I be obliged to get the doctor's permission?'

'Walk! Of course you can't. And what did my husband say to me before I started? Says he, "You'll have to get a conveyance to take him." "Leave me alone for that," says I; "although right you are." And I says to my cousin's husband, who drives a hackney coach, "Just you drop down and carry him home. It won't be ten minutes out of your time." So he'll be here in about a quarter of an hour. As for the doctor, I understand as much about you as he does, and, doctor or no doctor, you won't sleep in this bed to-night. I'll go and tell the head nurse or master, or somebody or the other, that you are off. You just put on your clothes.'

In a short time she returned, found Zachariah dressed, wrapped him round in shawls and rugs, helped him downstairs, put him into the coach, and brought him to her cousin's. It was a little house, in a long uniform street, but a good deal of pains had been taken with it to make it something special. There were two bedroom windows in front, on the upper story, and each one had flowers outside. The flower-pots were prevented from falling off the ledge by a lattice-work wrought in the centre into a little gate – an actual little gate. What purpose it was intended to answer is a mystery; but being there, the owner of the flower-pots unfastened it every morning when the sill was dusted, and removed them through it, although lifting them would have been a much simpler operation. There were flowers in the sitting-room downstairs, too; but they were inside, as the window was flush with the pavement. This sitting-room was never used except on Sundays. It was about nine feet square, and it had in it a cupboard on either side of the fireplace, a black horse-hair sofa alongside the wall on the right-hand side of the door, red curtains, a black horse-hair arm-chair, three other chairs to match, a little round table, two large shells, a framed sampler on the wall, representing first the letters of the alphabet, then the figures 1, 2, 3, etc., and, finally, a very blue Jesus talking to a very red woman of Samaria on a very yellow well – underneath, the inscription and date, 'Margaret Curtin, 10th March, 1785.' The only other decorations – for pictures were dear in those days – were two silhouettes, male and female, one at each corner of the mantelpiece, and two earthenware dogs which sat eternally looking at one another on the top of one of the cupboards. On the cupboard farthest away from the window was a large Bible with pictures in it and notes, and, strange to say, a copy of Ferguson's *Astronomy* and a handsome quarto edition in three volumes of *Cook's First Voyage*. Everything was as neat and clean as it could possibly be; but Mr. and Mrs. Hocking had no children, and had saved a little money.

Into this apartment Zachariah was brought. There was a fire burning, though it was not cold, and on the table, covered with a perfectly white cloth, stood a basin of broth, with some toast, a little brandy in a wine-glass, a jug of water, and a tumbler. The books, including the Bible, had apparently not been read much, and were probably an heirloom. As Zachariah began to recover strength he read the Ferguson. It was the first time he had ever thought seriously of Astronomy, and it opened a new world to him. His religion had centred all his thoughts upon the earth as the theatre of the history of the universe, and although he knew theoretically that it was but a subordinate planet, he had not realized that it was so. For him, practically, this little globe had been the principal object of the Creator's attention. Ferguson told him also, to his amazement, that the earth moved in a resisting medium, and that one day it would surely fall into the sun. That day would be the end of the world, and of everything in it. He learned something about the magnitude of the planets and the distances of the fixed stars, and noted that his author, pious as he is, cannot admit that planets or stars were created for the sake of man. He dwelt upon these facts, more especially upon the first, till the ground seemed to disappear under his feet, and he fell into that strange condition in which people in earthquake countries are said to be when their houses begin to tremble. We may laugh, and call him a fool to be disturbed by a forecast of what is not going to happen for millions of years; but he was not a fool. He was one of those unhappy creatures whom an idea has power to shake, and almost to overmaster. Ferguson was a Christian, and the thought of the destruction of our present dwelling-place, with every particle of life on it, did not trouble him. He had his refuge in Revelation. Zachariah, too, was a Christian, but the muscles of his Christianity were – now, at any rate, whatever they may once have been – not firm enough to strangle this new terror. His supernatural heaven had receded into shadow; he was giddy, and did not know where he was. He did not feel to their full extent the tremendous consequences of this new doctrine, and the shock which it has given to so much philosophy and so many theories, but he felt quite enough, and wished he had never opened the volume. There are many truths, no doubt, which we are not robust enough to bear. In the main, it is correct that the only way to conquer is boldly to face every fact, however horrible it may seem to be, and think and think till we pass it and come to a higher fact; but often we are too weak, and perish in the attempt. As we lie prostrate, we curse the day on which our eyes were opened, and we cry in despair that it would have been better for us to have been born oxen or swine than men. It is an experience, I suppose, not new that in certain diseased conditions some single fear may fasten on the wretched victim so that he is almost beside himself. He is unaware that this fear in itself is of no importance, for it is nothing but an index of ill health, which might find expression in a hundred other ways. He is unconscious of the ill health, except through his fancy, and regards it as an intellectual result. It is an affliction worse ten thousand times than any direct physical pain which ends in pain. Zachariah could not but admit that he was still physically weak; he had every reason, therefore, for supposing that his mental agony was connected with his sickness, but he could not bring himself to believe that it was so, and he wrestled with his nightmares and argued with them as though they were mere logical inferences. However, he began to get better, and forthwith other matters occupied his mind. His difficulty was not fairly slain, pierced through the midst by some heaven-directed arrow, but it was evaded and forgotten. Health, sweet blood, unimpeded action of the heart, are the divine narcotics which put to sleep these enemies to our peace and enable us to pass happily through life. Without these blessings a man need not stir three steps without finding a foe able to give him his death-stroke.

Zachariah longed to see his wife again, but he could not bring her to Liverpool until he had some work to do. At last the day came when he was able to say that he was once more earning his living, and one evening when he reached home she was there too. Mrs. Carter had herself brought her to Liverpool, but had gone back again to Manchester at once, as she could not stay the night. When he first set eyes on his wife he was astonished at the change in her. She was whiter, if possible, than ever, thin in the face, dark-ringed about the eyes, and very weak. But otherwise she was what she had always been. The hair was just as smooth, everything about her just as spotlessly clean and unruffled, and she sat as she always did, rather upright and straight, as if she preferred the discomfort of a somewhat rigid position to the greater discomfort of disarranging her gown. Zachariah had much to say. During the whole of the four hours before bedtime he did not once feel that drying-up of conversation which used to be so painful to him. It is true she herself said little or nothing, but that was of no moment. She was strengthless, and he did not expect her to talk. So long as he could speak he was happy. The next morning came, and with it came Hope, as it usually came to him in the morning, and he kissed her with passionate fervour as he went out, rejoicing to think that, although she was so feeble, she was recovering; that he could once more look forward, as in earlier days, to the evening, and forgetting every cloud which had ever come between them. Alas! when the night of that very day came he found his little store exhausted, and he and the companion of his life sat together for a quarter of an hour or more without speaking a word. He proposed reading a book, and took up the Ferguson, thinking he could extract from it something which might interest her; but she was so irresponsive, and evidently cared so little for it, that he ceased. It was but eight o'clock, and how to fill up the time he did not know. At last he said he would just take a turn outside and look at the weather. He went out and stood under the stars of which he had been reading. The meeting, after such a separation, was scarcely twenty-four hours old, and yet he felt once more the old weariness and the old inability to profit by her society or care for it. He wished, or half wished, that there might have existed such differences between them that they could have totally disregarded, or even hated, one another. The futility, however, of any raving was soon perfectly clear to him. He might as well have strained at a chain which held him fast by the leg, and he therefore strove to quiet himself. He came back, after being absent longer than he intended, and found she was upstairs. He sat down and meditated again, but came to no conclusion, for no conclusion was possible.

The next evening, after they had sat dumb for some moments, he said, 'My dear, you don't seem well.'

'I am not well, as you know. You yourself don't seem well.'

He felt suddenly as if he would have liked to throw himself on his knees before her and to have it all out with her; to say to her all he had said to himself; to expose all his misery to her; to try to find out whether she still loved him; to break or thaw the shell of ice which seemed to have frozen round her. But he could not do it. He was on the point of doing it, when he looked at her face, and there was something in it which stopped him. No such confidence was possible, and he went back into himself again.

'Shall I read to you?'

'Yes, if you like.'

'What shall I read?'

'I don't care; anything you please.'

'Shall it be Cook's Voyages?'

'I have just said I really do not care.'

He took down the Cook's Voyages; but after about ten minutes he could not go on, and he put it back in its place.

'Caillaud's trial is to take place next week,' he observed after a long pause.

'Horrible man!' she exclaimed, with a sudden increase of energy. 'I understand that it was in defending him Major Maitland lost his life.'

'My dear, you are quite wrong. He was defending Major Maitland, and shot the soldier who killed him.'

'Quite wrong, am I? Of course I am quite wrong!'

'I was at head-quarters, you remember.'

'Yes, you were; but you were not near Major Maitland.'

Zachariah raised his eyes; he thought he detected, he was sure he detected, in the tone of this sentence a distinct sneer.

'I was not with Major Maitland; my duties called me elsewhere; but I am more likely to know what happened than any gossiping outsider.'

'I don't believe in your foreign infidels.'

'*My* foreign infidels! You have no right to call them my infidels, if you mean that I am one. But let me tell you again you are mistaken. Besides, supposing you are right, I don't see why he should be a horrible man. He will probably be executed for what he did.'

'It was he and that daughter of his who dragged you and the Major into all this trouble.'

182

'On the contrary, Caillaud, as well as myself and the Major, did all we could to prevent the march. You must admit I understand what I am talking about. I was at every meeting.'

'As usual, nothing I say is right. It was to be expected that you would take the part of the Caillauds.'

Zachariah did not reply. It was supper-time; the chapter from the Bible was duly read, the prayer duly prayed, and husband and wife afterwards once more, each in turn, silently at the bedside, with more or less of sincerity or pathos, sought Him who was the Maker of both. It struck Zachariah during his devotions – a rather unwelcome interruption – that his wife as well as himself was in close communication with the Almighty.

CHAPTER FIFTEEN

End of the Beginning

*

THE trial took place at Lancaster. Zachariah was sorely tempted to go; but, in the first place, he had no money, and, in the second place, he feared arrest. Not that he would have cared two pins if he had been put into jail; but he could not abandon his wife. He was perfectly certain what the result would be, but nevertheless, on the day when the news was due, he could not rest. There was a mail coach which ran from Lancaster to Liverpool, starting from Lancaster in the afternoon and reaching Liverpool between eleven and twelve at night. He went out about that time and loitered about the coach-office as if he were waiting for a friend. Presently he heard the wheels and the rapid trot of the horses. His heart failed him, and he could almost have fainted.

'What's the news?' said the clerk to the coachman.

'All the whole d – d lot convicted, and one of 'em going to be hung.'

'One of them hung! Which one is that?'

'Why, him as killed the soldier, of course – the French-man.'

'A d – d good job too,' replied the clerk. 'I should like to serve every – Frenchman in the country the same way.'

Zachariah could not listen any longer, but went home, and all night long a continuous series of fearful images passed before his eyes – condemned cells, ropes, gallows, and the actual fall of the victim, down to the contortion of his muscles. He made up his mind on the following

184

day that he would see Caillaud before he died, and he told his wife he was going. She was silent for a moment, and then she said:

'You will do as you like, I suppose; but I cannot see what is the use of it. You can do no good; you will lose your place here; it will cost you something, and when you get there you may have to stop there.'

Zachariah could not restrain himself.

'Good God!' he cried, 'you hear that one of my best friends is about to be hung, and you sit there like a statue – not a single word of sympathy or horror – you care no more than a stone. *Use* of going! I tell you I will go if I starve, or have to rot in jail all my lifetime. Furthermore, I will go this instant.'

He went out of the room in a rage, rammed a few things into a bag, and was out of the house in ten minutes. He was excusably unjust to his wife – excusably, because he could not help thinking that she was hard, and even cruel. Yet really she was not so, or if she was, she was not necessarily so, for injustice, not only to others, but to ourselves, is always begotten by a false relationship. There were multitudes of men in the world, worse than Zachariah, with whom she would have been not only happier, but better. He, poor man, with all his virtues, stimulated and developed all that was disagreeable in her.

He was in no mood to rest, and walked on all that night. Amidst all his troubles, he could not help being struck with the solemn, silent procession overhead. It was perfectly clear – so clear that the heavens were not a surface, but a depth, and the stars of a lesser magnitude were so numerous and brilliant that they obscured the forms of the greater constellations. Presently the first hint of day appeared in the east. We must remember that this was the year 1817, before, so it is commonly supposed, men knew what it was properly to admire a cloud or a rock. Zachariah was not, therefore, on a level with the most ordinary subscriber to a modern circulating library. Nevertheless, he could not help noticing – we will say he did no more – the wonderful, the sacredly beautiful drama which noiselessly displayed itself before him. Over in the east the intense deep blue of the sky softened a little. Then the trees in that quarter began to contrast themselves against the background and reveal their distinguishing shapes. Swiftly, and yet with such even velocity that in no one minute did there seem to be any progress compared with the minute preceding, the darkness was thinned and resolved itself overhead into pure sapphire, shaded into yellow below and in front of him, while in the west it was still almost black. The grassy floor of the meadows now showed its colour, grey-green, with the dew lying on it, and in the glimmer under the hedge might be discerned a hare or two stirring. Star by star disappeared, until none were left, save Venus, shining like a lamp till the very moment almost when the sun's disk touched the horizon. Half a dozen larks mounted and poured forth that ecstasy which no bird but the lark can translate. More amazing than the loveliness of scene, sound and scent around him was the sense of irresistible movement. He stopped to watch it, for it grew so rapid that he could almost detect definite pulsations. Throb followed throb every second with increasing force, and in a moment more a burning speck of gold was visible, and behold it was day! He slowly turned his eyes away and walked onwards.

Lancaster was reached on the second evening after he left Liverpool. He could not travel fast nor long together, for he was not yet completely strong. He secured a bed in a low part of the town, at a public-house, and on the morning of the third day presented himself at the prison door. After some formalities he was admitted, and taken by a warder along a corridor with whitewashed walls to the condemned cell where Caillaud lay. The warder looked through a grating and said to Zachariah that a visitor was already there. Two were not allowed at a time, but he would tell the prisoner that somebody was waiting for him.

'Let's see, what's your name?' said the warder.

Then it suddenly struck him that he had been fool enough, in the excitement of entering the prison, to sign his real name in the book. There was no help for it now, and he repeated that it was Coleman.

'Ah, yes, Coleman,' echoed the man, in a manner which was significant.

'Who is the other visitor?' said Zachariah.

'It is his daughter.'

His first thought was to ask to be let in, but his next was that it would be profanity to disturb the intercourse of father and child, and he was silent. However, he had been announced, and Caillaud appeared at the grating,

187

begging permission for his friend to enter. It was at first refused; but presently something seemed to strike the jailer, for he relented with a smile.

'You won't want to come again?' he observed interrogatively.

'No; that is to say, I think not.'

'No; that is to say, I think not,' he repeated slowly, word for word, adding, 'I shall have to stay with you while you are together.'

Zachariah entered, the warder locking the door behind him and seating himself on the edge of the bedstead, where he remained during the whole of the interview, jingling his keys and perfectly unmoved.

The three friends spoke not a word for nearly five minutes. Zachariah was never suddenly equal to any occasion which made any great demands upon him. It often made him miserable that it was so. Here he was, in the presence of one whom he had so much loved, and who was about to leave him for ever, and he had nothing to say. That could have been endured could he but have *felt* and showed his feeling, could he but have cast himself upon his neck and wept over him, but he was numbed and apparently immovable. It was Caillaud who first broke the silence.

'It appears I shall have to console you rather than you me; believe me, I care no more about dying, as mere dying, than I do about walking across this room. There are two things which disturb me – the apprehension of some pain, and bidding good-bye to Pauline and you, and two or three more.'

There was, after all, but just a touch needed to break up Zachariah and melt him.

'You are happier than I,' he cried. 'Your work is at an end. No more care for things done or undone; you are discharged, and nobly discharged, with honour. But as for me!'

'With honour!' and Caillaud smiled. 'To be hung like a forger of bank-notes – not even to be shot – and then to be forgotten. Forgotten utterly! This does not happen to be one of those revolutions which men remember.'

'No! men will not remember,' said Pauline, with an elevation of voice and manner almost oratorical. 'Men will not remember, but there is a memory in the world which forgets nothing.'

'Do you know,' said Caillaud, 'I have always loved adventure, and at times I look forward to death with curiosity and interest, just as if I were going to a foreign country.'

'Tell me,' said Zachariah, 'if there is anything I can do.'

'Nothing. I would ask you to see that Pauline comes to no harm, but she can take care of herself. I have nothing to give you in parting. They have taken everything from me.'

'What a brute I am! I shall never see you again, and I cannot speak,' sobbed Zachariah.

'Speak! What need is there of speaking? What is there which *can* be said at such a time? To tell you the truth, Coleman, I hardly cared about having you here. I did not want to imperil the calm which is now happily upon me; we all of us have something unaccountable and uncontrollable in us, and I do not know how soon it may wake in me. But I did wish to see you, in order that your mind might be at peace about me. Come, good-bye!'

Caillaud put his hand on Zachariah's shoulder.

'This will not do,' he said. 'For my sake, forbear. I can face what I have to go through next Monday if I am not shaken. Come, Pauline, you too, my child, must leave me for a bit.'

Zachariah looked at Pauline, who rose and threw her shawl over her shoulders. Her lips were tightly shut, but she was herself. The warder opened the door. Zachariah took his friend's hand, held it for a moment, and then threw his arms round his neck. There is a pathos in parting which the mere loss through absence does not explain. We all of us feel it, even if there is to be a meeting again in a few months, and we are overcome by incomprehensible emotion when we turn back down the pier, unable any longer to discern the waving of the handkerchief, or when the railway train turns the curve in the cutting and leaves us standing on the platform. Infinitely pathetic, therefore, is the moment when we separate for ever.

Caillaud was unsettled for an instant, and then, slowly untwining the embrace, he made a sign to Pauline, who took Zachariah's hand and led him outside, the heavy, well-oiled bolt of the lock shooting back under the key with a smooth strong thud behind them. She walked down the corridor alone, not noticing that he had not followed her, and had just passed out of sight when an officer stepped up to him and said:

'Your name is Coleman?'

'Yes.'

'Sorry to hear it. My name is Nadin. You know me, I think. You must consider yourself my prisoner.'

Zachariah was in prison for two years. He had not been there three months when his wife died.

Let us now look forward to 1821; let us walk down one of the new streets just beginning to stretch northwards from Pentonville; let us stop opposite a little house, with a little palisade in front, enclosing a little garden five-and-twenty feet long and fifteen feet broad; let us peep through the chink between the blind and the window. We see Zachariah and Pauline. Another year passes; we peep through the same chink again. A cradle is there, in which lies Marie Pauline Coleman: but where is the mother? She is not there, and the father alone sits watching the child.

CHAPTER SIXTEEN
Cowfold
*

COWFOLD, half village, half town, lies about three miles to the west of the Great North Road from London to York. As you go from London, about fifty miles from the Post Office in St. Martin's-le-Grand – the fiftieth mile-stone is just beyond the turning – you will see a hand-post with three arms on it; on one is written in large letters, 'To LONDON'; on the second, in equally large letters, 'To YORK'; and on the third, in small italic letters, '*To Cowfold*.' Two or three years before the events narrated in the following chapters took place – that is to say, about twenty years after the death of Zachariah's second wife – a hundred coaches a day rolled past that hand-post, and about two miles beyond it was a huge inn, with stables like cavalry barracks, where horses were changed. No coach went through Cowfold. When the inhabitants wished to go northwards or southwards they walked or drove to the junction, and waited on the little grassy triangle till a coach came by which had room for them. When they returned they were deposited at the same spot, and the passengers who were going through from London to York or Scotland, or who were coming up to London, always seemed to despise people who were taken up or who were left by the roadside there.

There was, perhaps, some reason for this contempt. The North Road was at that time one of the finest roads in the world, broad, hard-metalled, and sound in the wet-test weather. That which led to Cowfold was under the control of the parish, and in winter-time was very bad indeed. When you looked down it, it seemed as if it led nowhere, and, indeed, the inhabitants of the town were completely shut off from any close communication with the outer world. How strange it was to emerge from the end of the lane and to see those wonderful words, 'To London,' 'To York'! What an opening into infinity! Boys of a slightly imaginative turn of mind – for there were boys with imagination even in Cowfold – would, on a holiday, trudge the three miles eastward merely to get to the post and enjoy the romance of those mysterious fingers. No wonder; for the excitement begotten by the long stretch of the road – London at one end, York at the other – by the sight of the *Star*, *Rover*, *Eclipse*, or *Times* racing along at twelve miles an hour, and by the inscriptions on them, was worth a whole afternoon's cricket or wandering in the fields. Cowfold itself supplied no such stimulus. The only thing like it was the mail-cart, which every evening took the letters from the post office, disappeared into the dark, nobody could tell whither, and brought letters in the morning, nobody could tell whence, before the inhabitants were out of bed. There was a vague belief that it went about fifteen miles and 'caught' something somewhere; but nobody knew for certain, except the postmistress and the mail-cart driver, who were always remarkably reticent on the point. The driver was dressed in red, carried a long horn slung at the side of the cart, and was popularly believed also to have pistols with him. He never accosted anybody; sat on a solitary perch just big enough for him; swayed always backwards and forwards a little in a melancholy fashion as he rode; was never

193

seen during the daytime, and was not, in any proper sense, a Cowfold person.

Cowfold had four streets, or more correctly, only two, which crossed one another at right angles in the middle of the town, and formed there a kind of square or open place, in which, on Saturdays, a market was held. The 'Angel' was in this square, and the shops grouped themselves round it. In the centre was a large pump with a great leaden spout that had a hole bored in it at the side. By stopping up the mouth of the spout with the hand it was possible through this hole to get a good drink, if a friend was willing to work the handle; and as the square was a public playground, the pump did good service, especially amongst the boys, all of whom preferred it greatly to a commonplace mug. On Sundays it was invariably chained up; for although it was no breach of the Sabbath to use the pump in the backyard, the line was drawn there, and it would have been voted by nine-tenths of Cowfold as decidedly immoral to get water from the one outside. The shops were a draper's, a grocer's, an ironmonger's, a butcher's, and a baker's. All these were regular shops, with shop-windows, and were within sight of one another. There were also other houses where things were sold; but these were mere dwelling-houses, and were at the poorer and more remote ends of Cowfold. None of the regular shops aforesaid were strictly what they professed to be. Each of them diverged towards 'the general.' The draper sold boots and shoes; the grocer sold drugs, stationery, horse and cow medicines, and sheep ointment; and the ironmonger dealt in crockery. Even the butcher was more than a butcher, for he was never to be seen at his chopping-block, and his wife did all the retail work. He himself was in the 'jobbing' line, and was always jogging about in a cart, in the hind part of which, covered with a net, was a calf or a couple of pigs. Three out of the four streets ran out in cottages; but one was more aristocratic. This was Church Street, which contained the church and the parsonage. It also had in it four red-brick houses, each surrounded with large gardens. In one lived a brewer who had a brewery in Cowfold, and owned a dozen beer-shops in the neighbourhood; another was a seminary for young ladies; in the third lived the doctor; and in the fourth old Mr. and Mrs. Muston, who had no children, had been there for fifty years, and this, so far as Cowfold was aware, was all their history. Mr. and Mrs. Muston and the seminary were the main strength of the church. To be sure, the doctor and the landlord of the 'Angel' professed devotion to the Establishment, but they were never inside the church, except just now and then, and were charitably excused because of their peculiar callings. The rest of Cowfold was Dissenting or 'went nowhere.' There were three chapels; one, *the* chapel, orthodox, Independent, holding about seven hundred persons, and more particularly to be described presently; the second, Wesleyan, new, stuccoed, with grained doors and cast-iron railing; the third, Strict Baptist, ultra-Calvinistic, Antinomian according to the other sects, dark, down an alley, mean, surrounded by a small long-grassed graveyard, and named ZOAR in large letters over the long window in front. The 'went nowhere' class was apparently not very considerable. On Sunday morning at twelve o'clock Cowfold looked as if it had been swept clean. It was only by comparison between the total number of church-goers and chapel-goers and the total population that it could be believed that there was anybody absent from the means of grace; but if a view could have been taken of the back premises an explanation would have been discovered. Men and women 'did up their gardens,' or found, for a variety of reasons, that they were forced to stay at home. In the evening they grew bolder, and strolled through the meadows. It is, however, only fair to respectable Cowfold to say that it knew nothing of these creatures, except by employing them on week-days.

With regard to the Wesleyan Chapel, nothing much need be said. Its creed was imported, and it had no roots in the town. The Church disliked it because it was Dissenting, and the Dissenters disliked it because it was half-Church and, above all, Tory. It was supported mainly by the brewer, who was drawn thither for many reasons, one of which was political. Another was that he was not in trade, and although he objected to be confounded with his neighbours who stood behind counters, the church did not altogether suit him, because there Mr. and Mrs. Muston and the seminary stood in his way. Lastly, as he owned beer-shops, supplied liquor which was a proverb throughout the county, and did a somewhat doubtful business according to the more pious of the Cowfold Christians, he preferred to be accredited as a religious person by Methodism than by any other sect, the stamp of Methodism standing out in somewhat higher relief.

As for Zoar, it was a place apart. Its minister was a big, large-jawed, heavy-eyed man who lived in a little cottage hard by. His wife was a very plain-looking person, who wore, even on Sundays, a cotton gown without any ornament, and who took her husband's arm as they walked down the lane to the chapel. The Independent minister, the Wesleyan minister, and, of course, the rector, had nothing to do with the minister of Zoar. This was not because of any heresy or difference of doctrine, but because he was a poor man, and poor persons sat under him. Nevertheless, he was not in any way a characteristic Calvinist. The Calvinistic creed was stuck in him as in a lump of fat, and had no organizing influence upon him whatever. He had no weight in Cowfold, took part in none of its affairs, and his ministrations were confined to about fifty sullen, half-stupid, wholly ignorant people who found in the Zoar services something sleepier and requiring less mental exertion than they needed elsewhere; although it must be said that the demands made upon the intellect in none of the places of worship were very extensive. There was a small endowment attached to Zoar, and on this, with the garden and house rent free, the minister lived. Once now and then – perhaps once in every three or four years – there was a baptism in Zoar, and at such times it was crowded. The children of the congregation, as a rule, fell away from it as they grew up; but occasionally a girl remained faithful and was formally admitted to its communion. In front of the pulpit was an open space, usually covered; but the boards could be taken up, and then a large kind of tank was disclosed, which was filled with water when the ceremony was performed. After hymns had been sung, the minister went down into the water, and the candidate appeared dressed in a long white robe very much like a night-gown. The dear sister, during a short address, stood on the brink of the tank for a few moments, and then descended into it beside the minister, who, taking her by the neck and round the waist, ducked her fairly and completely. She emerged and walked dripping into the vestry, where it was always said that hot brandy and water was ready.

Many of us have felt that we would give all our books if we could but see with our own eyes how a single day was passed by a single ancient Jewish, Greek, or Roman family; how the house was opened in the morning; how the meals were prepared; what was said; how the husband, wife and children went about their work; what clothes they wore, and what were their amusements. Would that the present historian could do as much for Cowfold! Would that he could bring back one blue summer morning, one afternoon and evening, and reproduce exactly what happened in Cowfold Square, in one of the Cowfold shops, in one of the Cowfold parlours, and in one Cowfold brain and heart. Could this be done with strictest accuracy, a book would be written, although Cowfold was not Athens, Rome, nor Jerusalem, which would live for many, many years longer than much of the literature of this century. But, alas! the preliminary image in the mind of the writer is faint enough, and when he comes to trace it the pencil swerves and goes off into something utterly unlike it. An attempt, however to show what the waking

198

hours in Cowfold Square were like may not be out of
place. The shopkeeper came into his shop at half-past
seven, about half an hour after the shutters had been taken
down by his apprentice. At eight o'clock breakfast was
ready; but before breakfast there was family worship, and
a chapter was read from the Bible, followed by an extempore prayer from the head of the household. If the master
happened to be absent, it was not considered proper that
the mistress should pray extempore, and she used a book
of 'Family Devotions.' A very solid breakfast followed,
and business began. It was very slow, but it was very
human – much more so than business at the present day
in the City. Every customer had something to say beyond
his own immediate errand, and the shop was the place
where everything touching Cowfold interests was abund-
antly discussed. Cowfold, too, did much trade in the
country round it. Most of the inhabitants kept a gig, and
two or three times, perhaps, in a week a journey somewhere or other was necessary which was not in the least
like a journey in a railway train. Debts in the villages were
collected by the creditor in person, who called and invited
his debtors to a most substantial dinner at the inn. At one
o'clock Cowfold dined. Between one and two nobody was
to be seen in the streets, and the doors were either fastened
or a bell was put upon them. After dinner the same duties
returned in the shop; but inside the house dinner was the
turning-point of the day. When the 'things were washed
up,' servant and mistress began to smarten themselves,
and disappearing into their bedrooms, emerged at four
to make preparations for tea, the meal most enjoyed in all

Cowfold. If any spark of wit slept in any Cowfoldian male or female, it appeared then. No invitations to dinner were ever heard of; but tea was the opportunity for hospitality, especially amongst women. The minister, when he visited, invariably came to tea. The news circulated at tea, and, in fact, at tea between five and six, Cowfold, if its intellect could have been measured by a properly constructed gauge, would have been found many degrees higher in the scale than at any other hour. Granted that the conversation was personal, trivial, and even scandalous, it was in a measure philosophical. Cowfold, though it knew nothing, or next to nothing, of abstractions, took immense interest in the creatures in which they were embodied. It would have turned a deaf ear to any debate on the nature of ethical obligation, but it was very keen indeed in apportioning blame to its neighbours who had sinned, and in deciding how far they had gone wrong. Cowfold, in other words, believed that flesh and blood, and not ideas, are the school and the religion for most of us, and that we learn a language by the examples rather than by the rules. The young scholar fresh from his study is impatient at what he considers the unprofitable gossip about the people round the corner; but when he gets older he sees that often it is much better than his books, and that distinctions are expressed by a washerwoman, if the objects to be distinguished eat and drink and sleep, which he would find it difficult to make with his symbols. Moreover, the little Cowfold clubs and parties understood what they were saying, and so far had an advantage over the clubs and parties which, since the days of penny newspapers, now discuss in Cowfold the designs of Russia, the graduation of the Income Tax, or the merits and demerits of the administration. The Cowfold horizon has now been widened, to use the phrase of an enlightened gentleman who came down and lectured there on the criminality of the advertisement duty; but unfortunately the eyes remain the same. Cowfold now looks abroad, and is very eloquent upon the fog in the distance, and the objects it thinks it sees therein; but, alas! what it has gained in inclusive breadth it has lost in definition. Politics, however, were not unknown in Cowfold; for before 1832 it was a borough, and after 1832 it was one of the principal polling-places for the county. Nevertheless, it was only on the eve of an election that anybody dabbled in them, and even then they were very rudimentary. The science to most of the voters meant nothing more than a preference of blue to yellow, or yellow to blue; and women had nothing whatever to do with it, excepting that wives always, of course, took their husbands' colours. Politics, too, as a rule, were not mentioned in private houses. They were mostly reserved for the 'Angel,' and for the brandies and water and pipes which collected there in the evening.

To return. After tea the master went back once more to his counter, and the shutters were put up at eight. From eight to nine was an hour of which no account can be given. The lights were left burning in the shops, and the neighbour across the way looked in, and remained talking till his supper was ready. Supper at nine, generally hot, was an institution never omitted, and, like tea, was convivial; but the conviviality was of a distinctly lower order. Everybody had whisky, gin, or brandy afterwards, and every male person who was of age smoked. There was, as a rule, no excess, but the remarks were apt to be disconnected and woolly; and the wife, who never had grog for herself but always sipped her husband's, went to sleep. Eleven o'clock saw all Cowfold in bed, and disturbed only by such dreams as were begotten of the previous liver and bacon and alcohol.

There were no villains amongst that portion of the inhabitants with which this history principally concerns itself, nor was a single adventure of any kind ever known to happen beyond the adventures of being born, getting married, falling sick, and dying, with now and then an accident from a gig. Consequently it might be thought that there was no romance in Cowfold. There could not be a greater mistake. The history of every boy or girl of ordinary make is one of robbery, murder, imprisonment, death-sentence, filing of chains, scaling of prison walls, recapture, scaffold, reprieve, poison, and pistols; the difference between such a history and that in the authorized versions being merely circumstantial. The Garden of Eden, the murder of Cain, the Deluge, the salvation of Noah, the exodus from Egypt, David and Bathsheba, with the murder of Uriah, the Assyrian invasion, the Incarnation, the Atonement, and the Resurrection from the Dead, to say nothing of the Decline and Fall of the Roman Empire, the tragedy of Count Cenci, the execution of Mary Queen of Scots, the Inquisition in Spain, and Revolt of the Netherlands, all happened in Cowfold, as well as elsewhere, and were perhaps more interesting there because they could be studied in detail and the records were authentic.

Church Street, Cowfold – that is to say, the street in which the church stood – was tolerably broad going east and west, so that the sun shone full on the white window-frames and red brick of Mr. Muston's house, in which everything seemed to sleep in eternal calm. On the opposite side was the seminary, also red brick and white paint, facing the north; but, to make amends, the garden had a southern aspect, and the back of the house was covered with a huge magnolia whose edges curled round to the western side, so that it could be seen by wayfarers. It was a sight not to be forgotten – the red brick, the white paint, the July sun, the magnolia leaves, the flanking elms on the east high above the chimneys, the glimpse of the acre of lawn through the great gates when they happened to be open, the peace, so profound, of summer noon! How lovely it looks as it hovers unsteadily before the eye, seen through the transfiguring haze of so many years! It was really, there is no doubt about it, handsomer than the stuccoed villa which stares at us over the way; but yet, if Cowfold Church Street, red brick, white paint, elms, lawn, and midsummer repose, could be restored at the present moment, would it be exactly what the vision of it is? What is the magic gift which even for the humblest of us paints and frames these enchanting pictures? It is nothing less than the genius which is common to humanity. If we are not able to draw or model, we possess the power to select, group, and clothe with an ideal grace, which is the very soul of art, and every man and woman, every bush, nay, every cabbage, cup and saucer, provided only it be not actually before us, becomes part of a divine picture. Would that we could do with the present what we do with the past! We *can* do something if we try.

At the end of Church Street came the vicarage, and then the churchyard, with the church. Beyond was the park, which half-embraced Cowfold, for it was possible to enter it not only from Church Street, but from North Street, which ran at right angles to it. The Hall was not much. It was a large plain stone mansion, built in the earlier part of the eighteenth century; but in front of the main entrance was a double row of limes stretching for a quarter of a mile, and the whole of the park was broken up into soft swelling hills, from whose tops, owing to the flatness of the country around, an almost immeasurable distance could be seen, gradually losing itself in deepening mist of tenderest blue. The park, too, was not rigidly circumscribed. Public roads led through it. It melted on two or three sides into cultivated fields, and even the private garden of the Hall seemed a part of it; for there was nothing between them but a kind of grassy ditch and an almost invisible fence. The domain of Cowfold Hall was the glory of Cowfold and the pride of its inhabitants. The modern love of scenery was not known in Cowfold, and still less was that worship of landscape and Nature known which, as before observed, is peculiar to the generation born under the influence of Wordsworth. We have learnt, however, from Zachariah that even before Wordsworth's days people were sometimes touched by dawn or sunset. The morning cheered, the moon lent pathos and sentiment, and the stars awoke unanswerable interrogations in Cowfold, although it knew no poetry, save Dr. Watts, Pollok's *Course of Time*, and here and there a little of Cowper. Under the avenue, too, whose slender columns, in triple rows on either side, rose to an immense height, and met in a roof overhead with all the grace of cathedral stone, and without its superincumbent weight and imprisonment – a roof that was not impervious to the sunlight, but let it pass and fall in quivering flakes on the ground – Cowfold generally took off its hat, partly, no doubt, because the place was cool, but also as an act of homage. Here and in the woods adjoining youths and maidens for three hundred years had walked and made love, for though the existing house was new, it stood on the site of a far older building. Dead men and women, lord and churl, gone to indistinguishable dust, or even beyond that – gone, perhaps, into vapour and gas, which had been blown to New Zealand and become men and women again – had burned with passion here, and vowed a union that was to last beyond the Judgment Day. They wept here, quarrelled here, rushed again into one another's arms here, swore to one another here, when Henry the Eighth was king; and they wept here, quarrelled here, embraced here, swore here, in exactly the same mad fashion, when William the Fourth sat upon the throne. Halfway up the avenue was a stone pillar commanding a gentle descent, one way to the Hall and the other way to the lodge. It set forth the anguish of a former lord of the time of Queen Anne, who had lost his wife when she was twenty-six years old. She was beneath him in rank, but very beautiful, and his affection for her had fought with and triumphed over the cruel opposition of father, mother, and relations, who had other designs. He had made enemies of them all; but he won his wife, and, casting her in the scale, father, mother and friends were as gossamer. She died two years after the wedding – to the very day. Rich in her love, he had never taken a thought to propitiate anybody, nor to make friends with the Mammon of Unrighteousness, and when she suddenly departed he turned round and found himself alone. So far from knocking at men's doors, he more fiercely hated those who now, touched with pity, would gladly have welcomed him. He broke from them all, lived his own life, was reputed to be a freethinker, and when he came to his estate, a long, long while afterwards, he put up the obelisk, and recorded in Latin how Death, the foul adulterer, had ravished his sweet bride – the coward Death whom no man could challenge – and that the inconsolable bridegroom had erected this monument in memory of her matchless virtues. That was all: no blessed resurrection nor trust in the Saviour. The Reverend John Broad, minister of Tanner's Lane Chapel, when he brought visitors here, regularly translated the epitaph. He was not very good at Latin, but he had somehow found out its meaning. He always observed that it was not classic, and consequently not easy to render. He pointed out, too, as a further curiosity, which somewhat increased the difficulty to any ordinary person, that V was used for U, and I for J. He never, as might be expected, omitted to enlarge upon the omission of any reference to the Atoning Blood and the Life to Come, and remarked how the poor man's sufferings would have been entirely 'assuaged' – a favourite word with Mr. Broad – if he had believed in 'those remedies.' At the same time Mr. Broad dwelt upon the 'associations' of the avenue, which, he thought, added much to its natural 'attractiveness'. Cowfold thought so too, and welcomed the words as exactly expressing what it felt. John Broad and Cowfold were right, and more right, perhaps, than they knew. The draper's young man who walked through the park with his arm round his young woman's waist looked up at the obelisk, repeated its story, and became more serious. Thus it came to pass that the old lord's love lived again somewhat in the apprentice, and that which to the apprentice seemed most particularly himself was a little bit of the self of the Queen Anne's earl long since asleep in the vault under Cowfold Church.

CHAPTER SEVENTEEN

When wilt thou Arise out of thy Sleep? Yet a Little Sleep

*

THE Reverend John Broad was minister of Tanner's Lane Chapel, or, more properly, Meeting-house, a three-gabled building, with the date 1688 upon it, which stood in a short street leading out of North Street. Why it was called Tanner's Lane nobody knew, for not in the memory of man had any tanner carried on his trade there. There was nothing of any consequence in it but the meeting-house, and when people said Tanner's Lane this was what they meant. There were about seven hundred and fifty sittings in it, and on Sundays it was tolerably full, for it was attended by large numbers of people from the surrounding villages, who came in gigs and carts and brought their dinners with them, which they ate in the vestry. It was, in fact, the centre of the Dissenting activity for a whole district. It had small affiliated meeting-houses in places like Sheepgate, Hackston Green, and Bull's Cross, in which service was held on Sunday evening by the deacons of Tanner's Lane, or by some of the young men whom Mr. Broad prepared to be missionaries. For a great many years the congregation had apparently undergone no change in character; but the uniformity was only apparent. The fervid piety of Cowper's time and of the Evangelical revival was a thing almost of the past. The Reverend John Broad was certainly not of the Revival type. He was a big, gross-feeding, heavy person with heavy ox-face and large mouth, who might have been bad enough for anything if Nature had ordained that he should have been born in a hovel at Sheepgate or in the Black Country. As it happened, his father was a woollen draper, and John was brought up to the trade as a youth; got tired of it, thought he might do something more respectable; went to a Dissenting College; took charge of a little chapel in Buckinghamshire; married early; was removed to Tanner's Lane, and became a preacher of the Gospel. He was moderate in all of what he called his 'views'; neither ultra-Calvinist nor Arminian; not rigid upon Baptism, and certainly much unlike his lean and fervid predecessor, the Reverend James Harden, M.A., who was educated at Cambridge, threw up all his chances there when he became convinced of sin, cast in his lot with the Independents, and wrestled even unto blood with the world, the flesh, and the devil in Cowfold for thirty years, till he was gathered to his rest. A fiery, ardent, untameable soul was Harden's, bold and uncompromising. He never scrupled to tell anybody what he thought, and would send an arrow sharp and swift through any iniquity, no matter where it might couch. He absolutely ruled Cowfold, hated by many, beloved by many, feared by all – a genuine soldier of the Cross. Mr. Broad very much preferred the indirect mode of doing good, and, if he thought a brother had done wrong, contented himself with praying in private for him. He was, however, not a hypocrite, that is to say, not an ordinary novel or stage hypocrite. There is no such thing as a human being simply hypocritical or simply sincere. We are all hypocrites, more or less, in every word and every action, and, what is more, in every thought. It is a question simply of degree. Furthermore, there are degrees of natural capacity for sincerity, and Mr. Broad was probably as sincere as his build of soul and body allowed him to be. Certainly no doubt as to the truth of what he preached ever crossed his mind. He could not doubt, for there was no doubt in the air; and yet he could not believe as Harden believed, for neither was Harden's belief now in the air. Nor was Mr. Broad a criminal in any sense. He was upright, on the whole, in all his transactions, although a little greedy and hard, people thought, when the trustees proposed to remit to widow Oakfield, on her husband's death, half the rent of a small field belonging to the meeting-house and contributing a modest sum to Mr. Broad's revenue. He objected. Widow Oakfield was poor; but then she did not belong to Tanner's Lane, and was said to have relations who could help her. Mr. Broad loved his wife decently, brought up his children decently, and not the slightest breath of scandal ever tarnished his well-polished reputation. On some points he was most peculiar, and no young woman who came to him with her experience before she was admitted into the church was ever seen by him alone. Always was a deacon present, and all Cowfold admitted that the minister was most discreet. Another recommendation, too, was that he was temperate in his drink. He was not so in his meat. Supper was his great meal, and he would then consume beef, ham, or sausages, hot potatoes, mixed pickles, fruit pies, bread, cheese, and celery in quantities which were remarkable even in those days; but he never drank anything but beer – a pint at dinner and a pint at supper.

On one Monday after noon in July, 1840, Mr. and Mrs.

Broad sat at tea in the study. This was Mr. Broad's habit
on Monday afternoon. On that day, after the three sermons on the Sunday, he always professed himself 'Mondayish'. The morning was given over to calling in the
town; when he had dined he slept in his large leathern
chair; and at five husband and wife had tea by themselves.
Thomas, the eldest son, and his two younger sisters,
Priscilla and Tryphosa, aged seventeen and fifteen, were
sent to the dining-room. Mr. Broad never omitted this
custom of spending an hour and a half on Monday with
Mrs. Broad. It gave them an opportunity of talking over
the affairs of the congregation, and it added to Mr. Broad's
importance with the missionary students, because they
saw how great were the weight and fatigue of the pastoral
office.

A flock like that which was shepherded by Mr. Broad
required some management. Mrs. Broad took the women,
and Mr. Broad the men; but Mrs. Broad was not a very
able tactician. She was a Flavel by birth, and came from
a distant part of the country. Her father was a Dissenting
minister; but he was Dr. Flavel, with a great chapel in a
great town. Consequently she gave herself airs, and occasionally let fall, to the great displeasure of the Cowfold
ladies, words which implied some disparagement of Cowfold. She was a shortish, stout, upright little woman, who
used a large fan and spoke with an accent strange to the
Midlands. She was not a great help to the minister, because she was not sufficiently flexible and insinuating for
her position; but nevertheless they always worked together, and she followed as well as she could the direc-

tions of her astuter husband, who, considering his bovine cast, was endowed with quite a preternatural sagacity in the secular business of his profession.

On this particular afternoon, however, the subject of the conversation was not the congregation, but young Thomas Broad, aged eighteen, the exact, and almost ridiculously exact, counterpart of his father. He had never been allowed to go to school, but had been taught at home. There was only one day-school in Cowfold, and his mother objected to the 'mixture'. She had been heard to say as much, and Cowfold resented this too, and the Cowfold youths resented it by holding Tommy Broad in extreme contempt. He had never been properly a boy, for he could play at no boyish games; had a tallowy, unpleasant complexion, went for formal walks, and carried gloves. But though in a sense incompletely developed, he was not incompletely developed in another direction. He was at what is called an awkward age, and both father and mother had detected in him an alarming tendency to enjoy the society of young women – a tendency much stimulated by his unnatural mode of life. Thomas was already a member of the church and was a teacher in the Sunday school; but his mother was uneasy, for a serious attachment between Thomas and anybody in the town would have been very distasteful to her. The tea having been poured out, and Mr. Broad having fairly settled down upon the buttered toast and radishes, Mrs. Broad began:

'Have you thought anything more about Thomas, my dear?'

Being a minister's son, he was never called Tom by either papa or mamma.

'Yes, my love; but it is very difficult to know how to proceed judiciously in such a case.'

'Mrs. Allen asked me, last Wednesday, when he was going to leave home, and I told her we had not made up our minds. She said that her brother in Birmingham wanted a youth in his office, but my answer was directly that we had quite determined that Thomas should not enter into any trade.'

'What did she say?'

'That she was not surprised, for she hardly thought Thomas was fitted for it.'

The minister looked grave and perplexed, for Mr. Allen was in trade, and was a deacon. Mrs. Broad proceeded –

"I am quite sure Thomas ought to be a minister; and I am quite sure, too, he ought to leave Cowfold and go to college.'

'Don't you think this event might be procrastinated; the expense would be considerable.'

'Well, my dear, Fanny Allen came here to tea the day before yesterday. When she went away she could not find her clogs. I was on the landing, and saw what happened, though they did not think it. Fanny's brother was waiting outside. Priscilla had gone somewhere for the moment – I don't know where – and Tryphosa was upstairs. Thomas said he would look for the clogs, and presently I saw him fastening them for her. Then he walked with her down the garden. I just went into the front bedroom and looked. It was not very dark, and, –

well, I may be mistaken, but I do believe –' The rest of the sentence was wanting. Mrs. Broad stopped at this point. She felt it was more becoming to do so. She shifted on her chair with a fidgety motion, threw her head back a little, looked up at the portrait of Dr. Flavel in gown and bands which hung over the fireplace, straightened her gown upon her knees, and pushed it forward over her feet so as to cover them altogether – a mute protest against the impropriety of the scene she had partly described. Mr. Broad inwardly would have liked her to go on; but he always wore his white neckerchief, except when he was in bed, and he was still the Reverend John Broad, although nobody but his wife was with him. He therefore refrained, but after a while slowly observed –

'Thomas has not made much progress in systematic theology.'

'They do not require much on admission, do they? He knows the outlines, and I am sure the committee will recollect my father and be glad to get Thomas. I have heard that the social position of the candidates is not what it used to be, and that they wish to obtain some of a superior stamp, who ultimately may be found adapted to metropolitan churches.'

'One of the questions last year, my dear, was upon the office of the Comforter, and you remember Josiah Collins was remanded. I hardly think Thomas is sufficiently instructed on that subject at present; and there are others. On the whole, it is preferable that he should not go till September twelvemonths.'

'His personal piety would have weight.'

'Undoubtedly.'

There was a pause, and Mrs. Broad then continued –

'Well, my dear, you know best; but what about Fanny? I shall not ask her again. How very forward, and indeed altogether –' Another stoppage, another twitch at her gown, with another fidget on the chair, the eyes going up to Dr. Flavel's bands as before. 'In *our* house too – to put herself in Thomas's way!'

Ah! Mrs. Broad, are you sure Thomas did not go out of his way – even in your house, that eminently respectable, eminently orthodox residence – even Thomas, your Samuel, who had been granted to the Lord, and who, to use his own words when his written religious autobiography was read at the church-meeting, being the child of pious parents, and of many prayers, had never been exposed to those assaults of the enemy of souls which beset ordinary young men, and consequently had not undergone a sudden conversion?

'But,' observed Mr. Broad, leaning back in his easy-chair, and half covering his face with his great broad fat hand, 'we shall offend the Allens if Fanny does not come, and we shall injure the cause.'

'Has George Allen, Fanny's brother, prayed at the prayer-meeting yet? He was admitted two months ago.'

'No.'

'Then ask his father to let him pray; and we need not invite Fanny till Thomas has left.'

The papa objected that perhaps Thomas might go to the Allens', but the mamma, with Dr. Flavel's bands before her, assured him that Thomas would do nothing of the kind. So it was settled that Mr. Broad should call at the Allens' to-morrow, and suggest that George should 'engage' on the following Thursday. This, it was confidently hoped, would prevent any suspicion on their part that Fanny had been put aside. Of course, once having begun, George would be regularly on the list.

CHAPTER EIGHTEEN

A Religious Picnic

*

OCCASIONALLY, in the summer months, Tanner's Lane indulged in a picnic; that is to say, the principal members of the congregation, with their wives and children, had an early dinner, and went in gigs and four-wheel chaises to Shott Woods, taking hampers of bread, cake, jam, butter, ham, and other eatables with them. At Shott Woods, in a small green space under an immense oak, a fire was lighted and tea was prepared. Mr. Broad and his family always joined the party. These were the days when Dissenters had no set amusements, and the entertainment at Shott mainly consisted in getting the sticks for the fire, fetching the water, and waiting on one another; the waiting being particularly pleasant to the younger people. Dancing, of course, was not thought of. In 1840 it may safely be said that there were not twenty Independent families in Great Britain in which it would have been tolerated, and, moreover, none but the rich learned to dance. No dancing-master ever came into Cowfold; there was no music-master there; no concert was ever given; and Cowfold, in fact, never 'saw nor heard anything,' to use a modern phrase, save a travelling menagerie with a brass band. What an existence! How *did* they live? It is certain, however, that they did live, and, on the whole, enjoyed their life.

The picnics were generally on a Monday, as a kind of compliment to Mr. Broad, who was supposed to need rest and change on Monday, and who was also supposed not to be able to spare the time on any other day. About

217

a month after the conversation recorded in the previous
chapter Tanner's Lane was jogging along to Shott on
one of its excursions. It was a brilliant, blazing afternoon
towards the end of August. The corn stood in shocks, and
a week with that sun would see it all stacked. There was
no dreary suburb round Cowfold, neither town nor
country, to shut out country influences. The fields came
up to the gardens and orchards at the back of half the
houses, and flowed irregularly, like an inundation, into
the angles of the streets. As you walked past the great
gate of the 'Angel' yard you could see the meadow at the
bottom belonging to Hundred Acres. Consequently all
Cowfold took an interest in agriculture, and knew a good
deal about it. Every shopkeeper was half a farmer, and
understood the points of a pig or a horse. Cowfold was not
a town properly speaking, but the country a little thick-
ened and congested. The conversation turned upon the
crops, and more particularly upon turnips and drainage,
both of them a new importation. Hitherto all the parishes
round had no drainage whatever, excepting along the
bottoms of the ridges, and the now familiar red pipes
had just made their appearance on a farm belonging to a
stranger to those parts – a young fellow from Norfolk.
Everybody was sceptical, and called him a fool. Everybody wanted to know how water was going to get through
fifteen inches of heavy land when it would lie for two days
where a horse trod. However, the pipes went in, and it so
happened that the first wet day after they were laid was a
Sunday. The congregation in Shott Church was very
restless, although the sermon was unusually short. One

by one they crept out, and presently they were followed
by the parson. All of them had collected in the pouring
rain and were watching the outfall in the ditches. To
their unspeakable amazement the pipes were all running.
Shott scratched its head and was utterly bewildered.
A new idea in a brain not accustomed to the invasion of
ideas produces a disturbance like a revolution. It causes
giddiness almost as bad as that of a fit, and an extremely
unpleasant sensation of having been whirled round and
turned head over heels. It was the beginning of new things
in Shott, the beginning of a break-down in its traditions;
a belief in something outside the ordinary parochial uni-
formities was forced into the skull of every man, woman
and child by the evidence of the senses; and when other
beliefs asked, in the course of time, for admittance, they
found the entrance easier than it would have been otherwise.

The elderly occupants of the Tanner's Lane gigs and
chaises talked exclusively upon these and other cognate
topics. The sons and daughters talked about other things
utterly unworthy of any record in a serious history.
Delightful their chatter was to them. What does it
signify to eighteen years what is said on such an afternoon
by seventeen years, when seventeen years is in a charming
white muslin dress, with the prettiest hat? Words are of
importance between me and you, who care little or nothing for one another. But there is a thrice blessed time
when words are nothing. The real word is that which
is not uttered. We may be silent, or we may be eloquent
with nonsense or sense – it is all one. So it was between

George Allen and Miss Priscilla Broad, who at the present moment were sitting next to one another. George was a broad, hearty, sandy-haired, sanguine-faced young fellow of one and twenty, eldest son of the ironmonger. His education had been that of the middle classes of those days. Leaving school at fourteen, he had been apprenticed to his father for seven years, and had worked at the forge down the backyard before coming into the front shop. On week-days he generally wore a waistcoat with sleeves and a black apron. He was never dirty; in fact, he was rather particular as to neatness and cleanliness; but he was always a little dingy and iron-coloured, as retail ironmongers are apt to be. He was now in charge of the business under his father; stood behind the counter; weighed nails; examined locks brought for repair; went to the different houses in Cowfold with a man under him to look at boiler-pipes, the man wearing a cap and George a tall hat. He had a hard, healthy, honest life, was up at six o'clock in the morning, ate well, and slept well. He was always permitted by his father to go on these excursions, and, in fact, they could not have been a success without him. If anything went wrong he was always the man to set it right. If a horse became restive, George was invariably the one to jump out, and nobody else thought of stirring. He had good expectations. The house in which the Allens lived was their own. Mr. Allen did a thriving trade, not only in Cowfold, but in all the country round, and particularly among the village blacksmiths, to whom he sold iron. He had steadily saved money, and had enlarged the original little back parlour into a

room which would hold comfortably a tea-party of ten
or a dozen.

Miss Priscilla Broad was framed after a different model.
Her face was not much unlike that of one of those women
of the Restoration so familiar to us in half a hundred
pictures. Not that Restoration levity and Restoration
manners were chargeable to Miss Priscilla. She never
forgot her parentage; but there were the same kind of
prettiness, the same sideways look, the same simper
about the lips, and there were the same flat unilluminated
eyes. She had darkish brown hair, which fell in rather
formal curls on her shoulder, and she was commonly
thought to be 'delicate.' Like her sister and brother, she
had never been to school, on account of the 'mixture,'
but had been taught by her mother. Her accomplishments
included Scripture and English history, arithmetic, geo-
graphy, the use of the globes, and dates. She had a very
difficult part to play in Cowfold, for she was obliged to
visit freely all Tanner's Lane, but at the same time to
hold herself above it and not to form any exclusive friend-
ships. These would have been most injudicious, because,
in the first place, they would have excited jealousy, and,
in the next place, the minister's daughter could not be
expected to be very intimate with anybody belonging to
the congregation. She was not particularly popular with
the majority, and was even thought to be just a bit of a
fool. But what could she have been with such surroundings? The time had passed when religion could be talked
on week-days, and the present time, when ministers,
children learn French, German, and Latin, and read

selected plays of Shakespeare, had not come. Miss Priscilla Broad found it very difficult, also, to steer her course properly amongst the young men in Cowfold. Mrs. Broad would not have permitted any one of them for a moment to dream of an alliance with her family. As soon might a Princess of the Blood Royal unite herself with an ordinary knight. Miss Broad, however, as her resources within herself were not particularly strong, thought about little or nothing else than ensnaring the hearts of the younger Cowfold males – that is to say, the hearts which were converted; and yet she encouraged none of them, save by a general acceptance of little attentions, by little mincing smiles, and little mincing speeches.

'Such a beautiful day,' said George, 'and such pleasant company!'

'Really, Mr. Allen, don't you think it would have been pleasanter for you in front?'

'What did you say, my dear?' came immediately from her mother, the ever-watchful dragon just before them. She forthwith turned a little round, for the sun was on her left hand, and with her right eye kept Priscilla well in view for the rest of the journey.

In the chaise behind pretty much the same story was told, but with a difference. In the back part were Mr. Thomas Broad and Miss Fanny Allen. The arrangement which brought these two together was most objectionable to Mrs. Broad; but unfortunately she was a little late in starting, and it was made before she arrived. She could not, without insulting the Allens, have it altered; but she consoled herself by avowing that it should not stand on the return journey in the dusk. Miss Fanny was flattered that the minister's son should be by her side, and the minister's son was not in the least deterred from playing with Miss Fanny by the weight of responsibility which oppressed and checked his sister. He did not laugh much; he had not a nature for wholesome laughter, but he chuckled, lengthened his lips, half shut his eyes; asked his companion whether the rail did not hurt her, put his arm on the top, so that she might lean against it, and talked in a manner which even she would have considered a little silly and a little odd, if his position, that of a student for the ministry, had not surrounded him with such a halo of glory.

Presently Shott Woods were reached; the parcels and hampers were unpacked, the fire was lit, the tea prepared, and the pastor asked a blessing. Everybody sat on the grass, save the reverend gentleman and his wife, who had chairs which had been brought on purpose. It would not have been considered proper that Mr. and Mrs. Broad should sit upon the grass, and indeed physically it would have been inconvenient to Mr. Broad to do so. He ate his ham in considerable quantities, adding thereto much plum-cake, and excusing himself on the ground that the ride had given him an appetite. The meal being over, grace was said, and the victuals that were left were repacked. About an hour remained before the return journey began. This was usually passed in sauntering about or in walking to the springs, a mile away, down one of the grass drives. Mrs. Broad never for a moment lost sight of Thomas, and pressed him as much as possible into her service; but when Mrs. Allen announced that the young people had all determined to go to the springs, Mrs. Broad could not hold out. Accordingly off they started, under strict orders to be back by eight. They mixed themselves up pretty indiscriminately as they left their seniors; but after a while certain affinities displayed themselves, George being found with Priscilla for example, and Thomas with Fanny. The party kept together; but Thomas and Fanny lagged somewhat till they came to a little opening in the underwood, which Thomas said was a short cut, and he pressed her to try it with him. She agreed, and they slipped out of sight nearly, but not quite, unobserved. Thomas professed himself afraid Fanny might be tired, and offered his arm. She again consented, not without a flutter, and so they reached a clearing with three or four paths branching from it. Thomas was puzzled, and as for Fanny, she knew nothing. To add to their perplexity some drops of rain were felt. She was a little frightened, and was anxious to try one of the most likely tracks which looked, she thought, as if it went to the springs, where they could take shelter in the cottage with the others. Thomas, however, was doubtful, and proposed that they should stand up in a shed which had been used for faggot-making. The rain, which now came down heavily, enforced his arguments, and she felt obliged to stay till the shower had ceased.

'Only think, Fanny,' he said, 'to be here alone with you!'

He called her Fanny now: he had always called her Miss Allen before.

'Yes,' said she, not knowing what answer to make.

'You are cold,' he added, with a little trembling in his voice and a little more light than usual in his eyes.

'Oh no, I am not cold.'

'I know you are,' and he took her hand; 'why, it is quite cold.'

'Oh dear no, Mr. Thomas, it is really not cold,' and she made a movement to withdraw it, but it remained.

The touch of the hand caused his voice to shake a little more than before.

'I say you are cold; come a little closer to me. What will your mamma say if you catch a chill?' and he drew Fanny a little nearer to him. The thick blood now drove through him with increasing speed; everything seemed in a mist, and a little perspiration was on his forehead. His arm found its way round Fanny's waist, and he pressed her closer and closer to him till his hot lips were upon her cheek. She made two or three futile attempts to release herself; but she might as well have striven with that brazen, red-hot idol who was made to clasp his victims to death. She was frightened and screamed, when suddenly a strong man's voice was heard calling 'Fanny, Fanny.' It was her brother. Knowing that she and Thomas had no umbrellas, he had brought them a couple.

'But, Fanny,' he cried, 'did I not hear you scream? What was the matter?'

'Nothing,' hastily interposed Thomas; 'she thought she saw it lighten.' Fanny looked at Thomas for a moment; but she was scared and bewildered, and held her peace.

The three went down to the rendezvous together, where the rest of the party had already assembled. Mrs. Broad had been very uneasy when she found that Thomas and Fanny were the only absentees, and she had urged George the moment she saw him to look for his sister without a moment's delay. The excuse of the rain was given and accepted; but Mrs. Broad felt convinced from Fanny's forward look that she had once more thrown herself in the way of her beloved child, her delicate Samuel. She was increasingly anxious that he should go to college, and his papa promised at once to transmit the application. Meanwhile, in the few days left before the examination, he undertook to improve Thomas where he was weakest, that is to say, in Systematic Theology, and more particularly in the doctrine of the Comforter.

CHAPTER NINETEEN

'The Kingdom of Heaven is Like unto Leaven'

★

MR. ISAAC ALLEN, Fanny's father, was an ardent Whig in politics – what in later years would have been called a Radical. He had been apprenticed in London, and had attended Mr. Bradshaw's ministrations there. He was the chosen friend of Zachariah Coleman; but although he loved Zachariah, he had held but little intercourse with him during his first marriage. There were family reasons for the estrangement, due principally to a quarrel between Mrs. Isaac and the first Mrs. Zachariah. But after Mrs. Zachariah died and her husband had suffered so much Isaac was drawn to him again. He was proud of him as a martyr for a good cause, and he often saw him when he went to London on business.

It was in consequence of these London visits that books appeared on the little book-shelf in Cowfold Square which were to be found nowhere else in the town, at any rate not in the Dissenting portion of it. It was a little bookcase, it is true, for people in country places were not great readers in those days; but Sir Walter Scott was there, and upstairs in Mr. Allen's room there was Byron – not an uncut copy, but one well used both by husband and wife. Mrs. Allen was not a particularly robust woman, although she was energetic. Often, without warning, she would not make her appearance till twelve or one o'clock in the day, and would have her fire alight in her bedroom and take her breakfast in bed. It was well understood when she was not at the table with the others that the house was to be kept quiet. After a cup of tea – nothing more – she rose and sat reading for a good two hours. It was not that she was particularly unwell – she simply needed rest. Every now and then retreat from the world and perfect isolation were a necessity to her. If she forced herself to come downstairs when she ought to be by herself she became really ill. Occasionally the fire was alight in the evening, too, and she would be off the moment tea was over, Isaac frequently joining her then, although he never remained with her in the morning. She was almost sure to escape on the day following any excitement or undue worry about household affairs. She knew Sir Walter Scott from end to end, and as few people knew him. He had been to her, and to her husband too, what he can only be to people leading a dull life far from the world. He had broken up its monotony and created a new universe! He had introduced them into a royal society of noble friends. He had added to the ordinary motives which prompted Cowfold action a thousand higher motives. Then there was the charm of the magician, so sanative, so blessed, felt directly any volume of that glorious number was opened. *Kenilworth* or *Redgauntlet* was taken down, and the reader was at once in another country and in another age, transported as if by some Arabian charm away from Cowfold cares. If anywhere in another world the blessings which men have conferred here are taken into account in distributing reward, surely the choicest in the store of the Most High will be reserved for His servant Scott! It may be said of others that they have made the world wise or rich, but of him it must be said that *he, more than all, has made the world happier* – wiser too, wiser through its happiness.

Of the influence of Byron nothing more need be said here, because so much has been said before. It may seem strange that the deacon of a dissenting chapel and his wife could read him, and could continue to wait upon the ministrations of the Reverend John Broad; but I am only stating a fact. Mrs. Allen could repeat page after page of *Childe Harold*, and yet she went diligently to Tanner's Lane. Part of what was read exhaled in the almost republican politics of the Allen household; but it had also its effect in another direction, and it was always felt by the Broads that the Allens were questionable members of the flock. They were gathered into the fold on Sunday, and had the genuine J.B. on their wool, but there was a cross in them. There was nothing which could be urged against them. No word of heresy ever escaped them, no symptom of disbelief was ever seen, and yet Mr. Broad often desired exceedingly that they were different, was never at ease with them, and in his heart of hearts bitterly hated them. After all that can be said by way of explanation, there was much in this concealed animosity of Mr. Broad which was unaccountable. It was concealed, because he was far too worldly-wise to show it openly; but it was none the less intense. Indeed, it was so intense as to be almost inconsistent with Mr. Broad's cast of character, and his biographer is at a loss to find the precise point where it naturally connects itself with the main stem from which branch off the rest of his virtues and vices. However, there it was, and perhaps some shrewder psychologist may be able to explain how such a passion could be begotten in a nature otherwise so somnolent.

For this literary leaven in the Allens' household, as we have said, Zachariah was answerable. Mrs. Allen loved him as she loved her father, and he wrote to her long letters, through which travelled into Cowfold Square all the thought of the Revolution. He never went to Cowfold himself, nor could he ever be persuaded to let little Pauline go. She had been frequently invited, but he always declined the invitation courteously, on the ground that he could not spare her. The fame of her beauty and abilities had, however, reached Cowfold, and so it came to pass that when Mr. Thomas Broad, junior, being duly instructed in the doctrine of the Comforter, entered the Dissenting College in London, he determined that at the first opportunity he would call and see her. He had been privately warned both by his father and mother that he was on no account to visit this particular friend of the Allens, firstly, because Zachariah was reputed to be 'inclined' towards infidelity, and secondly, because, summing up the whole argument, he was not 'considered respectable.'

'Of course, my dear, you know his history,' quoth Mrs. Broad, 'and it would very much interfere with your usefulness if you were to be intimate with him.'

Little Pauline had by this time grown to be a woman, or very nearly one. She had, as in nine times, perhaps, out of ten is the case, inherited her temperament from her mother. She had also inherited something more, for she was like her in face. She had the same luxuriantly dark hair – a wonder to behold when it was let down over her shoulders – the same grey eyes, the same singularly erect attitude, and lips which, although they were not tight and screwed up, were always set with decision. But her distinguishing peculiarity was her inherited vivacity, which was perfectly natural, but frequently exposed her – just as it did her mother – to the charge of being theatrical. The criticism was as unjust in her case as in that of her mother, if by being theatrical we mean being unreal. The unreal person is the half-alive languid person. Pauline felt what she said, and acted it in every gesture. Her precious promptitude of expression made her invaluable as a companion to her father. He was English all over and all through; hypochondriacal, with a strong tendency to self-involution and self-absorption. She was only half English, or rather altogether French, and when he came home in the evening he often felt as if some heavy obstruction in his brain and about his heart were suddenly dissolved. She and her mother were like Hercules in the house of Admetus. Before Hercules has promised to rescue Alcestis we feel that the darkness has disappeared. Pauline was loved by her father with intense passion. When she was a little child, and he was left alone with a bitter sense of wrong, a feeling that he had more than his proper share of life's misery, his heart was closed, and he cared for no friendship. But the man's nature could not be thus thwarted, and gradually it poured itself out in full flood – denied exit elsewhere – at this one small point. He rejoiced to find that he had not stiffened into death, and he often went up to her bedside as she lay asleep, and the tears came, and he thanked God, not only for her but for his tears. He could not afford to bring her up like a lady, but he did his best to give her a good education. He was very anxious that she should learn French, and as she was wonderfully quick at languages, she managed in a very short time to speak it fluently.

CHAPTER TWENTY

The Reverend Thomas Broad's Exposition of
Romans viii. 7

★

SUCH was the Coleman household when Mr. Thomas
Broad called one fine Monday afternoon about three
months after he had been at college. He had preached his
first sermon on the Sunday before, in a village about
twelve miles from London in a north-easterly direction,
somewhere in the flat regions of Essex. Mr. Thomas was
in unusually good humour, for he had not broken down,
and thought he had crowned himself with glory. The
trial, to be sure, was not very severe. The so-called
chapel was the downstairs living-room of a cottage holding at a squeeze about five-and-twenty people. Nevertheless, there was a desk at one corner, with two candles
on either side, and Mr. Thomas was actually, for the
first time, elevated above an audience. It consisted of
the wheelwright and his wife, both very old, half a dozen
labourers, with their wives, and two or three children.
The old wheelwright, as he was in business, was called
the 'principal support of the cause.' The 'cause,' however, was not particularly prosperous, nor its supporters
enthusiastic. It was 'supplied' always by a succession of
first-year's students, who made their experiments on the
corpus vile here. Spiritual teaching, spiritual guidance,
these poor peasants had none, and when the Monday
came they went to their work in the marshes and elsewhere, and lived their blind lives under grey skies, with
nothing left in them of the Sunday, save the recollection
of a certain routine performed which might one day save

233

them from some disaster with which flames and brim-stone had something to do. It was not, however, a reality to them. Neither the future nor the past was real to them; no spiritual existence was real; nothing, in fact, save the most stimulant sensation. Once upon a time, a man, look-ing towards the celestial city, saw 'the reflection of the sun upon the city (for the city was of pure gold), so exceeding glorious that he could not as yet with open face behold it, save through an instrument made for that purpose'; but Mr. Thomas Broad and his hearers needed no smoked glass now to prevent injury to their eyes. Mr. Thomas had put on a white neckerchief, had mounted the desk, and had spoken for three-quarters of an hour from the text, 'The carnal mind is at enmity with God.' He had received during the last three weeks his first lectures on the 'Scheme of Salvation,' and his discourse was a reproduction of his notes thereon. The wheelwright and his wife, and the six labourers with their wives, listened as oxen might listen, wandered home along the lanes heavy-footed like oxen, with heads towards the ground, and went heavily to bed. The elder student who had accompanied Mr. Thomas informed him that, on the whole, he had acquitted himself very well, but that it would be better, perhaps in future to be a little simpler, and avoid what 'may be called the metaphysics of Re-demption.'

'No doubt,' said he, 'they are very attractive, and of enormous importance. There is no objection to expound them before a cultivated congregation in London; but in the villages we cannot be too plain – that, at least, is my experience. Simply tell them we are all sinners, and deserve damnation. God sent His Son into the world. If we believe in Him we shall be saved; if not, we shall be lost. There is no mystery in that; everybody can understand it; and people are never weary of hearing the old old gospel.'

Mr. Thomas was well contented with himself, as we have said, when he knocked at Zachariah's door. It was opened by Pauline. He took off his hat and smiled.

'My name is Broad. I come from Cowfold, and know the Allens very well. I am now living in London, and having heard of you so often, I thought I should like to call.'

'Pray come in,' she said; 'I am very glad to see you. I wish my father were here.'

He was shown into the little front room, and after some inquiries about his relations Pauline asked him where was his abode in London.

'At the Independent College. I am studying for the ministry.'

Pauline was not quite sure what 'the ministry' meant; but as Mr. Thomas had yesterday's white tie round his neck – he always 'dirtied out' the Sunday's neckerchief on Monday, and wore a black one on the other weekdays – she guessed his occupation.

'Dear me! you must be tired with walking so far.'

'Oh no, not tired with walking; but the fact is I am a little Mondayish.'

'A little what?'

Mr. Thomas giggled a little. 'Ah, you young ladies, of

course, don't know what that means. I had to conduct a service in the country yesterday, and am rather fatigued. I am generally so on Mondays, and I always relax on that day.' This, it is to be remembered, was his first Monday.

Pauline regretted very much that she had no wine in the house; neither had they any beer. They were not total abstainers, but nothing of the kind was kept in their small store-closet.

'Oh, thank you; never mind.' He took a bottle of smelling-salts from the mantelpiece and smelt it. The conversation flagged a little. Pauline sat at the window, and Mr. Thomas at the table. At last he observed –

'Are you alone all day?'

'Generally, except on Sunday. Father does not get home till late.'

'Dear me! And you are not dull nor afraid?'

'Dull or afraid! Why?'

'Oh, well,' he sniggered, 'dull – why, young ladies, you know, usually like society. At least,' and he laughed a little greasy laugh at his wit, 'we like theirs. And then – afraid – well, if my sister were so attractive' – he looked to see if this pretty compliment was effective – 'I should not like her to be without anybody in the house.'

Pauline became impatient. She rose. 'When you come again,' she said, 'I hope my father will be here.'

Mr. Thomas rose too. He had begun to feel awkward. For want of something better to say, he asked whose was the portrait over the mantelpiece.

'Major Cartwright.'

'Major Cartwright! Dear me, is that Major Cartwright?' He had never heard of him before, but he did not like to profess ignorance of a Major.

'And this likeness of this young gentleman?' he inquired, looking at Pauline sideways, with an odious simper on his lips. 'Nobody I know, I suppose?'

'My father when he was one-and-twenty.' She moved towards the door. Mr. Thomas closed his fat eyes till they became almost slits, simpered still more effectively, as he thought, trusted he might have the pleasure of calling again, and departed.

Pauline returned, opened the window and door for ten minutes, and went upstairs. When she saw her father she told him briefly that she had entertained a visitor, and expressed her utter loathing of him in terms so strong that he was obliged to check her. He did not want a quarrel with any of Isaac's friends.

Mr. Thomas, having returned to the college, did not delay to communicate by mysterious hints to his colleagues that he was on visiting terms with a most delightfully charming person, and sunned himself deliciously in their bantering congratulations. About three weeks afterwards he thought he might safely repeat his visit; but he was in a difficulty. He was not quite so stupid as not to see that, the next time he went, it ought to be when her father was present, and yet he preferred his absence. At last he determined he would go about tea-time. He was quite sure that Mr. Coleman would not have returned then; but he could assume that he had, and would propose to wait for him. He therefore duly presented himself at half-past five.

'Good-evening, Miss Coleman. Is your father at home?'

'No, not yet,' replied Pauline, holding the door doubt-ingly.

'Oh, I am so sorry'; and, to Pauline's surprise, he entered without any further ceremony. She hardly knew what do do; but she followed him as he walked into the room, where she had just laid the tea-things and put the bread and butter on the table.

'Oh, tea!' he cried. 'Dear me, it would be very rude of me to ask myself to tea, and yet, do you know, Miss Coleman, I can hardly help it.'

'I am afraid my father will not be here till eight.'

He sat down.

'That is very unfortunate. You will tell him I came on purpose to see him.'

Pauline hesitated whether she should or should not inform Mr. Thomas that his presence was disagreeable, but her father's caution recurred to her, and she poured out a cup for her visitor.

It was one of his peculiarities that tea, of which he took enormous quantities, made him garrulous, and he expa-tiated much upon his college. By degrees, however, he became silent, and as he was sitting with his face to the window, he shifted his chair to the opposite side, under the pretence that the light dazzled his eyes. Pauline shifted too, apparently to make room for him, but really to get farther from him.

'Do people generally say that you take after your mother?' he said.

'I believe I am like my mother in many things.'

238

Another pause. He became fidgety; the half smile, half grin which he almost perpetually wore passed altogether from his face, and he looked uncomfortable and dangerous. Pauline felt him to be so, and resolved that, come what might, he should never set foot in the house again.

'You have such black hair,' he observed.

She rose to take away the tea-things.

'I am afraid,' said she, 'that I must go out; I have one or two commissions to execute.'

He remained seated, and observed that surely she would not go alone.

'Why not?' and having collected the tea-things, she was on the point of leaving. He then rose, and she bade him good-bye. He held out his hand, and she took it in hers, but he did not let it go, and having pulled it upwards with much force, kissed it. He still held it, and before the astonished Pauline knew what he was doing his arm was round her waist. At that moment the little front gate swung back. Nobody was there; but the Reverend Thomas was alarmed, and in an instant she had freed herself, and had placed the table between them.

'What do you mean, you Gadarene pig, you scoundrel by insulting a stranger in this way?' she cried. 'Away! My father will know what to do with you.'

'Oh, if you please, Miss Coleman, pray say nothing about it, pray do not mention it to your father; I do not know what the consequences will be; I really meant nothing; I really did not' – which was entirely true.

'You who propose to teach religion to people! I ought to stop you; but no, I will not be dragged into the mud.'

239

A sudden thought struck her. He was shaky, and was holding on by the table. 'I will be silent,' she cried – what a relief it was to him to hear her say that! – 'but I will mark you,' and before he could comprehend what she was doing she had seized a little pair of scissors which lay near her, had caught his wrist, and had scored a deep cross on the back of the hand. The blood burst out, and she threw him a handkerchief.

'Take that and be gone!'

He was so amazed and terrified, not only at the sight of the blood, but at her extraordinary behaviour, that he turned ghastly white. The pain, however, recalled him to his senses; he rolled the handkerchief over the wound, twisted his own round it too, for the red stain came through Pauline's cambric, and departed. The account current in the college was, that he had torn himself against a nail in a fence. The accident was a little inconvenient on the following Sunday, when he had to preach at Hogsbridge Corner; but as he reproduced the sermon on the carnal mind, which he knew pretty well by heart, he was not nervous. He had made it much simpler, in accordance with the advice given on a former occasion. He had struck out the metaphysics and had put in a new head – 'Neither indeed *can* be.' 'The apostle did not merely state a fact that the carnal mind was not subject to the law of God; he said, "Neither indeed *can* be." Mark, my brethren, the force of the *neither can*.'

CHAPTER TWENTY-ONE

The Wisdom of the Serpent

★

GEORGE ALLEN meanwhile, at Cowfold, languished in love with Priscilla Broad, who was now a comely girl of eighteen. Mrs. Broad had, of course, discovered what was in the wind, and her pride suffered a severe shock. She had destined Priscilla, as the daughter of a Flavel, for a London minister, and that she should marry a tradesman was intolerable. Worse still, a tradesman in Cowfold! What would become of their influence in the town, she continually argued with Mr. Broad, if they became connected with a member of their congregation? She thought it would be a serious hindrance to their usefulness. But Mr. Broad was not so sure, although he hated the Allens; and Priscilla, somehow or other, was not so sure, for, despite her mother's constant hints about their vulgarity, she not infrequently discovered that something was wanted from the shop, and bought it herself.

One Monday afternoon, Mr. Broad having thrown the silk handkerchief off his face and bestirred himself at the sight of the radishes, watercresses, tea, and hot buttered toast, thus addressed his wife –

'My love, I am not altogether inclined to discountenance the attentions which George pays to Priscilla. There are so many circumstances to be taken into account.'

'It is a great trouble to me, John, and I really think, if anything of the kind were to happen, at least you would have to seek another cause. Just consider the position in which I should stand towards Mrs. Allen. Besides, I am sure it will interfere with your duties here if we are obliged to take notice of the Allens more than of other people in the town.'

'To seek for another cause, my love? That is a very grave matter at my time of life. You remember, too, that there is an endowment here.'

'Quite so; and that is the more reason why we should not permit the attachment.'

'But, my love, as I observed, there are so many circumstances to be taken into account. You know as well as I do in what aspect I view the Allens, and what my sentiments with regard to them are – personally, that is to say, and not as minister of the gospel. Perhaps Providence, my dear, intends this opportunity as a means whereby the emotions of my poor sinful nature – emotions which may have been uncharitable – may be converted into brotherly love. Then we must recollect that Isaac is a prominent member of the church and a deacon. Thirdly, in all probability, if we do not permit Priscilla to marry George, offence will be taken, and they may withdraw their subscription, which, I believe, comes altogether to twenty pounds per annum. Fourthly, the Allens have been blessed with an unusual share of worldly prosperity, and George is about to become a partner. Fifthly and lastly' – Mr. Broad had acquired a habit of dividing his most ordinary conversation into heads – 'it is by no means improbable that I may need a co-pastor before long, and we shall secure the Allens' powerful influence in favour of Thomas.'

Mrs. Broad felt the full force of these arguments.

'I should think,' she added, 'that George, after marriage, cannot live at the shop.'

'No, that will not be possible; they must take a private house.'

So it was agreed, without any reference to the question whether Priscilla and George cared for one another, that no opposition should be offered. The Allens themselves, father and mother, were by no means so eager for the honour of the match as Mrs. Broad supposed them to be, for Mrs. Isaac, particularly proud of her husband, and a little proud of their comfortable business and their comfortable property, was not dazzled by the Flavel ancestry.

When George formally asked permission of Mr. Broad to sanction his addresses, a meeting between the parents became necessary, and Mrs. Broad called on Mrs. Allen. She was asked into the dining-room at the back of the shop. At that time, at any rate in Cowfold, the drawing-room, which was upstairs, was an inaccessible sanctuary, save on Sunday and on high tea-party days. Mrs. Broad looked round at the solid mahogany furniture; cast her eyes on the port and sherry standing on the sideboard, in accordance with Cowfold custom; observed that not a single thing in the room was worn or shabby; that everything was dusted with absolute nicety, for the Allens kept two servants; and became a little reconciled to her lot.

Mrs. Allen presently appeared in her black silk dress, with her gold watch hanging in front, and saluted the minister's wife with the usual good-humoured, slightly democratic freedom which always annoyed Mrs. Broad.

'My dear Mrs. Allen,' began Mrs. Broad, 'I have called

to announce to you a surprising piece of intelligence, although I dare say you know it all. Your son George has asked Mr. Broad to be allowed to consider himself as Priscilla's suitor. We have discussed the matter together, and I have come to know what your views are. I may say that we had destined – hoped – that – er – Priscilla would find her sphere as a minister's wife in the metropolis; but it is best, perhaps, to follow the leadings of Providence.'

'Well, Mrs. Broad, I must say I was a little bit disappointed myself – to tell you the plain truth; but it is of no use to contradict young people in love with one another.'

Mrs. Broad was astonished. Disappointed! But she remembered her husband's admonitions. So she contented herself with an insinuation.

'What I meant, my dear Mrs. Allen, was that, as the Flavels have been a ministerial family for so long, it would have been gratifying to me, of course, if Priscilla had bestowed herself upon – upon somebody occupying the same position.'

'That is just what my mother used to say. I was a Burton, you remember. They were large tanners in Northamptonshire, and she did not like my going to a shop. But you know, Mrs. Broad, you had better be in a shop and have plenty of everything, and not have to pinch and screw, than have a brass knocker on your door, and not be able to pay for the clothes you wear. That's my belief, at any rate.'

The dart entered Mrs. Broad's soul. She remembered some 'procrastination' – to use her husband's favourite word – in settling a draper's bill, even when it was diminished by the pew rent, and she wondered if Mrs. Allen knew the facts. Of course she did; all Cowfold knew every fact connected with everybody in the town. She discerned it was best to retreat.

'I wished to tell you, Mrs. Allen, that we do not intend to offer the least objection' – she thought that perhaps a little professional unction might reduce her antagonist – 'and I am sure I pray that God will bless their union.'

'As I said before, Mrs. Broad, neither shall we object. We shall let George do as he likes. He is a real good boy, worth a princess, and if he chooses to have Miss Broad, we shan't hinder him. She will always be welcome here, and it will be a consolation to you to know she will never want anything.'

Mrs. Allen shook her silk dress out a little, and offered Mrs. Broad a glass of wine. Her feelings were a little flustered, and she needed support, but she refused.

'No, thank you, Mrs. Allen. I must be going.'

CHAPTER TWENTY-TWO
The Oracle Warns – After the Event

★

IT is no part of my business to tell the story of the love-making between George and Priscilla. Such stories have been told too often. Every weakness in her was translated by George into some particularly attractive virtue. He saw nothing, heard nothing, which was not to her advantage. Once, indeed, when he was writing the letter that was for ever to decide his destiny, it crossed his mind that this was an epoch – a parting of the ways – and he hesitated as he folded it up. But no warning voice was heard; nothing smote him; he was doing what he believed to be best; he was allowed to go on without a single remonstrant sign. The messenger was dispatched, and his fate was sealed. His mother and father had held anxious debate. They believed Priscilla to be silly, and the question was whether they should tell George so. The more they reflected on the affair the less they liked it; but it was agreed that they could do nothing, and that to dissuade their son would only embitter him against them.

'Perhaps,' said Mrs. Allen, 'when she has a family she will be better.'

Mrs. Allen had a belief that children cured a woman of many follies.

Nevertheless the mother could not refrain, when she had to talk to George about his engagement, from 'letting out' just a word.

'I hope you will be happy, my dear boy. The great thing is not to have a fool for a wife. There has never, to my knowledge, been a woman amongst the Burtons or the Allens who was a fool.'

George felt nothing at the time, for he suspected nothing; but the words somehow remained with him, and reappeared later on in black intensity like invisible writing under heat.

So they were married, and went to live in a cottage, small, but very respectable, in the Shott Road. For the first six months both were in bliss. Priscilla was constantly backwards and forwards to her mother, who took upon herself at once the whole direction of her affairs; but there was no rupture with the Allens, for, whatever her other faults might be, Priscilla was not given to making quarrels, and there was little or no bitterness or evil temper in her. George came home after his work was over at the shop, and sometimes went out to supper with his wife, or read to her the newspaper, which came once a week. Like his father, he was an ardent politician, and, from the very beginning of the struggle, an enthusiastic Free Trader. The Free Trade creed was, indeed, the cause of serious embarrassment, for not only were the customers agricultural and Protectionist, but the deacons at Tanner's Lane, being nearly all either farmers or connected with the land, were also Protectionist, and Mr. Broad had a hard time of it. For himself, he expressed no opinion; but once, at a deacons' meeting, when it looked as if some controversy would arise, he begged Brother Allen to remember that, though we might be wise as serpents, we were also commanded to be harmless as doves. There was a small charity connected with the chapel, which was distributed, not in money, but in bread, and Brother Allen, not being able to contain himself, had let fall a word or two about the price of bread which would have raised a storm, if Mr. Broad had not poured on the troubled waters that oil of which he was a perfect reservoir.

George did his best to instruct his wife in the merits of the controversy, and when he found anything in his newspaper, read it aloud to her.

'You see, Priscilla,' he said one evening, 'it stands to reason that if foreign corn pays a duty, the price of every quarter grown here is raised, and this increased price goes into the farmer's or landlord's pocket. Why should I, or why should my men, pay twopence more for every loaf to buy Miss Wootton a piano?'

'Really, George, do you mean to say that they are going to buy Miss Wootton a piano?'

'My dear, I said that when they buy a loaf of bread twopence out of it goes to buy Miss Wootton's piano!' repeated George, laying an emphasis on every word. 'I did not mean, of course, that they put their twopences in her pocket. The point is, that the duty enables Wootton to get more for his corn.'

'Well,' said Priscilla triumphantly, 'I can tell you she is *not* going to have a piano. She's going to have a little organ instead, because she can play tunes better on an organ, and it's more suitable for her; so there's an end of that.'

'It doesn't matter whether it is an organ or piano,' said George; 'the principle is the same.'

'Well, but you said a piano; I don't think the principle is the same. If I were she I would sooner have the piano.'

A shade of perplexed trouble crossed George's face, and some creases appeared in his forehead; but he smoothed them away and laid down his paper.

'Priscilla, put away your work for a moment and just listen.'

Priscilla was making something in the shape of netting by means of pins and a long loop which was fastened under her foot.

'I can listen, George; there is no occasion to put it away.'

'Well then,' he answered, placing both his elbows on the table, and resting his face upon them, 'all corn which comes into this country pays a duty – that you understand. Consequently it cannot be sold here for less than sixty shillings a quarter. Of course, if that is the case, English wheat is kept up to a higher price than it would fetch if there were no duty. Therefore bread is, as I calculate, about twopence a loaf dearer than it ought to be. And why should it be? That's what I want to know.'

'I believe,' said Priscilla, 'we might save a good bit by baking at home.'

'Yes, yes; but never mind that now. You know that foreign corn pays a duty? You do know that?'

'Yes,' said Priscilla, because there was nothing else to be said.

'Well, then, you must see that, if that be so, farmers can obtain a higher price for English corn.'

Poor Priscilla really did her best to comprehend. She

stopped her knitting for a moment, put her knitting-pin to her lips, and answered very slowly and solemnly, 'Ye-es.'

'Ah; but I know when you say "Ye-es" like that you do not understand.'

'I do understand,' she retorted, with a little asperity.

'Well then, repeat it, and let us see.'

'No, I shall not.'

'Dear Priscilla, I am not vexed; but I only wanted to make it quite plain to you. The duty on foreign corn is a tax in favour of the farmer, or perhaps the landlord, just as distinctly as if the tax-collector carried the coin from our till and gave it them.'

'Of course it is quite plain,' she responded, making a bold stroke for her life. 'Of course it is quite plain we are taxed' – George's face grew bright, for he thought the truth had dawned upon her – 'because the farmers have to pay the duty on foreign corn.'

He took up his newspaper, held it open so as to cover his face, was silent for a few minutes, and then, pulling out his watch, declared it was time to go to bed. She gathered up her netting, looked at him doubtfully as she passed, and went upstairs.

The roof of George's house had a kind of depression or well in the middle of it, whence ran a rain-water pipe, which passed down inside, and so, under the floor, to the soft-water cistern. A bad piece of construction, thought he, and he wished, if he could have done so, to improve it; but there was no way of altering it without pulling the whole place to pieces. One day, a very short time after the talk about Free Trade, a fearful storm of rain broke over Cowfold, and he was startled by Ellen, his servant, running into the shop and telling him that the staircase was flooded, and missis wanted him at once. He put on his coat and was off in a moment. When he got there Priscilla met him at the door crying, and in a great fright. The well up aloft was full of water, and it was pouring in torrents through the little window. It had gone through the floor of the bedroom and into the dining-room, pulling down with it about half the ceiling, which lay in a horrid mess upon the dining table and the carpet. George saw in an instant what was the matter. He ran up the steps to the well, pulled out a quantity of straw and dirt which blocked up the entrance to the pipe; the water disappeared in two minutes, and all further danger was arrested.

'Why on earth,' he cried, in half a passion, 'did not you think to clear away the rubbish, instead of wasting your time in sending for me? It ought to have entered into anybody's head to do such a simple thing as that.'

'How was I to know?' replied Mrs. George. 'I am not an ironmonger. What have I to do with pipes? You shouldn't have had such a thing.'

Ellen stood looking at the wreck.

'We don't want you,' said George savagely; 'go into the kitchen,' and he shut the dining-room door. There the husband and wife stood face to face with one another, with the drip, drip, drip still proceeding, the ruined plaster, and the spoilt furniture.

'I don't care,' he broke out, 'one brass farthing for it all; but what I do care for is that you should not have had the sense to unstop that pipe.'

She said nothing, but cried bitterly. At last she sat down and sobbed out, 'O George, George, you are in a rage with me; you are tired of me; you are disappointed with me. Oh! what shall I do, what *shall* I do?' Poor child! her pretty curls fell over her face as she covered it with her long white hands. George was touched with pity in an instant, and his arms were round her neck. He kissed her fervently, and besought her not to think anything of what he had said. He took out his handkerchief, wiped her eyes tenderly, lifted one of her arms and put it round his neck as he pulled a chair towards him and sat down beside her. Nothing she loved like caresses! She knew what *their* import was, though she could not follow his economical logic, and she clung to him, and buried her face on his shoulder. At that moment, as he drew her heavy brown tresses over him, smothered his eyes and mouth in them, and then looked down through them on the white, sweet beauty they shadowed, he forgot or overlooked everything, and was once more completely happy.

Suddenly she released herself. 'What shall we do to-night, George, the bedroom will be so damp?'

He recovered himself, and admitted that they could not sleep there. There was the spare bedroom; but the wet had come in there too.

'I will sleep at father's, and you sleep at home too. We will have fires alight, and we shall be dry enough to-morrow. You be off now, my dear; I will see about it all.'

So George had the fires alight, got in a man to help him, and they swept and scoured and aired till it was dark. In a day or two the plasterer could mend the ceiling.

Priscilla had left, and, excepting the servant, who was upstairs, George was alone. He looked round, walked about – what was it? Was he tired? It could not be that; he was never tired. He left as soon as he could and went back to the shop. After telling the tale of the calamity which had befallen him he announced – it was now supper-time – that he was going to stay all night. Mother, father, and sister were delighted to have him – 'It looked like old times again'; but George was not in much of a mood for talking, and at ten o'clock went upstairs; his early departure being, of course, set down to the worry he had gone through. He turned into bed. Generally speaking he thought no more of sleep than he did of breathing; it came as naturally as the air into his lungs; but what was this new experience? Half an hour, an hour after he had laid down he was still awake, and worse than awake; for his thoughts were of a different cast from his waking thoughts; fearful forebodings; a horror of great darkness. He rose and bathed his head in cold water, and lay down again, but it was of no use, and he walked about his room. What an epoch is the first sleepless night – the night when the first wrench has been given us by the Destinies to loosen us from the love of life; when we have first said to ourselves that there are worse things than death!

George's father always slept well, but the mother stirred

at the slightest sound. She heard her boy on the other side of the wall pacing to and fro, and she slipped out of bed, put on her dressing-gown, and went to listen. Presently she knocked gently.

'George, my dear, aren't you well?'

'Yes, mother; nothing the matter.'

'Let me in.'

He let her in, and sat down. The moon shone brightly, and there was no need for any other light.

The mother came and sat beside her child.

'George, my dear, there is something on your mind? What is it? – tell me.'

'Nothing, mother; nothing indeed.'

She answered by taking his cold hand in both her own and putting it on her lap. Presently he disengaged himself and went to the window. She sat still for a moment, and followed him. She looked up in his face; the moonlight was full upon it; there was no moisture in his eyes, but his lips quivered. She led him away, and got him to sit down again, taking his hand as before, but speaking no word. Suddenly, without warning, his head was on his mother's bosom, and he was weeping as if his heart would break. Another first experience to him and to her; the first time he had ever wept since he was a child and cried over a fall or because it was dark. She supported that heavy head with the arm which had carried him before he could walk alone; she kissed him, and her tears flowed with his; but still she was silent. There was no reason why she should make further inquiry; she knew it all. By themselves there they remained till he became a little calmer, and then he begged her to leave him. She wished to stay, but he would not permit it, and she withdrew. When she reached her bedroom her husband was still asleep, and although she feared to wake him, she could no longer contain herself, and falling on her knees with her face in the bedclothes, so that she might not be heard, she cried to her Maker to have mercy on her child. She was not a woman much given to religious exercises, but she prayed that night such a prayer as had not been prayed in Tanner's Lane since its foundation was laid. For this cause shall a man leave father and mother and cleave to his wife? Ah yes! he does leave them; but in his heart does he never go back? And if he never does, does his mother ever leave him?

In the morning Mrs. Allen was a little pale, and was asked by her husband if she was unwell, but she held her peace. George too rose, went about his work, and in the afternoon walked up to the cottage to meet his wife there. She was bright and smiling, and had a thousand things to tell him about what her mamma said, and how mamma hoped that the nasty pipe would be altered and never ought to have been there; and how she was coming after tea to talk to him, and how she herself, Priscilla, had got a plan.

'What is it?' said George.

'Why, I would put a grating, or something, over the pipe, so that it shouldn't get stopped up.'

'But if the grating got stopped up that would be just as bad.'

'Well then, I wouldn't have a well there at all. Why don't you cover it over?'

'But what are you to do with the window? You cannot block out the light.'

So Priscilla's 'plans,' as she called them, were nothing. And though George had a plan which he thought might answer, he did not consult her about it.

CHAPTER TWENTY-THREE
Further Development
★

Six months afterwards Priscilla was about to give birth to her first-born. At Mrs. Allen's earnest request, old nurse Barton had been engaged, who nursed Mrs. Allen when George came into the world, and loved him like her own child. As a counterpoise, Mrs. Broad, who had desired a nurse from a distance whom she knew, installed herself with Priscilla. Nurse Barton had a great dislike to Mrs. Broad, although she attended Mr. Broad's ministrations at Tanner's Lane. She was not a member of the church, and never could be got to propose herself for membership. There was in fact, a slight flavour of Paganism about her. She was considered to belong to the 'world,' and it was only her age and undoubted skill which saved her practice amongst the Tanner's Lane ladies. There was a rival in the town; but she was a younger woman, and never went out to any of the respectable houses, save when Mrs. Barton was not available.

The child was safely born, and as soon as nurse Barton could be spared for an hour or two she went to Mrs. Allen, whom she found alone. The good woman then gave Mrs. Allen her opinions, which, by the way, she always gave with perfect frankness.

'Thank the Lord-i'-mercy this 'ere job, Mrs. Allen, is near at an end. If it 'adn't been my dear boy George's wife, never would I have set foot in that 'ouse.'

'Why not?'

'Why not? Now, Mrs. Allen, you know as well as I do. To see that there Mrs. Broad! She might 'ave ordered me about; that wouldn't a' been nothin'; but to see 'er a orderin' *'im*, and a ridin' on 'im like a wooden rockin'-'orse, and with no more feelin'! A nasty, prancin', 'igh-'eaded creatur'. Thinks I to myself often and often, if things was different I'd let yer know, that I would; but I 'eld my tong. It 'ud a been wuss for us all, p'r'aps, if I 'adn't.'

'I should think so,' said Mrs. Allen; 'remember she is the minister's wife.'

'Minister's wife!' repeated Mrs. Barton, and with much scorn. 'And then them children of hern. Lord be praised I never brought such things as them into the world. That was her fine nuss as she must get down from London; and pretty creaturs they are!'

'Hush, hush; George has one of them, and she is mine.'

'I can't 'elp it, ma'am, I must speak out. I say as he ought to 'ave married somebody better nor 'er; though I don't mind a-tellin' of yer she's the best of the lot. Why did the Lord in heaven, as sent Jesus Christ to die for our souls, let my George 'ave such a woman as that? What poor silly creaturs we all are!' and the old woman, bending her head down, shook it mournfully and rubbed her knees with her hand. She was thinking of him as he lay in her lap years and years ago, and pondering, in her disconnected, incoherent way, over the mysteries which are mysteries to us as much as to her.

Mrs. Broad, who was in constant attendance upon Priscilla, at the very earliest moment pronounced the baby a Flavel, and made haste to tell father and mother so. There was no mistaking a refinement, so to say, in the features and an expression in the eye. George, of course, was nearly banished for a time, and was much with his father and mother. At length, however, the hour arrived when the nurse took her departure, and, Mrs. Broad having also somewhat retired, he began to see a little more of his wife; but it was very little. She was altogether shut up in maternal cares – closed round, apparently, from the whole world. He was not altogether displeased, but he did at times think that she might give him a moment now and then, especially as he was greatly interested in the coming county election. It was rather too early in the day for a Free Trader to stand as a candidate, but two Whigs, of whom they had great hopes, had been put up, and both George and his father were most energetic in canvassing and on committees.

Mr. Broad had decided not to vote. He did not deny that his sympathies were not with the Tories, but as a minister of religion it would be better for him to remain neutral. This annoyed the Allens and damaged their cause. At a meeting held by the Tories one of the speakers called upon the audience to observe that all the respectable people, with very few exceptions, were on their side. 'Why,' cried he, 'I'll bet you, my friends, all Lombard Street to a china orange that they don't get even the Dissenting parson to vote for the Radicals. Of course he won't, and why? Just because he's a cut above his congregation, and knows a little more than they do, and belongs to the intelligent classes.'

George bethought himself that perhaps he might do something through Priscilla to influence her mother, and he determined to speak to her about it. He came home one evening after attending a committee, and found supper ready. Priscilla was downstairs, sitting with the door open.

'Hadn't we better shut the door?' said George; 'it is rather cold.'

'No, no, George; I shouldn't hear the baby.'

'But Ellen is upstairs.'

'Yes; but then she might go to sleep.'

'My dear,' began George, 'I wish your father could be got to vote straight. You see that by not doing so he goes against all the principles of the Independents. Ever since they have been in existence they have always stood up for freedom, and we are having the large yellow flag worked with the words, "Civil and Religious Liberty." It will be a bad thing for us if he holds aloof. I cannot understand,' he continued, getting eloquent, 'how a Dissenting minister can make up his mind not to vote against a party which has been answerable for all the oppression and all the wrongs in English history, and for all our useless wars, and actually persecuted his predecessors in this very meeting-house in which he now preaches. Besides, to say nothing about the past, just look at what we have before us now. The Tories are the most bitter opponents of Free Trade. I can't tell you how I feel about it, and I do think that if you were to speak to your mother she would perhaps induce him to change his mind.'

It was a long time since he had said so much all at once to his wife.

'George, George, I am sure he's awake!' and she was off out of the room in an instant. Presently she returned.

'Mamma came here this afternoon and brought his hood – a new one – such a lovely hood! – and she says he looks more than ever like a Flavel in it.'

'I don't believe you listened to a word of what I was saying.'

'Oh yes, I did; you always think I don't listen; but I can listen to you and watch for him too.'

'What did I say?'

'Never mind, I know.'

'I cannot understand,' he said sullenly, and diverted for a moment from his subject, 'why mamma should be always telling *you* he is a Flavel.'

'Well, really, George, why shouldn't she? Tryphosa said the other day that if you were to take away grandpapa Flavel's wig and bands from the picture in the *Evangelical Magazine* he would be just like him.'

'It seems to me,' replied George, 'that if there's any nonsense going about the town it always comes to you. People don't talk such rubbish to me.'

What the effect of this speech might have been cannot be told, for at this moment the baby did really cry, and Priscilla departed hastily for the night. She never spoke to her mother about the election, for, as George suspected, she had not paid the slightest attention to him; and as to exchanging with her mother a single word upon such a subject as politics, or upon any other subject which was in any way impersonal, she never did such a thing in her life.

It was the uniform practice of the Reverend John Broad to walk down the main street of Cowfold on Monday morning, and to interchange a few words with any of his congregation whom he might happen to meet. This pastoral perambulation not only added importance to him and made him a figure in Cowfold, but, coming always on Monday, served to give people some notion of a preoccupation during the other days of the week which was forbidden, for mental reasons, on the day after Sunday. On this particular Monday Mr. Broad was passing Mr. Allen's shop, and, seeing father and son there, went in. Mr. Allen himself was at a desk which stood near the window, and George was at the counter, in a black apron, weighing nails.

After an unimportant remark or two about the weather, Mr. Allen began in a cheery tone, so as to prevent offence:

'Mr. Broad, we are sorry we cannot persuade you to vote for the good cause.'

Mr. Broad's large mouth lengthened itself, and his little eyes had an unpleasant light in them.

'Brother Allen, I have made this matter the subject of much meditation, and I may even say of prayer, and I have come to the conclusion it will be better for me to occupy a neutral position.'

'Why, Mr. Broad? You cannot doubt on which side the right lies.'

'No; but then there are so many things to be considered, so many responsibilities; and my first care, you see, must be the ministerial office and the church which Providence has placed in my charge.'

'But, Mr. Broad, there are only two or three of them who are Tory.'

'Only old Bushel and another farmer or two,' interrupted George.

Mr. Broad looked severely at George, but did not condescend to answer him.

'Those two or three, Brother Allen, require consideration as much as ourselves. Brother Bushel is, I may say, a pillar of the cause, a most faithful follower of the Lord; and what are political questions compared with that? How could I justify myself if my liberty were to become a stumbling-block to my brother? The house of God without Brother Bushel to give out the hymns on Sunday would, I am sure, not be the same house of God to any of us.'

'But, Mr. Broad, do you think he will be so silly as to be offended because you exercise the same right which he claims for himself?'

'Ah, Brother Allen – offended! You remember, no doubt, the text, "Wherefore, if meat make my brother to offend, I will eat no flesh while the world standeth." '

It is a very good thing to have at one's elbow a Bible of rules for our guidance; but unfortunately we relieve ourselves very often of the most necessary inquiry whether the rule applies to the particular case in hand. Mr. Allen had the greatest possible respect for St. Paul, but he felt sure the apostle was where he had no business to be just at that particular moment. George also saw the irrelevance of the quotation, and discerned exactly where it did not fit.

'Mr. Broad, I am sure I don't pretend to know what St. Paul thought as well as you do – of course not – but do you think that voting is like eating meat? Is it not

263

a duty to express our convictions on such questions as those now before the country? It didn't much matter whether a man ate meat which had been offered to an idol or not, but it does matter how we are governed.'

Mr. Broad turned round on George and smiled with a smile which was certainly not a sign of affection, but otherwise did not notice him.

'Well, Mr. Broad,' continued Mr. Allen, 'all I can say is, I regret it; and I am sure you will excuse me if I also say that we, too, deserve some consideration. You forget that your refusal to declare yourself may be a stumbling-block to *us*.'

'I hope not, I hope not. George, how is Priscilla, and how is her child? Are they both quite well?' and with a pontifical benediction the minister moved away. When he got home he consulted the oracle – not on his knees, but sitting in his arm-chair – that is to say, Mrs. Broad at the Monday afternoon tea, and she relieved his anxiety. There was no fear of any secession on the part of the Allens, connected as they were with them through Priscilla. On the other hand, Brother Bushel, although he gave out the hymns, had already had a quarrel with the singing pew because they would not more frequently perform a tune with a solo for the double bass, which he always accompanied with his own bass voice, and Mr. Broad had found it difficult to restore peace; the flute and clarionet justly urging that they never had solos, and why the double bass, who only played from ear, and not half as many notes as they played, should be allowed to show off, they didn't know. Mr. Bushel, too, contri-

buted ten pounds a year to the cause, and Piddingfold
Green Chapel was but a mile farther off from him than
Cowfold. There were allies of the Allens in Tanner's
Lane, no doubt, but none of them would be likely to
desert so long as the Allens themselves remained. There-
fore Providence seemed to point out to Mr. and Mrs.
Broad that their course was clear.

CHAPTER TWENTY-FOUR

'I Came not to Send Peace, but a Sword'

★

MR. ALLEN, having business in London, determined to go on Saturday and spend the next day with Zachariah. Although he always called on his old friend whenever he could do so, he was not often away from home on a Sunday. He also resolved to take George with him. Accordingly, on Saturday morning they were up early and caught a coach on the North Road. The coaches by this time had fallen off considerably, for the Birmingham railway was open, and there was even some talk of a branch through Cowfold; but there were still perhaps a dozen, which ran to places a good way east of the line. Father and son dismounted at the 'George and Blue Boar,' where they were to sleep. Sunday was to be spent with the Colemans, whom George had seen before, but very seldom; never, indeed, since he was a boy.

Zachariah still went to Pike Street Chapel, but only in the morning to hear Mr. Bradshaw, who was now an old man and could not preach twice. On that particular Sunday on which Zachariah, Pauline, Mr. Allen, and George heard him he took for his text the thirteenth verse of the twelfth chapter of Deuteronomy: 'Take heed to thyself that thou offer not thy burnt offerings in every place thou seest.' He put down his spectacles after he had read these words, for he never used a note, and said: 'If your religion doesn't help you, it is no religion for you; you had better be without it. I don't mean if it doesn't help you to a knowledge of a future life or of the way to heaven. Everybody will say his religion does that.

266

What I do mean is that the sign of a true religion, true for *you*, is this – Does it assist you to bear your own private difficulties? –does it really? – not the difficulties of the schools and theology, but those of the parlour and counting-house; ay, difficulties most difficult, those with persons nearest to you? . . . Everybody ought to have his *own* religion. In one sense we are all disciples of Christ, but nevertheless each man has troubles peculiar to himself, and it is absurd to expect that any book system will be sufficient for each one of us at all points. You must make your own religion, and it is only what you make yourself which will be of any use to you. Don't be disturbed if you find it is not of much use to other persons. Stick to it yourself if it is really your own, a bit of yourself. There are, however, in the Book of God universal truths, and the wonderful thing about them is that they are at the same time more particularly adapted to you and me and all our innermost wants than anything we can discover for ourselves. That is the miracle of inspiration. For thousands and thousands of years some of the sayings here have comforted those who have well-night despaired in the desert of the world. The wisdom of millions of apostles, of heroes, of martyrs, of poor field labourers, of solitary widows, of orphans, of the destitute, of men driven to their last extremity, has been the wisdom of this volume – not their own, and yet most truly theirs. . . . Here is a word for us this morning: "*Take heed to thyself that thou offer not thy burnt offerings in every place thou seest.*" Ah! what a word it is. You and I are not idolaters, and there is no danger of our

267

being so. For you and me this is not a warning against idolatry. What is it for us, then? Reserve yourself; discriminate in your worship. Reserve yourself, I say; but what is the implication? What says the next verse? "*In the place which the Lord shall choose*"; that is to say, keep your worship for the Highest. Do not squander yourself, but, on the other hand, before the shrine of the Lord offer all your love and adoration. What a practical application this has! . . . I desire to come a little closer to you. What are the consequences of not obeying this Divine law? You will not be struck dead nor excommunicated; you will be simply *disappointed*. Your burnt offering will receive no answer; you will not be blessed through it; you will come to see that you have been pouring forth your treasure and, something worse, your heart's blood – not the blood of cattle – before that which is no God – a nothing, in fact. "Vanity of vanities," you will cry, "all is vanity." My young friends, young men and young women, you are particularly prone to go wrong in this matter. You not only lay your possessions, but yourselves, on altars by the roadside.'

It was the first time George had ever heard anything from any public speaker which came home to him, and he wondered if Mr. Bradshaw knew his history. He interpreted the discourse after his own way, and Priscilla was ever before him.

They came back to the little house and sat down to dinner in the little front room. There were portraits on the walls – nothing else but portraits – and the collection at first sight was inconsistent. Major Cartwright was still there; there were also Byron, Bunyan, Scott, Paine, Burns, Mr. Bradshaw, and Rousseau. It was closely expressive of its owners. Zachariah and Pauline were private persons; they were, happily for them, committed to nothing, and were not subsidized by their reputations to defend a system. They were consequently free to think at large, and if they admired both Bunyan and Rousseau, they were at liberty to do so. Zachariah, in a measure, and a very large measure, had remained faithful to his earliest beliefs – who is there that does not? – and although they had been modified, they were still there; and he listened to Mr. Bradshaw with the faith of thirty years ago. He also believed in a good many things he had learned without him, and perhaps the old and the new were not so discordant as at first sight they might have seemed to be. He was not, in fact, despite all his love of logic, the 'yes *or* no' from which most people cannot escape, but a 'yes *and* no'; not immorally and through lack of resolution, but by reason of an original receptivity and the circumstances of his training. If he had been merely a student the case would have been different; but he was not a student. He was a journeyman printer, and hard work has a tendency to demolish the distinctions of dialectics. He had also been to school outside his shop, and had learned many lessons, often confusing and apparently contradictory. Blanketeer marches; his first wife; the workhouse; imprisonment; his second wife; the little Pauline, had each come to him with its own special message, and the net result was a character, but a character disappointing to persons who

269

prefer men and women of linear magnitude to those of three dimensions.

After dinner the conversation turned upon politics, and Mr. Allen described his interview with Mr. Broad, regretting that the movement in the district round Cowfold would receive no countenance from the minister of the very sect which ought to be its chief support.

'A sad falling off,' said Zachariah, 'from the days, even in my time, when the Dissenters were the insurrectionary class. Mr. Bradshaw, last Sunday, after his sermon, shut his Bible and told the people that he did not now interfere much in political matters; but he felt he should not be doing his duty if he did not tell those whom he taught which way they *ought* to vote, and that what he had preached to them for so many years would be poor stuff if it did not compel them into a protest against taxing the poor for the sake of the rich.'

'Yes,' replied Mr. Allen; 'but then, Broad never has taught what Bradshaw teaches; he never seems to me to see anything clearly; at least, he never makes me see anything clearly; the whole world is in a fog to him.'

'From what I have heard of Mr. Broad,' said Pauline, 'I should think the explanation of him is very simple; he is a hypocrite – an ordinary hypocrite. What is the use of going out of the way to seek for explanations of such commonplace persons?'

'Pauline, Pauline,' cried Zachariah, 'you surely forget, my child, in whose company you are!'

'Oh, as for that,' said George, 'Miss Coleman needn't mind me. I haven't married Mr. Broad, and my father is quite right. For that matter, I believe Miss Coleman is right too."

'Well,' said Mr. Allen, 'it is rather strong to say a man is an ordinary hypocrite, and it is not easy to prove it.'

'Not easy to prove it,' said Pauline, shifting a little in her chair and looking straight at Mr. Allen with great earnestness; 'hypocrisy is the one thing easiest to prove. I can tell whether a man is a hypocrite before I know anything else about him. I may not for a long time be able to say what else he may be, but before he speaks, almost, I can detect whether he is sincere.'

'You women,' said Zachariah with a smile, 'or you girls, rather, are so positive. Just as though the world were divided like the goats and the sheep in the gospel. That is a passage that I never could quite understand. I never hardly see a pure breed either of goat or sheep. I never see anybody who deserves to go straight to heaven or who deserves to go straight to hell. When the judgment day comes it will be a difficult task. Why, Pauline, my dear, I am a humbug myself.'

'Ah well, I have heard all that before; but, nevertheless, what I say is true. Some men, using speech as God meant men to use it, are liars, and some are not. Of course, not entirely so, nor at all times. We cannot speak mere truth; we are not made to speak it. For all that, you are not a liar.'

'Anyhow, I shall go on,' said Mr. Allen. 'We shall have a desperate fight, and shall most likely lose; but no Tory shall sit for our county if I can help it.'

'Of course you will go on,' said Zachariah. 'So shall I go on. We are to have a meeting in Clerkenwell to-morrow night, although, to tell you the truth, I don't feel exactly the interest in the struggle which I did in those of five-and-twenty years ago, when we had to whisper our treasons to one another in locked rooms and put sentries at the doors. You know nothing about those times, George.'

'I wish I had,' said George with an unusual passion, which surprised his father and caused Pauline to lift her eyes from the table and look at him. 'I only wish I had. I can't speak as father can, and I often say to myself I should like to take myself off to some foreign country where men get shot for what they call conspiracy. If I knew such a country, I half believe I should go to-morrow.'

'Which means,' said Pauline, 'that there would be an end of you and your services. If you care anything for a cause, you can do something better than get shot for it; and if you want martyrdom, there is a nobler martyrdom than death. The Christians who were trundled in barrels with spikes in them deserve higher honour than those who died in a moment, before they could recant. The highest form of martyrdom, though, is not even living for the sake of a cause, but living without one, merely because it is your duty to live. If you are called upon to testify to a great truth, it is easy to sing in flames. Yes, yes, Mr. George, the saints whom I would canonize are not martyrs for a cause, but those who have none.'

George thought that what Pauline said – just as he had thought of Mr. Bradshaw's sermon – seemed to be said for

272

him; and yet, what did she know about him? Nothing. He was silent. All were silent, for it is difficult to follow anybody who pitches the conversation at so high a level; and Zachariah, who alone could have maintained it, was dreaming over his lost Pauline and gazing on the sacred pictures which were hung in the chamber of his heart. Just at that moment he was looking at the one of his wife as a girl; the room in which he was sitting had gone; he was in the court near Fleet Street; she had cleared the space for the dance; she had begun, and he was watching her with all the passion of his youth. The conversation gradually turned to something more indifferent, and the company broke up.

On the Monday George and his father went home. It is very depressing, after being with people who have been at their best, and with whom we have been at our best, to descend upon ordinary existence. George felt it particularly as he stood in the shop on Tuesday morning and reflected that for the whole of that day – for his father was out – he should probably not say nor hear a word for which he cared a single straw. But there was to be an election meeting that evening, and Mr. Allen was to speak, and George, of course, must be there. The evening came, and the room at the Mechanics' Institute which had just been established in Cowfold was crowded. Admission was not by ticket, so that, though the Whigs had convened it, there was a strong muster of the enemy. Mr. Allen moved the first resolution in a stirring speech, which was constitutionally interrupted with appeals to him to go home and questions about a grey mare – '*How about old*

Pinfold's grey mare?' – which seemed conclusive and humorous to the last degree. Old Pinfold was a well-known character in Cowfold, horse-dealer, pig-jobber, attendant at races, with no definite occupation, and the grey mare was an animal which he managed to impose upon Mr. Allen, who sued him and lost. When Mr. Allen's resolution had been duly seconded, one Rogers, a publican, got up and said he had something to say. There was indescribable confusion, some crying, 'Turn him out,' others 'Pitch into 'em, Bill.' Bill Rogers was well known as the funny man in Cowfold, a half-drunken buffoon whose wit, such as it was, was retailed all over the place; a man who was specially pleased if he could be present in any assembly collected for any serious purpose and turn it into ridicule. He got upon a chair, not far from where George sat, but refused to go upon the platform. 'No, thank yer, my friends, I'm best down here; up there's the place for the gentlefolk, the clever uns, them as buy grey mares' – (roars of laughter) – 'but, Mr. Chairman, with your permission' – and here Bill put his hat upon his chest and made a most profound bow to the chair, which caused more laughter – 'there is just one question I should like to ask – not about the grey mare, sir' – (roars of laughter again) – 'but I see a young gentleman here beknown to us all' – (pointing to George) – 'and I should just like to ask him, does his mother-in-law – not his mother, you observe, sir – does his mother-in-law know he's out?' Once more there was an explosion, for Mr. Broad's refusal to take part in the contest was generally ascribed to Mrs. Broad. George sat still for a moment, hardly realizing his position, and then the blood rose to his head; he crashed across the forms, and before the grin had settled into smoothness on Bill's half-intoxicated features there was a grip like that of a giant on his greasy coat-collar; he was dragged amidst shouts and blows to the door, George nothing heeding, and dismissed with such energy that he fell prostrate on the pavement. His friends had in vain attempted to stop George's wrathful progress; but they were in a minority.

Next Saturday a report of the scene appeared in the county newspaper, giving full particulars, considerably exaggerated; and Mr. Broad read all about it to Mrs. Broad on Saturday afternoon, in the interval between the preparation of his two sermons. He had heard the story on the following day; but here was an authentic account in print. Mrs. Broad was of opinion that it was shocking; so vulgar, so low; her poor dear Priscilla, and so forth. Mr. Broad's sullen animosity was so much stimulated that it had overcome his customary circumspection, and on the Sunday evening he preached from the text, 'Pure religion and undefiled before God and the Father is this, To visit the fatherless and widows in their affliction, and to keep himself unspotted from the world.' Mr. Broad remarked that the Apostle James made no mention here of the scheme of redemption; not because that was not the chief part of religion, but because he was considering religion in the aspect – he was very fond of this word 'aspect' – which it presented to those outside the Church. He called upon his hearers to reflect with him for a few moments, in the first place, upon what religion was not;

secondly, upon what it was; and thirdly, he would invite their attention to a few practical conclusions. He observed that religion did not consist in vain strife upon earthly matters, which only tended towards divisions in the Body of Christ. 'At such a time as this, my brethren, it is important for us to remember that these disputes, especially if they are conducted with unseemly heat, are detrimental to the interests of the soul and give occasion to the enemy to blaspheme.' When Mr. Broad came to the secondly, and to that subdivision of it which dealt with freedom from worldly spots, he repeated the words with some emphasis, ' "Unspotted from the world." Think, my friends, of what this involves. Spots! The world spots and stains! We are not called upon to withdraw ourselves from the world – the apostle does not say that – but to keep ourselves unspotted, uncontaminated he appears to mean, by worldly influence. The word unspotted in the original bears that interpretation – uncontaminated. Therefore, though we must be in the world, we are not to be *of* the world, but to set an example to it. In the world! Yes, my brethren, we must necessarily be in the world; that is the condition imposed upon us by the Divine Providence, because we are in a state of probation; we are so constituted, with a body and with fleshly appetites, that we must be in the world; but we must be separate from it and its controversies, which are so unimportant compared with our eternal welfare.'

Mr. Bushel sat on high at his desk, where he gave out the hymns, and coughed every now and then, and looked straight at the pew where the Allens and George sat. Mr. Bushel knew well enough that, although he was just as ardent on the other side, the sermon was not meant for him, and not one of Mr. Broad's remarks touched him. He thought only of the Allens, and rejoiced inwardly. George walked home with Priscilla in silence. At supper-time he suddenly said:

'I think your father might have found something better to do than preach at me.'

Priscilla was shocked. She had never heard a criticism of her father before.

'Really, George, what are you thinking of to talk in that way about a sermon, and on a Sunday night, too?'

'He did preach at me; and if he has anything to say against me, why doesn't he come and say it here or at the shop?'

'Oh, George, this is dreadful! Besides, mamma *did* come and talk to me.'

'What has that got to do with it? Well, what did your mother say?'

'Why, she told me all about this meeting, and how you fought a man and nearly killed him, and you a member at Tanner's Lane, and how you oughtn't to have been there at all, and what Mr. Bushel was going to do.'

'Oughtn't to have been there at all? Why not? I don't believe you know any more than this table why I was there.'

'Oh yes, I do. You never tell me anything, but Mrs. Bushel told me. You want to get them all turned out of their farms.'

'Bosh! There you are again! – the pains I took the

277

other night again to make you comprehend what Free Trade meant. I knew you didn't understand a word about it; and if you did understand, you wouldn't believe me. You never take any notice of anything I say; but if Mrs. Bushel or any other blockhead tells you anything, you believe that directly.'

Priscilla's eyes filled; she took out her handkerchief and went upstairs. George sat still for a while, and then followed her. He found her sitting by the baby's cradle, her head on her hands, and sobbing. It touched him beyond measure to see how she retreated to her child. He went to her; his anger was once more forgotten, and once more he was reconciled with kisses and self-humiliation. The next morning, however, as he went to the square, the conversation of the night before returned to him. 'What does it all mean?' he cried to himself. 'Would to God it were either one thing or another! I could be happy if I really cared for her; and if I hated her downright, I could endure it like any other calamity which cannot be altered; but this is more than I can bear!'

The Allens, father and mother, held anxious debate whether they should take any notice of the attack by their pastor, and in the end determined to do nothing. They considered, and rightly considered, that any action on their part would only make George's position more difficult, and he was the first person to be considered.

Next Saturday there was some business to be done in London, and George went, this time by himself. On the

Sunday morning he called on the Colemans, and found Zachariah at home, but Pauline away. Mr. Bradshaw, too, was not to preach that day. It was wet, and Zachariah and George sat and talked, first about the election, and then about other indifferent subjects. Conversation – even of the best, and between two friends – is poor work when one of the two suffers from some secret sorrow which he cannot reveal, and George grew weary. Zachariah knew what was the matter with him, and had known it for a long while, but was too tender to hint his knowledge. Nevertheless, remembering his own history, he pitied the poor boy exceedingly. He loved him as his own child, for his father's sake, and loved him all the more for an experience so nearly resembling another which he recollected too well.

'How is it Mr. Bradshaw is not preaching to-day?' said George.

'He is ill; I am afraid he is breaking up; and latterly he has been worried by the small attacks made upon him by people who are afraid to say anything distinctly.'

'What kind of attacks?'

'Well, they insinuate that he is Arian.'

'What is that?'

Zachariah explained the case as well as he could, and George was much interested.

'Arian or not, I tell you one thing, Mr. Coleman, that Mr. Bradshaw, whenever I have heard him, seems to help me as Mr. Broad never does. I never think about what Mr. Broad says except when I am in chapel, and sometimes not then.'

'Bradshaw speaks from himself. He said a thing last Sunday which stuck by me, and would have pleased a country lad like you more than it did three parts of his congregation, who are not so familiar with country life as he is. He told us he was out for a holiday, and saw some men hoeing in a field –"Hoeing the charlock," he said to himself; but when he came nearer he found they were hoeing turnips – hoeing up the poor plants themselves, which lay dying all around; hoeing them up to let the other plants have room to grow.

'I have known men,' added Zachariah after a pause, 'from whose life so much – all love, for example has – been cut out; and the effect has been, not ruin, but a growth in other directions which we should never have seen without it.'

Zachariah took down a little book from his shelf, and wrote George's name in it.

'There, my boy, it is not much to look at, but I know nothing better, and keep it always in your pocket. It is the *Imitation of Christ*. You will find a good deal in it which will suit you, and you will say, as I have said a thousand times over it, that other people may write of science or philosophy, but this man writes about *me*.'

He put it on the table, and George opened it at the sentence '*He that can best tell how to suffer will best keep himself in peace. That man is conqueror of himself, and lord of the world, the friend of Christ, and the heir of heaven.*' He turned over the leaves again – '*He to whom the Eternal Word speaketh is delivered from a world of unnecessary conceptions.*' Zachariah bent his head near him and gently expounded the texts. As the exposition grew George's heart dilated, and he was carried beyond his troubles. It was the birth in him – even in him, a Cowfold ironmonger, not a scholar by any means – of what philosophers call *the idea*, that Incarnation which has ever been our Redemption. He said nothing to Zachariah about his own affairs, nor did Zachariah, as before observed, say anything to him; but the two knew one another, and felt that they knew one another as intimately as if George had imparted to his friend the minutest details of his unhappiness with his wife.

Towards the end of the afternoon Pauline returned, and inquired how the battle went in Cowfold.

'I am afraid we shall be beaten. Sometimes I don't seem to care much about it.'

'Don't care! Why not?'

'Oh, we talk and talk, father and I, and somehow people's minds are made up without talking, and nobody ever changes. When we have our meetings, who is it who comes? Does Bushel come? Not a bit of it. We only get our own set.'

'Well,' said Zachariah, the old man's republican and revolutionary ardour returning, 'this is about the only struggle in which I have felt much interest of late years. I should like to have cheap bread, and what is more, I should like to deprive the landlords of that bit of the price which makes the bread dear. I agree with you, my boy. Endless discussion is all very well – forms "public opinion," they say; but I wish a stop could be put to it when it has come round to where it began; that one side could say to the other, "You have heard all our logic, and we have heard all yours; now then, let us settle it. Who is the strongest and best drilled?" I believe in insurrection. Everlasting debate – and it is not genuine debate, for nobody really ranges himself alongside his enemy's strongest points – demoralizes us all. It encourages all sorts of sophistry, becomes mere manœuvring, and saps people's faith in the truth. In half an hour, if two persons were to sit opposite one another, they could muster every single reason for and against Free Trade. What is the use of going on after that? Moreover, insurrection strengthens the belief of men in the right. A man who voluntarily incurs the risk of being shot believes ever afterwards, if he escapes, a little more earnestly than he did before. "Who is on the Lord's side, let him come unto me," says the flag. Insurrection strengthens, too, the faith of others. When a company of poor men meet together and declare that things have got to such a pass that they will either kill their enemies or die themselves, the world then thinks there must, after all, be *some* difference between right and wrong.'

'Father, that is all past now. We must settle our quarrels in the appointed way. Don't say anything to discourage Mr. Allen. Besides, people are not so immovable as you think. How they alter I don't know; but they do alter. There is a much larger minority in favour of Free Trade than there was ten years ago.'

'All past now, is it? You will see one of these days.'

It was time for tea, and Pauline left to get the tea-things. In the evening they strolled out for a walk through

Barnsbury and up Maiden Lane, then a real and pretty lane stretching north-westwards through hedges to Highgate. After they had gone a few hundred yards Zachariah went back; he had forgotten something, and George and Pauline walked on slowly together. The street was crowded, for it was just about church time, but on the opposite side of the road George saw somebody whom he knew, but who took no notice of him.

'How odd!' he said to Pauline; 'that is Tom Broad! What is he doing here, I wonder?'

Pauline made no answer, and at that moment Zachariah rejoined them.

The reason for Mr. Thomas Broad's appearance in that quarter will be best explained by the following letter, which he had received the day before from his father: –

'MY DEAR THOMAS, – I was very glad to hear of your success at Mr. Martin's chapel, at Hackney, on Sunday afternoon. Although it was nothing more than an afternoon service, you must remember that it is the first invitation to a metropolitan pulpit which you have received. It would be as well if you were to call on Mr. Martin at your earliest convenience, and also on Mr. Chandler, in Leather Lane, whom you mentioned to me, and who, I believe, is a prominent deacon. The choice of your subject was judicious, although it is not so easy to fix the character of a discourse for the afternoon as for the morning or evening. "*I will give him a white stone*" is a text I have used myself with great profit. A young minister, I need hardly say, my dear Thomas, ought to confine himself to what is generally accepted, and not to particularize. For this reason he should avoid not only all disputed topics, but, as far as possible, all reference to particular offences. I always myself doubted the wisdom, for example, of sermons against covetousness, or worldliness, or hypocrisy. Let us follow our Lord and Master, and warn our hearers against sin, and leave the application to the Holy Spirit. I only mention this matter now because I have found two or three young students err in this direction, and the error, I am sure, militates against their usefulness.

'Your dear mamma and Tryphosa are both quite well. Not so Priscilla. I grieve to say she is *not* well. George's conduct lately has been very strange. I am afraid that he will be a trouble, not only to us, but to the Church of Christ. Both he and his father have kindled strife amongst us in this unhappy election contest, from which, as a minister of God's Word, I have held aloof. For one or two Sundays the Allens have absented themselves from Divine service in the evening, and we know that there has been no sickness in the house. I feel certain that before long they will withdraw their subscription. I have good reason to believe that their friend, Mr. Coleman, exercises a very baleful influence upon them. However, God's will be done! These are the trials which His servants who minister to His flock must expect. Goodbye, my dear Thomas. Mamma and Tryphosa send their love. Give diligence to make your calling and election sure. – Your affectionate father,

'JOHN BROAD.

'*P.S.* – It will be as well, perhaps, if you can ascertain whether the Allens visit the Colemans, and more particularly if George goes there. The Coleman household consists, I believe, of a father and daughter. You will remember that Coleman has been a convict, and, I have heard, has tendencies towards infidelity. Priscilla informs me that Mr. Allen and George will be in London to-morrow; but she does not know what they are going to do there. You will doubtless be able to obtain the information I desire, and on future occasions I will also advise you when either George or his father is in the metropolis.'

Mr. Thomas Broad had his own reasons for complying with his father's request. He hated the Colemans and George with as much active malignity as was possible to his heavy unctuous nature. Why he should hate the Colemans is intelligible, and his hatred to George can also be explained, partly through sympathy between father and son, and partly because the hatred of a person like Thomas Broad to a person like George Allen needs no explanation.

CHAPTER TWENTY-FIVE

'And a Man's Foes shall be They of His own Household'

*

THE county polling day meanwhile drew near, and with
its approach party spirit rose and the mutual exasperation
of both sides increased. George and his father were out
every evening at the Institute or canvassing, and George's
first attempts at public speaking were a success. At length
the day dawned which was to decide their fate. Cowfold
was the polling station for a large district, and both
sides fully recognized its importance. The Democratic
colour was orange, and the Tory was purple. Everybody
wore rosettes and bands of music went about the town,
carrying flags and banners, which had such an effect
upon the Cowfold population, more particularly upon
that portion of it which knew nothing whatever of the
questions at issue, that the mere sound of the instruments
or sight of a bit of bunting tied to a pole was sufficient
to enable them to dare a broken head, or even death.
Beer may have been partly the cause of this peculiar
mental condition, but not entirely, for sober persons felt
the contagion. We may laugh at it if we please, and no
doubt it is evidence of the weakness of human nature; but
like much more evidence of the same order, it is double-
voiced, and testifies also to our strength.

Priscilla was staying that night with her mother. Mr.
Broad's house, at the end of the town, was very quiet,
and George did not care to leave her alone with the servant. Those were the days when the state of the poll was
published every hour, and as Cowfold lay near the centre

of the county, a very fair opinion could be formed of the progress of the voting. By three o'clock it was known that up to eleven parties were neck and neck, and the excitement grew more and more intense. Every public-house in Cowfold was free, and soon after dinner-time there was not a single person in the place who was ever drunk before who had not found it necessary to get drunk then in order to support the strain on his nerves. Four o'clock came, and the polling-booth was shut; the numbers were made up, and the two committees now anxiously awaited the news from the outlying districts. The general impression seemed to be that the popular candidate would win by about a dozen, and by eight o'clock a crowd had assembled before the 'Cross Keys' to give due welcome to the desired announcement. Ten o'clock came, and the mob began to get impatient and unruly. Then there was a stir and a roar, and the whole assemblage rushed off to the 'Angel,' in the square. On the balcony was a huge placard, with the purple hero at the top – 1837 – and below was the orange favourite, in small and ignominious figures – 1831. Bushel stood at the open window waving his hat, apparently half frantic. Just underneath him was a smaller crowd of the purple faction, who were cheering and bawling with all their might as the enemy came in sight. In an instant the conflict had begun. The purple banners were the first objects of attack, and disappeared every one of them, in less than five minutes, under foot. Seen from one of the upper stories of the houses, the square looked like a great pot full of boiling confusion. By degrees the wearers of purple were driven hard against the 'Angel' yard gates, which opened to receive them; some who were not successful in securing admittance escaping, with bloody heads, down the side lane, and so out across the fields. There was great difficulty in shutting the gates again; but the 'Angel' hostlers appeared on the scene with pitchforks and other weapons, which caused an ebb of the tide for a moment. They managed in the nick of time to swing the gates together, and the heavy wooden bar was thrown across them. The orange party was now triumphant, but very unhappy, because it was able to do no further mischief. Suddenly Bushel was seen again at the window, and, as it was afterwards averred, made some insulting gesture. A stone was the prompt response, and in five minutes there was not a whole pane of glass left in the front of the building. 'Have old Bushel out! Smoke 'em out!' was shouted, and a rush followed towards the door. But the insurgents had no siege train for such a fortress, and the sight of two or three fowling-pieces somewhat damped their courage. They therefore turned off, wrecked the brewer's house, and forced the 'Angel' tap, which was separated from the main building. The spirit-casks were broached, and men turned the gin and brandy taps into their mouths without waiting for glasses. Many of them, especially those who first entered, were at once overcome and dropped, lying about in the room and in the gutter perfectly insensible. The remainder, who could only drink what was left, became more and more riotous, and a general sack of all purple property was imminent. Mr. Allen was at the 'Cross Keys,' but George was at home, and as he watched the scene he saw the mob take a kind of lurch and sway along the street which led to Mr. Broad's. He thought he heard Mr. Broad's name, and in an instant he had buttoned up his coat, taken the heaviest stick he could find, and was off. He had the greatest difficulty in forcing his way, and he did not reach the front of the crowd till it was opposite Mr. Broad's and the destruction of the windows had begun. He leaped over the iron railing, and presented himself at the gate with the orange rosette on his coat and the stick in his right hand. He was just in time, for yells of 'Psalm-singing old hypocrite!' were already in the air, and the fence was being stormed. George administered to the foremost ruffian a blow on the shoulder which felled him on the path outside, and then, standing on the low brick wall on which the railings rested, showed his rosette, brandished his club, and made some kind of inarticulate expostulation, which, happily for him and Mr. Broad, was received with cheers. Whether taken by itself it would have been effectual or not cannot be said, for just at that moment a more powerful auxiliary appeared. When the 'Angel' was abandoned the imprisoned garrison, amongst whom were one or two county magistrates, held a brief consultation. They organized their forces and marched out, the well-to-do folk in front and abreast, armed with bludgeons, the 'Angel' dependents and about fifty more of the refugees coming in the rear, every garden and stable weapon of offence being distributed amongst them. They had the advantage, of course, of being sober. They advanced at a run, and their tramp was heard just as George was beginning to try the effect of his eloquence. Panic and scattering flight at once followed, not, however, before some dozen or so of the fugitives had recovered what little sense they ever had by virtue of sundry hard knocks on their skulls, and a dozen more or so had been captured. By twelve o'clock Cowfold was quiet and peaceable. Citizens were left to wonder how their town, lying usually so sleepily still, like a farmyard on a summer Sunday afternoon, could ever transform itself after this fashion. Men unknown and never before seen seemed suddenly to spring out of the earth, and as suddenly to disappear. Who were they? Respectable Cowfold, which thought it knew everybody in the place, could not tell. There was no sign of their existence on the next day. People gathered together and looked at the mischief wrought the night before, and talked everlastingly about it; but the doers of it vanished, rapt away apparently into an invisible world. On Sunday next, at one o'clock, Cowfold Square, save for a few windows not yet mended, looked just as it always looked; that is to say, not a soul was visible in it, and the pump was, as usual, chained.

The band of rescuers had passed George as he stood in the garden, and when they had gone he knocked at the door. It was a long time before anybody came, but at last it was partly opened, just as far as the chain would permit, and the Reverend John Broad, looking very white and with a candle in his hand, appeared.

'It is I, George, Mr. Broad. Please tell me how Priscilla is, and – how you all are after your fright. I will not come in if you are all well.'

'No, Mr. George, you will not come in. I little thought that a member of Tanner's Lane Church, and my daughter's husband, would associate himself with such disgraceful proceedings as those we have witnessed this evening.'

'But, Mr. Broad, you are quite mistaken. I was not with the mob. I came here as soon as I could to protect you.'

Mr. Broad, terrified and wrathful, had, however, disappeared, and George heard the bolts drawn. He was beside himself with passion, and knocked again and again, but there was no answer. He was inclined to try and break open the door at first, or seek an entrance through a window, but he thought of Priscilla, and desisted.

He was turning homewards, when he reflected that it would be useless to attempt to go to sleep, and he wandered out into the country towards Piddingfold, pondering over many things. The reaction of that night had been too severe. His ardour was again almost entirely quenched when he saw the men for whom he had worked, and who professed themselves his supporters, filthily drunk. A noble sentence, however, from the *Idler* came into his mind – his mother had a copy of the *Idler* in her bedroom, and read and re-read it, and oftentimes quoted it to her husband and her son – '*He that has improved the virtue or advanced the happiness of one fellow-creature . . . may be contented with his own performance; and, with respect to mortals like himself, may demand, like Augustus, to be dismissed at his departure with applause.*' He reflected that he, an ironmonger's son, was not born to save the world, and if the great Dr. Johnson could say what he did, with how little ought not a humble Cowfold tradesman to be satisfied! We all of us have too vast a conception of the duty which Providence has imposed upon us; and one great service which modern geology and astronomy have rendered is the abatement of the fever by which earnest people are so often consumed. But George's meditations all through that night were in the main about his wife, and as soon as he reached his shop in the morning, the first thing he did was to write a note to her telling her to come home. This she did, although her mother and father objected, and George found her there at dinner-time. She looked pale and careworn, but this, of course, was set down to fright. She was unusually quiet, and George forbore to say anything about her father's behaviour. He dreaded rather to open the subject; he could not tell to what it might lead. Priscilla knew all about George's repulse from her father's door, and George could tell she knew it.

His father and he had determined that Cowfold would not be a pleasant place for them on the following Sunday, and that business, moreover, demanded their presence in London. Thither, accordingly, they went on the Saturday, as usual; and Priscilla naturally communicating their intention to her mother, Mr. Thomas Broad received an epistle from his father something like one we have already read, but still more imperative in its orders that the dutiful son should see whether the Allens made Zachariah's house their headquarters. That they did not sleep there was well known, but it was believed they had constant intercourse with that unregenerate person, a disciple of Voltaire, as the Reverend John Broad firmly believed, and it would be 'advantageous to possess accumulated evidence of the fact.' Priscilla knew that they lodged always at the 'George and Blue Boar'; and how they spent their time on Sunday she did not know. There was also a postscript, this time with a new import: –

'It has been reported that Coleman's daughter is a young female not without a certain degree of attractiveness. It may perhaps, my dear Thomas, be some day of service to me and to the Church if you were to inform me whether you have observed any tendencies towards familiarity between George and this person. I need not at the present moment give you my reasons for this inquiry. It will be sufficient to say that I have nothing more in view than the welfare of the flock which Divine Providence has committed to my charge.'

Mr. Thomas did his duty, and a letter was received by his father on the following Tuesday, which was carefully locked up in the drawer in which the sermons were preserved.

The next day – that is to say, on Wednesday – George was at work, as usual, when his little maid came to say that his mistress was very bad, and would he go home directly? She had been unwell for some days, but it was not thought that there was anything serious the matter with her. George followed the girl at once, and found Priscilla in bed with a violent headache and very feverish. The doctor came, and pronounced it a case of 'low fever,' a disease well enough known in Cowfold. Let us make the dismal story as brief as possible. Nurse Barton, hearing of her 'dear boy's' trouble, presented herself uninvited that evening at ten o'clock, and insisted that George should not sit up. She remained in the house, notwithstanding Mrs. Broad's assurances that she really was not wanted, and watched over Priscilla till the end came.

About a week afterwards, just when Priscilla seemed to be getting a little better – she had been delirious, but her senses had returned – and Mrs. Allen, who had been in the house all day, had departed, a change for the worse took place, and the doctor was summoned. George, sitting in the parlour alone, heard nurse Barton come downstairs.

'My dear boy,' she said as she entered, 'God in His mercy strengthen you in this trial as He has laid upon you, but I thought I'd just come and tell you myself. The doctor wor a-comin', but I said "No; my boy shall hear it from me." I don't think as your wife will get better; she don't seem to pull herself up a bit. She a'nt got no strength no more than a fly. You'd better see her, I think.'

'Who is there?'

'Her mother and the doctor.'

'Can't you get rid of them?'

'All right, my dear. I must stay with you both, but you won't mind me – God bless you!' and the old woman put her arms round George's neck and kissed him tenderly.

She returned, and presently she redeemed her promise, for she actually got Mrs. Broad away. At first she was obstinate, but Priscilla whispered that she wished to see her husband alone, and the doctor took upon himself to warn Mrs. Broad that resistance on her part might be dangerous. She then retreated with him, and George found himself by the bedside. His wife was so prostrate that she was hardly able to make herself heard, but she lifted up her finger and made a sign that he should bend his head down to her. He bent it down, and her damp brown hair – the beautiful brown hair he had loved so – lay on his forehead, and its scent was all about him once more.

'George, my dear,' she just breathed out, 'I am a poor silly girl, but I always loved you.'

He stopped her instantly with his kisses, but Death had stopped her too. He recoiled for a moment, and with a sudden scream, 'O God, she's gone!' he fell into the arms of his nurse, who stood behind him.

CHAPTER TWENTY-SIX

A Professional Consultation

★

THREE months passed, during which the Allens' pew was vacant at Tanner's Lane. George remained at home with his only child, or was at his mother's, or, shocking to relate, was in the fields, but not at chapel; nor were any of his family there. During the whole of those three months one image was for ever before his eyes. What self-accusations! Of what injustice had he not been guilty? Little things, at the time unnoticed, turns of her head, smiles, the fall of her hair – oh, that sweet sweet brown hair! – all came back to him, and were as real before him as the garden wall. He thought of her lying in her grave – she whom he had caressed – of what was going on down there, under the turf, and he feared he should go mad. Where was she? Gone, for ever gone – gone before he had been able to make her understand how much he really loved her, and so send her to sleep in peace. But was she not in heaven? Would he not see her again? He did not know. Strange to say, but true, he, a member of Tanner's Lane Church, who had never read a sceptical book in his life, was obliged to confess, perhaps not consciously, but none the less actually, he did not know.

In those dark three months the gospel according to Tanner's Lane did nothing for him, and he was cast forth to wrestle with his sufferings alone. It is surely a terrible charge to bring against a religious system, that in the conflict which has to be waged by every son of Adam with disease, misfortune, death, the believers in it are provided with neither armour nor weapons. Surely a real religion, handed down from century to century, ought to have accumulated a store of consolatory truths which will be of some help to us in time of need. If it can tell us nothing, if we cannot face a single disaster any the better for it, and if we never dream of turning to it when we are in distress, of what value is it? There is one religious teacher, however, which seldom fails those who are in health, and, at last, did not fail him. He was helped by no priest and by no philosophy; but Nature helped him, the beneficent Power which heals the burn or scar and covers it with new skin.

At the end of the three months the Reverend John Broad received a brief note from Mr. Allen announcing that their pew at the chapel could be considered vacant, and that the subscription would be discontinued. Within a week Mr. Broad invited Brother Bushel, Brother Wainwright the cart-builder and blacksmith, and Brother Scotton the auctioneer, to a private meeting at his own house. In a short speech Mr. Broad said that he had sought a preliminary conference with them to lay before them the relationship in which the Allens stood to the church in Tanner's Lane. They had formally ceased to attend his ministrations, but of course, as yet, they remained on the church books. It was a matter which he, as the minister of the flock, felt could not any longer be overlooked. He would say nothing of the part which the Allens had taken in the late unhappy controversies which had distracted the town, excepting that he considered they had displayed a heat and animosity inconsistent with their professions and detrimental to the best interests of the cause.

'I agree with that, Mr. Broad,' interrupted Mr. Bushel; 'and I may say that, as you know, if you had done nothing, *I should;* for how any member of the – gospel – could live in – and go on – peace and harmony with all men in the Church of Christ, I, at least – that's my opinion.' Mr. Bushel was short-necked, and shook his head always while he was talking, apparently in order to disengage his meaning, which consequently issued in broken fragments.

Mr. Broad resumed – 'I may, however, observe that George Allen was in company with the intoxicated mob which devastated Cowfold; and although he has asserted that he merely endeavoured to control its excesses – and such appears to be the view taken by the civil authorities who have prosecuted the perpetrators of the outrages – we, as members, my dear brethren, of Christ's Body, have to be guided by other considerations. While upon this subject of George Allen, I may say, with as much delicacy as is permissible to a faithful minister of God's holy Word, that I fear George has been – a – h'm – what shall I say? – at least led astray by an unhappy intimacy with a female residing in the metropolis who is an infidel. I have no doubt in my own mind that the knowledge of this fact accelerated the departure of my dear daughter, whose sorrow was of a twofold character – sorrow, in the first place, with regard to her husband's unfaithfulness, causing her thereby much personal affliction, which, however, endureth but for a moment, for she now inherits a far more exceeding weight of glory' – Mr. Broad's week-day and extempore quotations from the Bible were always rather muddled – 'and, in the second place, sorrow for her husband's soul. I think we have distinct evidence of this intimacy, which I shall be able to produce at the proper moment. We have all observed, too, that whilst the Allens have not latterly attended Divine Service at Tanner's Lane, they have not seceded to another place of worship. Finally, and by way of conclusion, let me remark that I have wrestled long with the Lord to know what was my duty towards these apostates and towards the Church of Christ. I considered at first I ought to remonstrate privately with Mr. Allen; but, alas! he has shown a recalcitrant disposition whenever I have attempted to approach him. I have consulted Brother Bushel on the subject; indeed, I may say that Brother Bushel had previously intimated to me the necessity of taking some steps in the matter, and had assured me that he could not any longer occupy the prominent position which he now occupies in the church – so much, I may say, to our own edification and advantage – if something were not done. We think, therefore, that the church should be privately convoked for deliberation. Brother Wainwright, what counsel have you to give?'

Brother Wainwright always had a heavy account with Brother Bushel. He was a little man, with a little round head covered with straggling hair, which came over his forehead. He sat with his hat between his knees, looked into it, scratched his head, and said with a jerk, 'Oi agree with Brother Bushel.'

'Brother Scotton, what do you say?'

Brother Scotton was a Cowfold man, tall and thin, superintendent of the Sunday school, and to a considerable extent independent of village custom. He was not only an auctioneer, but a land surveyor; he also valued furniture, and when there were any houses to be let, drew up agreements, made inventories, and had even been known to prepare leases. There was always, therefore, a legal flavour about him, and he prided himself on his distant professional relationship to full-blown attorney-hood. It was tacitly understood in Cowfold that his opinion in certain cases was at least equal to that of Mortimer, Wake, Collins & Mortimer, who acted as solicitors for half the county. Mr. Scotton, too, represented Cowfold urban intelligence as against agricultural rusticity; and another point in his favour was, that he had an office – no shop – with a wire blind in the window with the words, 'Scotton, Land Agent, Auctioneer, and Appraiser,' painted on it. On Mr. Broad's present appeal for his verdict, he put himself in a meditative attitude, stretched out his legs to their full length, threw his head back, took his lower lip in his left hand, pulled up his legs again, bent forward, put his hands on his knees, and looked sideways at Mr. Broad.

'I suppose that Mr. Allen and his son will have the charges communicated to them, Mr. Broad, and be summoned to attend the meeting?'

'What do you say, Brother Bushel?'

'Don't see no use in it. All very well them lawyers' – a snap at Scotton – 'come and argyfy – I hate argyfying, I do myself – never seed no good on it. Get rid of a man – I do. "Sickly sheep infects the flock and pisons all the rest." ' These last words formed part of a hymn of which Brother Bushel was very fond.

'What do you say, Brother Wainwright?'

Brother Wainwright, although he could do nothing but agree with Brother Bushel, and never did anything but agree with him, preferred to make a show of reflection. He again looked in his hat, shut his mouth fast; again scratched his head; again shook it a little, and with another jerk, as if announcing a conclusion at which he had arrived with great certainty, but after a severe mental effort, he said –

'Oi go with Brother Bushel, *Oi* do.'

'Well,' said Scotton, extending his legs again and gazing at the ceiling, 'I must nevertheless be permitted to adhere –'

'Adhere,' interrupted Bushel. 'What's the use of talking like that? You always adhere – what for I should like to know.'

Scotton went on with dignity, not noticing the attack –

'Adhere, I was about to say, Mr. Broad, to my previously expressed opinion. I am not at all sure that the Allens have not a legal status, and that an action would not lie if we proceeded without due formalities. Tanner's Lane, you must recollect, is in a peculiar position, and there is an endowment.'

Mr. Scotton had this advantage over Cowfold generally, that if he knew nothing about the law himself, excepting so far as bids at a sale were concerned, Cowfold knew less, and the mention of the endowment somewhat disturbed Mr. Broad's mind.

'Brother Bushel is no doubt quite justified in his anxiety to avoid discussion, which will in all probability lead to no useful result; but, on the other hand, it will be as well, perhaps, to proceed with caution.'

'Well,' ejaculated Bushel, 'do as yer like; you'll see you'll get in an argyfication and a mess, you take my word on it.'

'Suppose,' said Mr. Broad, his face shining as he spoke, 'we hit upon a third course, the *via media*, you know, Brother Scotton' – (Brother Scotton nodded approvingly, as much as to say, '*I* know; but how about Bushel?') – 'the *via media*, and have a friendly meeting of the most influential members of the church – a majority – and determine upon a course of action, which we can afterwards ratify at the formal meeting, at which the Allens will be present. We shall in this way, it seems to me, prevent much debate, and practically arrive at a conclusion beforehand.'

'Yes,' said Scotton, very slowly. 'I don't see, at the present moment, any particular objection; but I should not like to commit myself.'

'How does it strike you, Brother Bushel?'

'Arter that, I suppose Scotton ull want some sort of a dockyment sent. I'm agin all dockyments. Why, what'll Allen do? Take it over to Collins – Mortimer – stamp it, ten-and-sixpenny stamp. What will yer do then?'

'No, Brother Bushel; I apprehend that it will be my duty as pastor to write to the Allens a simple letter – a simple pastoral letter – announcing that a church meeting will be convened at a certain hour in the vestry, to consider some statements – charges – naming them – not going into unnecessary detail, and requesting their attendance.'

'That's better; that wouldn't be a dockyment, I s'pose; and yet p'raps he might stamp that. Resolution arterwards. Time they were out of it. Come on, Wainwright, gettin' dark.'

'Well then, we agree,' said Mr. Broad – 'happily agree; and I trust that the Lord will yet prosper His Zion, and heal the breaches thereof. Will any of you take any refreshments before you go? Will you, Brother Bushel?'

Brother Bushel did not believe in Mr. Broad's refreshments, save those which were spiritual, and declined them with some abruptness, preferring much a glass of hot brown brandy and water at the inn where his horse was. Brother Wainwright would have taken anything, but was bound to follow Brother Bushel, who was about to give him a lift homewards; and Brother Scotton was a teetotaller, one of the first who was converted to total abstinence in Cowfold, and just a trifle suspected at Tanner's Lane, and by Bushel in particular, on that account. Water-drinking was not a heresy to which any definite objection could be raised; but Tanner's Lane always felt that if once a man differed so far from his fellows as not to drink beer and spirits, there was no knowing where the division might end. 'It was the thin end of the wedge,' Mr. Broad observed confidentially to Bushel once when the subject was mentioned.

The preliminary meeting, therefore, was held, and Mr.

Broad having communicated the charges against the Allens
– absenting themselves from public worship, disturbance
of the peace of the church, intercourse with infidel associ-
ates, and finally, so far as George was concerned, 'questionable behaviour,' as Mr. Broad delicately put it, 'with
an infidel female' – it was determined to call them to
account. There was some difference of opinion, however.
It was thought by some that all reference to the election,
direct or indirect, should be avoided, for the majority
in Tanner's Lane was certainly not Tory. But Brother
Bushel seemed to consider this the head and front of
the offence, and declared that if this were not part of the
indictment he would resign. He also was opposed to giving the Allens any information beforehand, and, if he had
been allowed to have his own way, would not have permitted them to attend. He would have them 'cut off,' he
said, 'there and then, summararlilly.' He got into great
difficulties with this last word, and before he could get
rid of it had to shake his head several times. Others
thought it would be dangerous to act in this style; and
there seemed no chance of any agreement, until Mr.
Broad once more 'healed the incipient division' by pro-
posing another *via media*, which was carried. It was determined that there should be only an allusion to the political
charge. It was to be subsidiary. In fact, it was not to be
a political charge at all, but a moral charge, although, as
Mr. Broad privately explained to Brother Bushel, it would
come to the same thing in the end. Then Mr. Broad, as
he had suggested at an earlier stage, was himself to write
a letter to the Allens, stating in 'general terms' the dis-

satisfaction felt by the church and its minister with them, and requesting their appearance in the vestry on the day named. Brother Scotton was still malcontent, but as he was in a minority he held his peace. He resolved, however, on his own account, to acquaint the Allens with what had happened, and prepare them. They were no particular friends of his, but Bushel also was no particular friend, and his auctioneering trade had at least educated him, in the disputes amongst buyers, to hold the scales of justice a little more evenly than they were held by Bushel's hands.

Neither George nor his father were much disturbed by any of the items in Scotton's information, nor by Mr. Broad's letter, save the reference to Pauline. It is true it was very remote, but the meaning, especially after Scotton's explanation, was obvious, and George was in a fury which his father found it very difficult to repress. For himself George did not care, but he did care that Pauline's name should not be dragged into the wretched squabble. Father and son both agreed that the case should be laid before Zachariah; but when Mr. Allen came back from London he merely said, in answer to George's inquiries, that Zachariah and himself were in perfect accord, and that at the meeting George was not to interfere.

CHAPTER TWENTY-SEVEN

Mr. Broad's last Church Meeting – Latimer Chapel

*

THE eventful evening at last arrived. It had been announced from the pulpit on the Sunday before that a
special meeting of the church would be held on the following Wednesday to consider certain questions of discipline – nothing more – as it was not thought proper
before the general congregation to introduce matters with
which the church alone was qualified to deal. Everybody,
however, knew what was intended, and when Wednesday
night came the vestry was crowded. Mr. Broad sat in a
seat slightly elevated at the end of the room, with a desk
before him. On his right hand was Brother Bushel, on
the left was Brother Scotton, and on the front bench were
Brother Wainwright and a few of the more important
members, amongst whom was Thomas Broad, who, although it was a week-day, was in full ministerial costume;
that is to say, he wore his black – not pepper-and-salt –
trousers and a white neckerchief. Mr. Allen and George
were at the back of the room. There were no women
there, for although women were members as well as men,
it was always an understood thing at Tanner's Lane that
they were to take no part in the business of the community. Seven o'clock having struck, Mr. Broad rose and
said, 'Let us pray.' He prayed for about ten minutes, and
besought the Almighty to shed abroad His Holy Spirit
upon them for their guidance. As the chosen people had
been brought through the wilderness and delivered from
the manifold perils therein, so God, he hoped, would lead
His flock then assembled through the dangers which en-

compassed them. Oh, that they might be wise as serpents and harmless as doves! Might they for ever cleave to the faith once delivered to the saints! Might they never be led astray to doubt the efficacy of the Blood of the Atonement once offered by the Son of God! Might they, through their Saviour's merits, secure at last an entrance into those mansions where all the saints of God, those faithful souls whom He had elected as His own, of His own eternal foreknowledge, would abide for ever, in full fruition of the joys promised in His Word.

The prayer over, Mr. Broad rose and said that he was there that night to discharge a most painful duty – one which, if he had taken counsel with flesh and blood, he would most gladly have avoided. But he was a humble servant of their common Lord and Master. It behoved him to cease not to warn every one night and day; to remember that the Holy Ghost had made him an overseer to feed the church of God which He had purchased with His precious blood. He had done nothing in this matter without constant recurrence to the footstool of grace, and he had also consulted with some of his dear brethren in Christ whom he saw near him. They would have observed that Brother Allen and his family had for some time absented themselves from the means of grace. He should have said nothing upon this point if they had joined any other Christian community. If even they had attended the Established Church, he would have been silent, for he was free to confess that in other religious bodies besides their own God had faithful servants who held fast to the fundamental doctrines of His Book. But it was notorious, alas! that his dear brother had gone NOWHERE! In the face of the apostolic command not to forsake the assembling of themselves together, what could they do but suspect that his dear brother's belief had been undermined – sapped, he would say? But to that point he would return presently. Then again, they were all familiar with the circumstances attending the late political contest in the county. He knew that many of his dear brethren differed one from another concerning matters relating to this world, although they were all, blessed be God, one in Christ, members of His Body. He himself had thought it better to follow, as far as he could, the example of his Lord and Master, to render unto Cæsar the things that are Cæsar's, and to lead a quiet and peaceable life in all godliness and honesty. He would not for a moment, however, condemn any who differed from him in carnal policy. But his dear Brother Allen and his son had overstepped the line; and, considering this was a mixed church, he was of opinion that they should have acted – what should he say? – with more Christian consideration. More than this, Mr. George Allen was known to have abetted an unruly mob, a position highly unbecoming, he might say, to one occupying the position of member at Tanner's Lane. But he might, perhaps, be permitted to dwell for a moment on another point. His dear Brother Allen and his son had – there was no doubt of it – consorted with infidels, one of whom had been convicted by the laws of his country – a *convict* – and it was through their instrumentality that his brethren had been led to wander from the fold. This was the secret of the calamity which had overtaken the church.

Wolves, he would say – yes, wolves, grievous wolves – had entered in, not sparing the flock. Let them consider what an Infidel was! It meant a man who denied his Maker, Revelation, a life beyond the grave, and who made awful jests upon the Holy Scriptures! He had evidence that in this miserable household there was a portrait of that dreadful blasphemer Voltaire, who on his death-bed cried out in vain for that salvation which he had so impiously refused, and amidst shrieks of despair, which chilled with terror those who stood by him, was carried off by the Enemy of Souls to the lake that burneth with brimstone, where their worm dieth not and the fire is not quenched. – (Sensation.) (This was a famous paragraph in one of Mr. Broad's sermons preached on great occasions, and particularly when he supplied a metropolitan pulpit. The story had been contradicted twice in the county paper by a Frenchman, a retired teacher of his native language, who had somehow heard of the insult offered to his great countryman, and a copy of the contradiction had been sent to Mr. Broad. He was content with observing that its author was a Frenchman, and therefore probably an atheist, 'with no consciousness of moral obligation.' Voltaire's diabolic disappearance continued, therefore, to be one of Mr. Broad's most striking effects.) – This was a subject of great delicacy. They knew how closely related he was to Brother Allen through that dear saint now in glory. He did not, he could not – (Mr. Broad seemed to be affected) – allude in any detail to what had happened; but still it was his duty to point out that Mr. George Allen had been in constant intercourse with a female in

309

an infidel family – yes, before his wife's death he had been seen with her *alone*! *Alone* with an infidel female! He only hoped that the knowledge of this fact did not accelerate the departure of his blessed daughter – daughter in the flesh and daughter in Christ. He could not measure the extent of that intercourse; the Searcher of hearts alone could do that, save the parties concerned; but, of course, as she was an unbeliever, they must fear the worst. For himself, he had felt that this was the root of everything. They would judge for themselves how fervently he must have appealed to the Mercy-seat, considering his position and relationship with his dear brother, before he had seen his way to take the present course; but at last God had revealed Himself to him, and he now committed the case to them. Might God have mercy on them, and His Spirit lead them.

Mr. Allen and George had scarcely restrained themselves, and George, notwithstanding his father's injunction, leapt up before the concluding sentences were out of Mr. Broad's mouth. Mr. Scotton, however, rose, and Mr. Allen pulled George down. Mr. Scotton wished to say just one word. They could not, he was sure, over-estimate the gravity of the situation. They were called together upon a most solemn occasion. Their worthy pastor had spoken as a minister of the gospel. He, Mr. Scotton, as a layman, wished just to remind them that they were exercising judicial functions, – (Brother Bushel fidgeted and got very red) – and that it was necessary they should proceed in proper order. With regard to two of the charges, the evidence was fully before them; that is to say, absence from public worship and what might perhaps be thought want of consideration for the peace of the church. – ('P'raps,' grunted Bushel – 'p'raps, indeed.') – But with regard to the third charge, the evidence was *not* before them, and as this was the most important of the three, he would suggest before going any further that they should hear what Mr. Broad could produce.

Brother Bushel objected. It was very seldom indeed that he offered any remarks in public; but this time he could not refrain, and introduced himself as follows:

'Brother Scotton says "p'raps." I don't say "p'raps," when people go settin' class agin class. P'raps nobody's windows was broke! Evidence! Hasn't our minister told us George Allen has been to London? He wouldn't tell us an untruth. Due respec', Brother Scotton – no lawyering – none of that – of them functions – 'specially when it's infidels and ricks may be afire – aught I know.'

Mr. Broad interposed. He quite understood Brother Bushel's ardour for the truth, but he was prepared to produce some simple corroboration of what he had affirmed, which would, he thought, satisfy Brother Scotton and the brethren generally. 'Thomas,' quoth Mr. Broad, 'will you please step forward and say what you know?'

Mr. Thomas thereupon advanced to the table, and said it would ill become him to expatiate on the present occasion. He would confine himself to obeying the mandate of his father. He then reported that he had been led to visit the Colemans at first as friends of the Allens, and not knowing their devilish tendencies. God had, however, he hoped, mercifully protected him. If it had not been for God's grace, where might he not have been that day? It was true that they were disciples of the French sceptic; his likeness was on the walls; his books were on the bookshelves! Mr. George Allen had been in the habit of associating not only with Mr. Coleman, but with his daughter, and with the daughter *alone!* as had already been stated. She was also an infidel – more so, perhaps, than her father, and Satan had a way, as they all knew, of instilling the deadly poison so seductively that unwary souls were often lost, lost, lost beyond recall, before they could truly be said to be aware of it. He wished, therefore, that evening to confess again, as, indeed, he had just confessed before, that by grace he had been saved. It was not of him that willeth, nor of him that runneth, but of God that showeth mercy. He trembled to think how near he himself had been to the pit of destruction, lured by the devices of the great Enemy of Souls; but praise be to God he had been saved, not through his own merits, but through the merits of his Redeemer.

Mr. Broad purred with pleasure during this oration, and looked round on the audience for their approval.

Mr. Allen was now completely quieted. The speech had acted like a charm. He rose immediately.

'Mr. Broad,' he said deliberately, but with much emphasis – you might have heard a pin drop – 'the value of the testimony just given depends upon the character of the witness. May I ask him to explain *how he came by that scar on the back of his hand*?'

Mr. Allen remained standing. There was no sign of an

312

answer. He sat down for a moment, but still there was no movement. He rose again.

'Mr. Broad, as there is no reply, will you permit me to give the explanation?'

Mr. Thomas Broad then slowly erected himself near the table at which his father was sitting. He held on by it hard, and gulped down half a glass of water which was there. His tallowy face looked more tallowy than ever, and his voice shook most unpleasantly as he was just heard to say that he did not know with what object the question was put – that it – that it – seemed – seemed – irrel – irrelev – and these were the last syllables ever heard from the lips of Mr. Thomas in Tanner's Lane, for he dropped into his seat and apparently fainted. There was great confusion while his recovery was attempted. He was conveyed into the chapel, more water was given him, smelling-salts applied, and in due time he regained his senses; but his father, on his return to the vestry, announced that after what had happened the meeting had perhaps better be adjourned. He felt it impossible to go any further just then. Tanner's Lane Church, therefore, departed, much musing, and was never again summoned on that business. Mr. Allen had some thoughts of demanding another meeting and a formal acquittal, but the pastor was suddenly struck with paralysis, and although he lingered for nearly two years, he preached no more. So it came to pass that George and his father are on the church books till this day. There was, of course, endless gossip as to the meaning of Mr. Allen's appeal. Whether George ever knew what it was is more than I can say, but it is certain that

Cowfold never knew. Mr. Allen always resolutely repelled all questions, saying that it would be time enough to go further when he was next attacked. The Broads, mother and daughter, asserted that no doubt Thomas had a mark upon the back of his hand, but that it had been caused by a nail in a fence, and that he had fainted through indisposition. This theory, however, was obviously ridiculous, for Mr. Allen's reference had no meaning if Thomas had met with a simple accident. Mrs. Broad saw that her son's explanation, greatly as she trusted him, was weak, and at last Thomas, with Christian compunction, admitted that the fence was the palings of the College garden, over which he had once clambered when he was too late for admittance at the College gates. This was true. Mr. Thomas, on the very evening of his interview with Pauline, had obtained admission over the palings, had been detected, and there had been an inquiry by the authorities; but the scar, as we know, had another origin. Mrs. Broad was compelled to circulate this story, and accompanied it with many apologies and much regret. It was the sorrow of her life, she said; but, at the same time, she must add that her son was delayed by no fault of his. The President had investigated the matter, and had contented himself with a reprimand. Her friends would understand that Thomas would prefer, under the circumstances, not to visit Cowfold again, and, considering her dear husband's sickness, she could not advise that the prosecution of the Allens should be pressed.

Cowfold, however, was not satisfied. Mr. Allen would not, as a man of the world, have thought so much of such an indiscretion. Why was Mr. Thomas late? Cowfold could not endure simple suspense of judgment. Any theory, however wild, is more tolerable than a confession that the facts are not sufficient for a decision, and the common opinion, corroborated, it was declared, by surest testimony, was that Mr. Thomas had been to the theatre. There was not a tittle of evidence to support this story, but everybody was certain it was true. Everybody repeated it, and constant repetition will harden the loosest hearsay into a creed far more unshakable than faith in the law of gravity.

Just before Mr. Broad's last illness, the secession of the Allens was imitated by about twenty of the younger members of the congregation, who met together on Sunday, under Mr. Allen's guidance, and worshipped by themselves, each of them in turn making some attempt at an exposition of the Bible and a short address. By the time Mr. Broad died, Tanner's Lane had sunk very low; but when his successor was chosen the seceders exercised their rights, and were strong enough to elect a student fresh from college, who had taken an M.A. degree at the University of London. He preached his first sermon from the text, 'I am crucified with Christ,' and told his hearers, with fluent self-confidence, that salvation meant perfect sympathy with Christ – 'Not I, but Christ liveth in me'; that the office of Christ was not to reconcile God to man, but man to God; and this is effected in proportion as Christ dwells in us, bringing us more and more into harmony with the Divine. The Atonement is indeed the central doctrine, the pivot of Christianity but it is an at*one-*

315

ment, a making of one mind. To which Tanner's Lane listened with much wonderment, and not without uncomfortable mental disturbance, the elder members complaining particularly that this was not the simple gospel, and that the trumpet gave an uncertain sound. But the opposition gradually died out; the meeting-house was rebuilt, and called Latimer Chapel. The afternoon service was dropped and turned into a service for the Sunday-school children; an organ was bought and a choir trained; the minister gave week-day lectures on secular subjects, and became a trustee of the Cowfold charity schools, recently enlarged under a new scheme. He brought home a wife one day who could read German; he joined the County Archæological Society, and wrote a paper on the discoveries made when the railway station was built on what was supposed to be an ancient British encampment. For Cowfold was to become an important junction on the new line to the north, and Mr. Bushel's death had been accelerated by vexation through seeing a survey carried across his own fields.

As for Mrs. Broad and Tryphosa, they left Cowfold and went into Lancashire, to be near uncle Flavel. George, notwithstanding the new doctrine in Latimer Chapel and the improvement in the Cowfold atmosphere, was restless, and before the revolution just described was completed had been entirely overcome with a desire to emigrate with his child. His father and mother not only did not oppose, but decided to accompany him. Mr. Allen had saved money, and though he and his wife were getting on in years, there was nothing in either of them of that subsidence into indifferent sloth which is the great mistake of advancing age. Both were keen in their desire to know the last new thing, eager to recognize the last new truth, forgetful of the past, dwelling in the present, and, consequently, they remained young. They were younger, at any rate, just now than George; and it was his, not exactly melancholy, but lack of zest for life, which mainly induced them so readily to assent to his plans. One bright June morning, therefore, saw them, with their children, on the deck of the Liverpool vessel which was to take them to America. Oh, day of days, when, after years of limitation, monotony, and embarrassment, we see it all behind us, and face a new future with an illimitable prospect! George once more felt his bosom's lord sit lightly on his throne; once more felt that the sunlight and blue sky were able to cheer him. So they went away to the West, and we take leave of them.

What became of Zachariah and Pauline? At present I do not know.

THE HOGARTH PRESS

A New Life For A Great Name

This is a paperback list for today's readers – but it holds to a tradition of adventurous and original publishing set by Leonard and Virginia Woolf when they founded The Hogarth Press in 1917 and started their first paperback series in 1924.

Now, after many years of partnership, Chatto & Windus · The Hogarth Press are proud to launch this new series. Our choice of books will not echo that of the Woolfs in every way – times have changed – but our aims will be the same. Some sections of the list will be light-hearted, some serious: all will be rigorously chosen, excellently produced and energetically published, in the best Hogarth Press tradition. We hope that the new Hogarth Press paperback list will be as prized – and as avidly collected – as its illustrious forebear.

Some of our forthcoming titles follow. If you would like more information about Hogarth Press books, write to us for a catalogue:

40 William IV Street, London WC2N 4DF

Please send a large stamped addressed envelope

HOGARTH FICTION

The Revolution in Tanner's Lane by Mark Rutherford,
New Introduction by Claire Tomalin

Chance by Joseph Conrad,
New Introduction by Jane Miller

The Whirlpool by George Gissing,
New Introduction by Gillian Tindall

Mr Weston's Good Wine by T. F. Powys,
New Introduction by Ronald Blythe

HOGARTH HUMOUR

Mrs Ames by E. F. Benson,
New Introduction by Stephen Pile

Paying Guests by E. F. Benson,
New Introduction by Stephen Pile

The Amazing Test Match Crime by Adrian Alington,
New Introduction by Brian Johnston

HOGARTH CRIME

The Saltmarsh Murders by Gladys Mitchell

The Mysterious Mickey Finn by Elliot Paul

Death By Request by Romilly and Katherine John

The Hand In The Glove by Rex Stout

HOGARTH BIOGRAPHY AND AUTOBIOGRAPHY

The Journal of a Disappointed Man & A Last Diary by
W. N. P. Barbellion,
Original Introduction by H. G. Wells and New Introduction
by Deborah Singmaster

Pack My Bag by Henry Green,
New Introduction by Paul Bailey

Being Geniuses Together by Robert McAlmon and Kay
Boyle,
New Afterword by Kay Boyle

Samuel Johnson by Walter Jackson Bate

Flush by Virginia Woolf,
New Introduction by Trekkie Ritchie

HOGARTH TRAVEL

The Spanish Temper by V. S. Pritchett,
New Introduction by the Author

The Amateur Emigrant by Robert Louis Stevenson,
New Introduction by Jonathan Raban

HOGARTH LITERARY CRITICISM

The Common Reader, First Series by Virginia Woolf,
edited and introduced by Andrew McNeillie

The Common Reader, Second Series by Virginia Woolf,
edited and introduced by Andrew McNeillie

The English Novel from Dickens to Lawrence
by Raymond Williams

The Common Pursuit by F. R. Leavis

Seven Types of Ambiguity by William Empson

HOGARTH BELLES-LETTRES

Ivor Gurney: War Letters,
a selection edited by
R. K. R. Thornton

By Way of Sainte Beuve by Marcel Proust,
translated by Sylvia Townsend Warner,
New Introduction by Terence Kilmartin

HOGARTH POETRY

Collected Poems, C. P. Cavafy,
translated by Edmund Keeley and Philip Sherrard, edited by
George Savidis

Collected Poems, William Empson